Dark Hearts and Tattletales

A Collection by Poe's Sparrow

Jane Gwaltney

Also Edited by Sandra Murphy

Chris Bauer likes his stories short and furnished with twists and turns readers won't see coming.

Those in this collection range from out-of-control Thanksgiving turkeys to a bomber pilot's fateful flight, and take the reader from a pizza delivery joint to a homemade backyard rocket ship.

Even his machines seem to have minds of their own, with a love for pranks — or even more deadlier plans.

But, if you're lucky, sometimes serendipity solves the problem.

And let's face it, whichever way you serve it, Revenge is *always* sweet. Unless you're a squirrel. In which case it's just plain nutty.

So, sit back and enjoy a variety of locations, plots, and an introduction to some of the very strange people and the worlds they live in.

Paperback ISBN: 9781963479348
eBook ISBN: 9781963479331

Dark Hearts and Tattletales
A Collection by Poe's Sparrow
Jane Gwaltney

Sandra Murphy Presents is an imprint of
Misti Media LLC
https://whitecitypress.com
Available in both Paperback and eBook Editions
1 2 3 4 5 6 7 8 9 10
Text Copyright © 2024 Jane Gwaltney
Paperback ISBN: 9781963479621
eBook ISBN: 9781963479614

CONTENTS

ᑫᘐᕋ

* Honorable Mention by Ellen Datlow in The Year's Best Fantasy and Horror

** First Place in "Impaired" contest

***Honorable Mention in The Best Horror of the Year, Volume One, edited by Ellen Datlow

Introduction

When you love to write short stories and Edgar Allan Poe lives in your house (or at least in your mind), those stories are bound to be a bit...weird. Unusual. Not many happy endings but always a good read.

Jane Gwaltney shares a dozen previously published stories and four never before seen tales to grab the imagination and run away with it. She is a member of a critique group called Writers Under The Arch (WUTA) in St. Louis, Missouri and the Horror Writers Association.

Dive into the pages if you dare. You've been warned.

By Default

She sat in the dark...waiting. In her hand, two tiny beads glowed, ember orange. She giggled...

The cowbell clanged, bludgeoning the oak frame. Drury hesitated as the door swung open, then took care in closing it. Nevertheless, flakes of paint rained from splintered wood. He looked about him, conscience stricken.

It was impossibly quiet. His ears felt as if they'd been stuffed with cotton wool. Mold simmered with a hodge-podge of aromatic substances, gouging his nostrils. He sneezed. Panic washed over him. He wasn't prone to histrionics, but the impulse to back step through that weathered door was non-negotiable.

It wouldn't budge.

"May I help you, sir?"

The polite query dripped down his back with the merciful speed of molasses. The sunny road which had brought him leered through the dusty windowpane, daring him to reclaim his confidence. "Uhhh..." he said.

The woman was grandmotherly from the neck up. He felt a twinge of guilt as his eyes took in the proportions of the mounds beneath the words on her tee shirt.

"You'll need one of our shirts to take home as a souvenir." Her chin bobbed.

He felt like a pure idiot, nodding in unison. "It's our...*fault*," he read out loud. "I saw that painted on a billboard at the New Madrid city limits. It's on tee shirts, *too?* I'm afraid I don't understa—"

"Young man, you don't know about the earthquakes? The New Madrid fault?" She winked, with a disturbing familiarity. "It's *our* fault...*get it?* The tourists keep me in business, at least 'til Missouri's next 'big one' hits."

His mouth opened—

"Now, what sort of book were you looking for? Even the browsers don't leave my shop empty handed. I'm networked online to used book dealers worldwide. If you don't see that special rarity, I can order it, just like that!"

Her finger-snap got Drury talking. "Gulliver's Travels. An early limited-edition copy is what I want. A birthday present for my daughter."

"Ah, yes." The shopkeeper motioned for him to follow. "Only *one* birthday per year. Very special, indeed. All those *un*-birthdays going to waste. Truly a crime...and do call me Vera."

The "used car" sales approach was irritating, but something about her went far beyond that. He was convinced an empty chair at The Mad Tea Party table was waiting, reserved exclusively for Vera.

"What did you say your daughter's name is?" Vera chirped.

"I didn't say." Drury flinched. Overhead, a mounted cast iron gargoyle bared its teeth. The stomach held a timepiece inset, the hands rusted to a stop at nine o'clock.

"You're not a small towner. One can tell *that* easily enough." Vera turned a corner.

He raised his sleeve to check his watch, then double stepped for a moment, feeling like a sluggish caboose tagged to the end of an outdated train. "True. I'm based in New York City, and I'm a world traveler by occupation. Look, I'm on a tight schedule. My rental car's due back, plane to catch. Do you have that book?"

"Well, I grew up in England, myself. Lancashire," she drawled, toddling on at the same unhurried pace. "But I'm much at home in New Madrid."

Drury raised an eyebrow. She'd divulged the origins of her Brit-Hick accent, even though he'd expressed no interest. Worse, his question remained unanswered...and he wasn't used to *waiting*. Wandering around the spooky place unassisted was decidedly the lesser of two evils at this point.

"Oh!" Vera exclaimed. The 180-degree spin was startling, considering her age. Her complexion had paled, a near match for her snowy French Twist.

Drury came to a halt much closer than he would've preferred.

"I remember now," she said. "We do have one such edition, but it's...it's still with the latest acquisitions, in the basement storeroom. It's very untidy there right now. Perhaps I can *send* the book to you through the post as soon as I locate it?" She brought her hands together in front of her midriff, lacing them in a knot, her index fingers erecting a steeple. "Especially since you're in a rush."

He submerged his relief. "Actually, I see no reason I can't find a replacement. I'll give myself a tour. Plenty of treasures here. Shouldn't take long, and I'll let you know if I need help," he lied. A fleeing glimpse showed Vera rooted in place, arms akimbo, her brow furrowed...

* * *

"Basement. No Admittance," the sign challenged. Drury passed, perusing nearby. His impatience flamed higher with each disappointing volume he plucked from the shelves. "I know what's hoarded down there," he grumbled to a dour-faced elderly man.

Deep facial creases took the shape of a gaping toothless mouth. Steel gray eyes darted to the basement door. "You seen 'em, *too?*" An accusatory finger sliced air, as Drury backed away. "They're down there...eatin' the world from the inside out. Scat!"

The old man stomped, and a hissing ball of fur ejected itself from behind a tall upright vacuum cleaner. "Damned cat. Always sneakin' around."

His gnarled hands fumbled with the power cord, and after a laborious battle, jammed the plug into an outlet. The machine roared and launched forward, devouring carpet, oblivious to Drury's attempts to continue the conversation.

"Cats are downstairs eating the world?" Drury aimed the ludicrous summation at the man's retreating back. He'd seen more than enough New Madrid loonies. Did seismic activity affect human sensibilities? He smirked, thinking of the San Francisco Bay Area. *Case closed.*

The skin on the back of his neck prickled, and the sign taunted again. His hand fondled the doorknob. A euphoric surge greeted him as the door opened, the sound squelched by the vacuum's racket. He thought it unlikely that Vera's little hole-in-the-wall was rigged with surveillance equipment. Besides...he was merely doing a good deed for a senior citizen. He'd find that book on his own.

Shutting the door behind him, he stood motionless, with a tight grip on the railing. His pupils struggled to make adjustments. Several blinks later, the dim outlines of stairs coaxed his feet downward.

Whoosh! He reeled at the bottom step, a flash of something solid brushing his leg as it passed. Opaque black, with a rippling of *fur*. He fought to slow his breaths, wondering if he'd cried out. His eyes danced from side to side, his mind craving a harmless explanation, a sight to make him laugh at his own foolishness.

Nothing moved. Anywhere.

But what a sight to behold. Never in his life had he seen so many books crammed into such a small area. The low ceiling and claustrophobia enveloped him. Overwhelmed by the smell of humid cinderblock, he was held fast by curiosity.

He'd been seeing "things" from the corners of his eyes for as long as he could remember, enticed by subtleties beneath the varnish of reality. But as his mother had aptly pointed out, there was no money in ghost-chasing. A respectable career gathering facts had cured his fiction fever.

Or *had* it?

Excitement tickled the soles of his feet. It had been ages since he'd gone exploring. A row of painted-in windows off to his left caught his attention. Stiletto spokes of daylight threaded pocks left by fallen chips of green enamel, casting eerie jagged stripes across towering heaps of books.

"*Untidy* ain't the word for this," he snorted. "Sure wouldn't want to be down here when that 'big one' hits." He navigated a short distance with shuffling baby-steps and upraised arms, in search of an artificial light source. His heart leapt as he spotted an evenly rounded glow in a far-off corner. He wormed his way toward it.

A sudden thought lifted hairs along his scalp. *He might not be alone.* "Cats," he reminded himself. He'd already encountered that skittish black one, and country folks usually kept at least a few around to control the rodents—

A noise riveted him to the floor. It paused, in unison. He gritted his teeth...it began again: a soft thump, then peculiar rustlings. He edged closer, a silly refrain rattling in his head. *Are you a man or a mouse?*

"Did you find your book, mister?"

He figured his eyes were popping from his sockets, *literally*, cartoon-character style. He swallowed a gasp and laughed, suspense escaping like air from a blown-out tire. "No, sure didn't," he grinned.

Just a little girl. He watched her finish her game. The ball bounced once, and her hand deftly swept the floor clean of all ten jacks. Then, her triumphant catch. "Would you like to play?" she asked.

Her arena was a spotlight bubble projected from a dingy overhead bulb. She was kneeling on a folded rug, and her waist-length black hair gave the illusion of a hooded cape. *Strange* little girl.

"Sorry, I don't have time...um, don't tell on me, okay? I saw the sign, but...well, it's just that I wanted a certain book for my daughter. Bet she's about your age, too."

"I won't tell." She rose and dusted her knees. Her patent leather "Mary Jane" shoes gleamed. "I like the classics best."

"Great! My daughter isn't exposed to fine literature, in my opinion. Her mother indulges her with the latest trendy tripe. I'm looking for Gulliver's Travels, a *wholesome* book. Even the classics should be carefully chosen for developing minds. Hmm, besides...this edition'll be a collector's item. Good investment, even if she doesn't read it. Of course, my *main* concern is that some books are dangerous for children."

"How so?" The little imp's dark eyes flashed. She settled herself on a low stool and struck a prim and proper pose. "We might learn something we aren't meant to know?"

Drury began to itch under the collar. "I don't support censorship, but society's values have...*changed.* Some books aren't appropriate for enlightened people of *any* age. Er, how old *are* you, anyway? You seem—"

"The answers to all questions are in the classics." Delicately, she licked a fingertip and used it to preen her eyebrows. "Someday, shops like my granny's will be the only places to find out what's real. New books don't really say anything new. By the way, what do you do for a living?"

Nosy brat. Drury stuck his wrist into the spotlight and glared at his watch. "Vera sure fed you the sales pitch, I see. Probably has you peddling shirts, too. My occupation? Statistician. I collect facts about things you're too young to understand." A vague rumble distracted him, the source impossible to pinpoint. He looked at the ceiling. *Just Vera rolling carts of books,* he assured himself.

"Gulliver's Travels was said to be a political satire, in disguise." The girl took a jewelry box from the pocket of her crisply starched apron and dumped in the ball and jacks. "Also, the Lilliputians might be deemed offensive to the stature-challenged, methinks. Are you sure you should allow Beth to read it?"

"How...how do you know my daughter's name? Oh, never mind." *Sly trickery,* he thought. Somehow, weird ol' Vera had put the little smart-ass up to this.

Squeaking. He heard squeaking. It wasn't upstairs. It was very close to his right ear. He didn't want to turn his head. But he *had* to.

His chin trembled, but words wouldn't come. Eye level with the shelf, the titles jumped out at him. *Gulliver's Travels,* every last one of them riddled with nickel-sized holes...

From the holes oozed a stream of pink naked rodents.

Drury's knees knocked together, and the jolt released his tongue. "Mice...*incredible*—could be hundreds—"

A cough interrupted. "No..."

He could hear her yawn.

"We don't have mice at all, anymore. The rats ate them."

Drury was breathing hard. Embarrassed, too. Apparently, the girl's words had tapped a reflex. He was now cringing behind her, yet he could barely remember moving.

"You're very edgy," she said. "You found our batch of late-edition Gulliver's, though. Schoolbook overstock. The illustrations are boring. Fitting, that they be ruined."

Drury salvaged the remnants of his composure. "I think I'd better scrap this and go. Don't want to miss Beth's birthday, like I did *last* year."

"Did she cry?"

He could see his reflection in the girl's enormous brown eyes. "Yes. I... I travel so much, and her mother and I are divorced." His throat felt tight. "I'm sure I don't see her often enough. Now, I even failed to get her that special storybook."

"You should *tell* her a story, mister. It would mean more. I can *show* you a true adventure story, and it would be special because it's the kind only children believe." She added a conspirator wink, her pale hand reaching into her apron again. It returned as a loosely closed fist. "But if she's prone to nightmares, and you want to spare her, you could tell her it's just a scary fiction tale."

He was intrigued. *The poor waif should be outside, playing in the sunshine with other children.* Her giggle tugged at a guilt-laden heartstring. *Yes, he missed the sound of Beth's laughter.* "Okay, so what do you have in your hand, young lady?"

It opened, revealing a tiny hairless rodent. His repulsion almost brought up his breakfast, but he couldn't tear himself from the critter's eyes...*ember orange...*

Drury felt a blank wave wash over him, aware he was following the girl as she slowly backed out of the spotlight. Finger-puppet shadows tickled the walls until they were snuffed by semi-darkness. When she turned, her curtain of hair swirled in a slow-motion arc. He continued to follow, captivated…

She stopped.

Her hand rose, and he stood by, heart thumping. The rat wriggled off the ends of her fingers, joining a hazy row of duplicates slithering along a ledge. One by one, they disappeared into a small hole in the wall...

The next thing Drury knew, he was focusing on the girl again. In her hand, an oil lamp shimmered. "This used to be a coal room," he mumbled, shaking his head in hopes of clearing it.

"I wrote a poem today." Her voice lilted with childish exuberance. "It's called *Guilt*. Listen. I'll recite it."

> I have been cheated,
> whimsical meanderings cut short
> by your avenging blade.
> You shatter my smooth surface,
> charging amidst furry creatures,
> crushing a few each time,
> leaving the rest to crouch in terror...
> knowing you will return.

For the first time, she broke into a wide grin. The tip of her tongue flicked over a gap where the buds of two adult teeth had emerged.

A quiver crept up Drury's legs, advancing until it included the top of his head. He sickened as he heard a rumbling, much louder than before. *It was beneath his feet.* "Earthquake!" he gasped.

"No, silly," she said, glancing toward the partially open coal chute.

His eyes goggled. A large slinky dark shape seemed to extrude from the floor. It bounded upward, slamming against the chute, then *out* it.

"A d-dog?"

"*Rat.*"

A scream was trapped in that place the human psyche reserves for utter disbelief. He'd just seen a rat with a tail resembling a full-size boa constrictor? *No way...*

"Merlin is naughty," the mini sorceress clucked. "Don't worry, he's the only one who sneaks out in the daytime. The other big ones are sleeping. They feed at night in the cornfields. The little albinos from the lab aren't allowed out at all, of course."

"Uh, from the lab?" A calm had settled over him. This couldn't be real. Why not delve for details?

"They tunneled all the way from St. Louis, following the fault line," she answered, matter of factly. "Some significant quakes are coming soon, if the virus doesn't kill off the big ones fast enough."

"*Virus*? They're spreading a virus?"

"They were, but just amongst themselves. By nature, their life spans are short. Much shorter since they were infected by the lab rats from Jefferson University Medical School. Remember the so-called 'harmless minor explosion' in the viral research facility? It registered on the Richter Scale—"

"Rumor!"

"*Fact*," she corrected. "That's when the rats nesting in Gulliver's Travels started growing so huge. Anyway, the big ones die off faster than they can multiply, just like the virus did. Only five big ones are still living...so those crop circles out there will gradually disappear. No more 'aliens' to entertain the locals and tourists. The pinkies don't even grow or mature at all anymore. They die in a few weeks, poor things." She shrugged. "Strange, huh? Granny will lose a lot of business."

Drury eyed the coal chute. "I'm leaving now, little girl. I'm going back up the stairs, getting in my car—"

"Granny *knows* you came down here. If you go back upstairs..." She shook her head. "I don't think you want to see granny angry."

Sweat beaded on his forehead. She was right. It made no damned sense, but the thought of facing a firing squad was less intimidating. Or even a pack of rats the size of St. Bernards. "Get me out of here," he whined.

"Sure." She dragged a chair and centered it under the coal chute. "It's the only way out, unless you use one of their tunnels."

Drury was amazed at his speed in reaching the chair. He balanced, peering out the shaft. "My shoulders," he panted. "I know they won't fit!"

"We shall see."

She had pulled up a hefty table and was standing at an almost even height beside him. Her hands suddenly grasped his shoulders. With the strength of a Sumo wrestler, she wedged him into the opening like a corkscrew.

"Who are...*wh-what* are you?" he whispered. His teeth chattered so violently, he feared he would wake the rats.

"Just a little girl," she replied sweetly. She gave his backside a mighty shove, and he transformed into a cork, popping free, into the daylight.

* * *

Dust kicked up along the road leading out of New Madrid. Drury leaned into the gas pedal. He was miles down the interstate before he detected an unfamiliar bulge in his coat pocket. *He had to know...*

Taking the next exit, he found a secluded patch of countryside and stopped to examine the object.

A brown bottle, labeled "New Madrid Book and Souvenir Shop." Inside, a curly strip of paper. His eyes blurred with moisture as he unrolled it:

I wish Beth a wonderful birthday. Enjoy your trip, mister.
Love,
Alyce

The Night She Left Our World

"I can't hear myself think!" David shouts. He shakes his fist at the churning blackened sky and marches into the house.

The ravens' fragile hierarchy is in vociferous disarray. Surely they number in the hundreds now. The decibel level of vibrato *kraas* and piercing shrieks threatens to split the earth. I clutch at my throat. Tree tops writhe, dislodging all but the fiercest participants in this latest insurrection. The dethroned swirl above, a striking contrast against cotton clouds.

I can *feel* the noise. It pelts like a hailstorm, stinging me senseless. If I did not know better, I would swear my feet have left the ground...

My cheeks burn as I open the back door. The clash between the cacophony outside and David's music locks me in suspension for a moment. I force the door closed and pour myself a large glass of cold water before joining him in the living room.

Coincidence? Or has he been playing Pink Floyd's "Learning To Fly" over and over? It is loud and hypnotic. I do not bother to ask.

Can't keep my eyes from the circling sky...

His smile is cooler than my drink. It douses the fire raging inside me.

Just an earthbound misfit...

We dance.

* * *

Early the next morning I find her. A squadron of ravens mob me as I approach, beaks and claws ripping my jacket. I construct a tight tent of it, covering my head, and peer through a narrow opening. They abandon the chase when I stoop beside her.

I know without touching her that she is as broken as I once was. A wing dangles, bloodied and useless. But she stands and meets my gaze, her spirit intact.

Her eyes sizzle.

* * *

Lenore is tolerating the stiffened gauze swathed appendage with dignity. But her neck ruff shoots out like spiked umbrellas when David intrudes. She emits a low growl.

"I thought you only knew *human* medicine." David backs up and his hand rests uneasily on the shed door's corroded latch.

"A wound is a wound. A bone, a bone," I say.

"And this is a wild animal. They *attack* when they're in pain."

I shrug. "So do human beings."

Our thoughts collide and center on my war-decimated homeland. His eyes flash pity, then settle back into a hard-won notch: our truce of mutual respect. "How do you know Hitchcock's pal is a ladybird?" he asks playfully.

"Educated guess. She is smaller than most, but definitely an adult."

"Well, I'm calling 'her' *Lenny*, just in case."

* * *

David is 'eating crow', so to speak.

"Lenore is almost fully mended." I smile. "Yesterday she received a *second* cautious visit from her ardent suitor. What an incredible wingspan! He is the largest of the flock."

David checks his watch, then sits down to feast on sausages and fresh eggs. "Is she as impressed with him as *you* are?"

"Oh, yes. She is ecstatic! I am certain they have met before. He must be her mate."

After breakfast, I check on my recovering patient. My plan is to prop open the shed door for longer periods each day while keeping a watchful eye. "We have become friends, Lenore, have we not?"

She preens her injured wing hesitantly, not quite trusting it yet. At present we both realize I am her crutch. But I must encourage the return of her confidence. "He is very handsome, this husband of yours." I tilt my head and she does the same.

A chuckling rises from her throat. I laugh and her volume increases. She struts, then pauses to close her chunky beak gently over my wedding band. "He should buy you one of your own." I wink at her.

Awkwardly she shuts both jelly-marble eyes and re-opens them. I feel like applauding, charmed by her attempts to imitate my gestures. She releases my finger and searches my apron pocket for leftovers. Her pleasure is unconcealed as she tears apart and devours three plump sausages...

* * *

We turn from the winding side road, into our driveway, the tires crunching gravel—

"There, David—look! Stop here or we will scare him away."

He kills the engine. "Got frozen food in the back, remember? Romeo the Crow had better make it quick."

"*Raven.*"

"I'm joking, Lora."

David's elbow wriggles against my ribs, but I am engrossed in the huge bird's courting display. Brazen and majestic, he bobs his head rhythmically and raises his wings. Sunlight ripples across the iridescent purple sheen on his "tuxedo."

Suddenly he erupts in bawdy laughter, slowing to a hoarse rattle. Finally it smooths into an expertly rendered *purr*, with the grating eroticism of a jungle cat.

I gasp and hold in a breath. Lenore is emerging from the shed! Her gait is strong, due to repeated test runs. Today there is no coy retreat. She stretches her wings in a graceful arc and prances to where her lover waits.

A warbling series of *quorks* precede her slightly asymmetrical lift-off, and she lands on a low bough, he in instant pursuit. They tangle then sail away together, gaining equal altitude en route to the uppermost limbs of a towering spruce.

"She is beautiful," I say. She is my pride. *Soaring...*

David kisses warm tears from my face.

* * *

There is far too much time to think lately. I am restless, unfocused. Soapy casserole dishes slip from my fingers and make me angry.

David brings a dustpan and squats to fill it with shimmering pieces of glass. "There's another one we'll never have to wash again."

Shooing him, I finish the job myself. "It is doubtful that your parents will want to have dinner with us—with *me* again anyway."

"What? They *like* you," he protests.

"They look at me as if I were a Zoo exhibit."

"And you look at *them* like they were the people who dropped bombs on your family!"

His "knife" embeds itself in my back and I pivot, eager to retaliate. Instead, we just stare at each other...both sorry.

I speak first, desperate to close the gap between us. "My mother used to refer to my rage as 'blood heat'. But that is what got me through medical school. I wanted to exhale one fiery breath and turn evil to ashes. Now, my homeland is barren, a glacier. Those I left behind—*they have frozen their tears*. But compromised survival is not for *me*."

David takes a step toward me but I take one quick step backward. "Lora, you'll be practicing medicine again. We'll cut through this bureaucratic 'red tape' bullshit...and that *is* what you want, right? No compromise?"

I have lowered my head. "My *own* family perished while my hands were busy saving others—"

"You can't be everywhere at once."

"Why not?" I lift my head. We have had this talk many times, and I know I respond as a child would. Mournful. Disbelieving. But tonight the tone of these two words has changed to *defiance*.

I surprise myself. "Mourning is bitter cold, like Winter. Until this moment, I saw no chance for Spring."

* * *

David and I start all over, constructing our world together. Strategic phone calls, letters... Soon there are hints of progress. The instruments in my medical bag are organized and polished. I have recently subscribed to several professional journals.

It rains frequently now and mornings are nippy. I am still outside as much as possible. How *easily* I can pick out Lenore and her husband from the frenzied rabble—

"Look, there in the cedar!" I point, and David pretends to see them too.

The moments I treasure most are when Lenore slips away, when neither of our husbands are watching, and ransacks my apron pockets for delicacies.

I never disappoint her...

* * *

Then one night, Lenore leaves our world.

The trees combust with a deafening mimicry of human warfare. The sounds are not those of beast or fowl, but of shells exploding, guttural wailing, and merciless slaughter. By the following morning the flock has vanished, except for an unlucky few, who, like spent casings lay dead on the ground.

The trees are gleaned bare. Black flapping-shutter wings had swollen to hundreds, then evaporated to none. Overnight. Two weeks later, the trees remain bare...

The sight of it terrifies me.

Coincidence, I am told, by he who possesses no personal knowledge of ravens. But I know them well now. Habitual creatures who *reason*. They do not alter rituals on whim. Their "human" attributes have long elicited my wonder. What lies beneath takes me far beyond that.

David calls this "obsession."

"I call it 'peripheral awareness'." I squeeze out a dollop of honey and dissolve it in my tea. "Do stop referring to them as *crows*."

He pops an ice cube into his mouth. His tongue holds it against the backs of his upper front teeth. So perfect and white.

So unnatural. I hope they break this time when he bites down. He knows I cannot bear to hear him chew ice.

But scarcely an hour later, I marvel at the emotional bond between the two of us. At the way it flourishes in the quiet. He cools the boiling terror inside me with his hands, with those perfect white teeth, that frosty tongue. "At this moment I do not mind being human. I do not even mind being alive."

"*In* this moment," David answers. "That's where *we* live."

His lips touch my closed eyelids. This means he is content too. Ready to close his *own* eyes and float with me into slumber.

Just as I begin to drift, he speaks again. "Lora, you belong to another century."

The words are soft and sad. I want to lift my head but cannot. "No. I belong to another *world*, maybe. Cruelty and pain rule *every* century."

* * *

In the morning I roll to his side of the bed and wind myself tightly in the blankets. His absence always leaves me cold, quite literally. The aching hollow spot beneath my breastbone is still there too, enlarging each day I mourn. I grope for my robe, compelled to convince myself anew. I must go to the shed and then to her grave—and for twenty-four hours more, I shall *know* Lenore has died...

Winter is coming. The chill etches my marrow and my shoes plaster dew dampened foliage into cracks of the brick walkway. "I will *not* look at the trees," I tell myself, but my head lifts as the vow is spoken—

Empty. Only silence, where the birds had clustered. The leaves are varied shades of flame, straight out of Van Gogh's "Allee des Alyscamps". Since the day we moved to our private plot of land, textured splotches of ravens would pepper the bobbing limbs with their cocky brashness.

Two weeks...and I have yet to understand what has happened. I will *never* accept it.

The shed door is propped open, as I left it. I will tear it from its hinges if David dares to close it again. Lingering at the threshold, I make believe she is inside waiting for my healing magic. Our secret ceremonies—

My heart pounds and I turn away. Walking fast, I shudder at the memory of her defiled body, heart gouged from her gaping chest cavity in a manner suggestive of one or more hawks. But their "meal" had obviously been interrupted...and from *somewhere*, while I buried my courageous Lenore, I could feel eyes—

My strides have taken me far beyond the shed, into the browning grass of the meadow. Her resting place is deep, marked with heavy flat stones. During the first week, while her scent was fresh, my "bed" was a sleeping bag beside her grave.

I drop to my knees. "I am here this time to apologize, my dear sister. Someday I will learn how to be *everywhere*."

My lengthy sigh only bundles my tensions, but at last the words are forming. "I have been almost silent since you left me, placid on the outside. I cannot express what smolders within, not to you, not to David. I have not cried. *My tears are frozen—*"

My mouth opens wide and a sound escapes, a raw tumbling howl I did not know my voice could make. A tingle across my scalp prompts me to raise my head and gaze upward.

Behind him, the sun's brilliance is white-hot. He is coasting. Alone.

Abruptly he dips, with the velocity and precision of a fighter jet. In seconds I meet his luminous eyes—and recoil at the contradiction of dull frosted brown pupils. His beak skims my wedding band as I sprawl, my head hitting a pillow of stone.

A hum is circling, like the beating of thousands of wings in a booming funnel cloud. It reminds me of an orchestra come to climax—

The ebony flock drops from the sky, but not to mob me this time. *At last* I know they bear me no malice.

I am aware of an odd sensation in both arms. A lifting, tickling sensation. Pain without measure sears my shoulders for one exquisite moment, then I feel Lenore's husband kiss the tears from my eyes...

Obsession? Obsessions are *weighty* devices, shackles of gravity that hold one down.

But I am weightless.

I fly.

Bring Good Things to Life

No one could figure it out...

Some days they ventured from their homes. Small groups clustered on the high spots where the grass was still green, necks twisting in corkscrew fashion...a simile for their question-marked eyes.

Of course they were frightened. But human beings tend to deny the unfolding of catastrophe. At the very least, they postpone. Acknowledgement is a slow cancer.

Even when the obvious is out of control.

* * *

Jarod caught a glimpse of his wife's face just before she flitted from view. "Isn't there something left in the pantry to use for flavoring?" he griped.

The edge of his plate fried his fingers as a canister of red paprika dinged the wall. He retrieved it from the floor, saying nothing, and casually sprinkled scarlet dots across his meal's shiny grey "skin." The ooze sucked them downward. The effect was like watching supernovas smolder to a dull maroon, growing cold...inert. *Dead.*

Jarod's appetite was gone, but he speared the largest mushroom and stuffed it into his mouth. *Tasteless.* "Damn, Tess, I *know* we had potatoes in the cellar. Why—"

"They're for Tara and Julian!" She re-emerged from the sleep-room. His anger evaporated. Guilt gnawed. "I'm sorry."

The void between them filled with the sound of rain drumming the roof. Feeble rays of green light cast a pulsating mosaic pattern over the kitchen, as unrelenting drops splattered the mold-etched window glass.

"Sorry" wasn't enough. "I'll go over to see Barry. Right now," he said, rising from his chair. He plucked another mushroom from his plate. *Sustenance*, to fuel his determination.

"Will you pay him for his help with no job? He never had much use for you before. He *despises* you now...and so do I."

"Tess..." The way she'd said it ruled out future amendment. Not that it mattered anymore. Her words were justified and her retreat finalized them.

He followed, her path leading to the Tele-Scan. No use competing with its encapsulating drone. News Views was dominating all wavelengths. He pitied those in the lower regions without access. Their hysteria had to be reaching a peak...

Jarod groaned. It was evident media information would be useless to them now. "It's *w-worse*," he babbled. "It's..." His fists tightened, fingernails gouging his palms. Floods had claimed victims beyond estimation, the rains distributed in an even, impenetrable cloud...blanketing the Earth.

Shock parted Tess' puffy eyelids. She flipped through the screens, stopping to alternate between the Sudanese and Australian reports. Isolated camps of drought-stricken Sudanese danced outside their tents, ecstatic children cupping their hands to drink the water falling from the sky.

Her laugh dripped acid. "No more drought. No more famine, Jarod. The world is saved. *Amazing* what thirty-two days of constant rain'll do, isn't it?"

He couldn't speak. Words had never been his domain. He knew only the hieroglyphic language of statistical research, mathematical formulas. *Precise and predictable.* He was a scientist, not a philosopher...and certainly no prophet.

The screen switched to Australia. The announcer's pale hair

reflected the overhead lights, and her vermillion mouth moved in perfect symmetry. Tess frowned, increasing the alternator to Rapid Pace.

The Sudanese announcer's face merged. *The same poreless skin, aquiline nose...*only the backdrop footage varied. Both women's eyes syncopated a rhythm of blinks and blanks, in tune with each syllable.

"They're *cloning* them now," Tess said. "I just know it."

"No. Don't be ridiculous." Jarod eased a foot inside one of his boots and braced, pulling hard.

Tess threw up her hands. "You're so *right!*" She slapped her knees. "The *last* thing I need is to be ridiculous." The Australia screen steadied. Her grin vanished.

He winced and looked down again, positioning his toes strategically. A sharp tug finished the job.

"Australia...Australia is *gone*," Tess wailed, fleeing the room.

Jarod's pulse throbbed beneath his temples. He choked on a sob as he yanked at the second boot. Then, raising his head, he allowed himself a peek...

* * *

Already, his hands were beginning to callous. The boat glided downhill for at least thirty seconds, after the last push from his oar. *Two stops to make*, he reminded himself. The image of the watery grave that had been Australia rattled about in his head, adding another layer to the horrors disguised within curtains of rain.

Each day, each *hour* compounded the assault on one's eyes and ears. *Midday*...and visibility was five feet at best. He saw only vague outlines of rooftops as he completed his descent. The water had risen dramatically, licking the base of the mountain. *Their* mountain, where he and Tess had built their home...and their dreams. He lurched forward, his elbow twisting as he nosedived and clung to the crisscrossed oars.

The boat had slammed into a solid object. He fought the rocking and swaying and reached out to shove an exposed chimney. Cockroaches scuttled from its rim. Shaking his arms violently, he dislodged his craft and flung the glistening insects into the murky depths.

He shuddered. An intermingled sense of awe and repulsion had developed toward the loathsome creatures, one of the few species to succeed at scaling the mountains in increased swarms. Some residents had resorted to utilizing them as a food source, pulverizing and mixing the paste into substances their children would accept.

Not *my* babies, Jarod promised. He adjusted his hat at a slight tilt, directing the rivulets away from his line of vision. In the absence of wind, liquid arrows pierced the mustard-hued heavens. A ghoulish mystery…or *was* it?

He willed his mind to blot the flesh crawling anxiety. The stench of rotting organic matter offended far beyond his olfactory perceptions. The stagnant pool teemed with a soup of decomposing plants, animals, and *human* fodder. He'd turned his head…silently retching these past weeks, when the Tele-Scan zoomed in on such scenes. There was no longer a choice but to wade through the worst of it. He knew the mountain peaks stubbornly jutted skyward. *Illusions of sanctuary*, he thought, but prayed he was still on course.

The occasional *whirr* of an airship cut into the muddle of destruction. He pulled harder on the oars, steeling himself against the pleas from neighbors with whom he'd always exchanged polite small talk. He would slither through the gully, unseen…

The boat pitched to one side and a face exploded from its edge, dipping and sloshing behind a stranger's firmly latched knuckles. "Let me in, damn you—help me!"

Water rushed in, snatching the oar from Jarod's right hand. He clawed, lodging his body between the seat and hull until he'd recovered the handle. Without hesitation, he lifted and swung, concentrating his strength as he brought the oar down on the man's arm.

The head bobbed again. "My kids…" The mouth filled with garbled sounds.

Jarod's second blow bashed the man squarely between the eyes. The grip released…

* * *

The dwellings appeared untouched by the mayhem, almost idyllic. During his arduous trek up Barry's mountain, Jarod had questioned his own sanity. Decay and decline had peeled away, layer by layer—*impossible!*

As he stood outside the compound, heaving and lightheaded, Barry's voice confirmed reality. Jarod did as instructed, turning his face into the Security Sentinel's red beam until his identity was established.

Beyond the gate was a virginal Eden. A cool mist anointed him with the fragrance of lilacs and honeysuckles. He squinted, making his way through a dreamlike intensity of color.

Barry closed the entrance panel behind them. The subdued lighting revealed a half-smile. "You don't look good at all. How are Tess and the children?"

Brackish liquid from Jarod's slumped shoulders spattered the floor. He forced pride down his parched throat. "Dying, unless you help them."

"Tess chose *you*, even after—"

"She regrets it. You've *won*, do you hear me?" Jarod's eyes went wild. "*How*...how did you manage this-this...do you *know* how widespread this mess is? Why is it skipping over you? Our homes are at the same elevation. This isn't logical."

"How did you get through the valley?" Barry motioned to a young man passing the interior doorway. "Please bring us a pitcher of juice. Whatever's freshest...and a tray from the afternoon meal for this gentleman."

"Boat," Jarod said flatly. "No other way left. They're floating thicker than flies. Sometimes, you dump the dead from them or fight the living to steal them. Sometimes you don't even bother to dump out the dead."

"Sit *here*. The sunroom's furniture is washable." Barry's forehead was lined.

Uncertainty? Compassion? Jarod took a seat, exhaustion stilling his tongue.

"So you say I've won. I would have to disagree. *No*," Barry emphasized, "I come in second. *Always*."

Jarod's anger imploded. *Too much at stake*. "I've lost *everything*. This is no time to let rivalry get in the way. We *all* stand to lose. This is *real*!" He waved his arms in expansive circles. "The whole planet is dying, but there's a chance—only *you* can get me in to see Terbrock."

"You expect him to give you your job back?" Barry roared with laughter.

"*Job?* Hell, no!" Jarod's fist hit the armrest. "There'll be no more 'jobs', no *anything* if he doesn't let me try to *undo* this."

Barry sat back, wearing a residual smirk, and Jarod quickly hid his hands beneath the tabletop. Dishes were placed before them, the server's movements exhibiting an athletic grace. His exit, like his entrance, was made in silence.

The aroma of a savory stew mingled with the tropical fruit essence from a frosty ceramic jug.

"Go ahead. Eat." Barry helped himself to a large cup of juice. He stood, pausing to sip, then resumed. "Your guilt is self-defeating when it reaches martyrdom. I'll leave you to ponder that while I make arrangements to send food to your family. Yes, I have an airship in working order. *Two*, in fact." He glanced over his shoulder. "Oh, and you'll have a tour of the hydroponic gardens when I return."

* * *

It was an orgy for the gourmand, its grandeur obscene. Jarod had eaten his fill, yet his mouth watered. He stifled a response, unsure if he was on the verge of laughter or tears.

"It's so simple, really." Barry led the way between two concise rows of mango trees.

Jarod tracked his magnetic footfalls, steered by radar, his eyes goggled with wonder...

"The answers were there, laid out before us. But only the chosen have ears and eyes. It comes down to *that*, Jarod, my friend." Barry pulled a ripened summer squash from a vine which bore resemblance to a weighty green power cord. Dense etchings of shade crawled across his face. "We were once the best of friends, were we not?"

"We *were*." Their games of chess had become habit in early childhood. *Contests, without the need for words.* Jarod remained undefeated.

Barry's steps took them into the brightest sector. Pineapples towered above their heads, their topaz insets gloating perfection. Jarod chafed. "Water has proven itself an excellent growth medium," Barry pointed out. "The delivery of nutrients is flawless."

"I had no idea." Jarod took in the dimensions of the clear domed ceiling. "The expansion is incredible."

"Enough to feed an army, yes. Or a *colony*."

Jarod felt a flush of clammy heat. "Humidity's highest here."

"Sensor controlled, the entire operation. Your prototype was right on target, Jarod."

"But I—"

"The last millennium was a 'figurative' washout." Barry smiled. "The year 3000 will arrive *literally* fresh and clean."

"Clean? It's a cesspool out there! What are you babbling about?"

"You asked to speak to Terbrock," Barry cut in crisply. "Correct? I agree it's fair, and now's the time." He pressed a touchpad on his wristband. "I *am* the only one who can arrange it. True. I'm *second* in command...always second, you know."

"What..."

"It's up to Terbrock to tell you what's happening. Or *not*. *His* call."

Jarod snatched at Barry's arm. "Tell me what? *What?*"

"It could have been different," Barry mumbled, backing away. "*I wish*..." His hand rose, swiping Jarod's shoulder in a distinct gesture of affection. Then he was gone...

Jarod felt a curt tug on his sleeve. "The ship's ready to depart, sir. I'm the navigator."

* * *

I wish... Barry's unfinished phrase paralyzed Jarod with dread. The view out the porthole reinforced his anxiety as the airship floated beyond the mountain's line of demarcation. Fog, then leaden bolts of rain slowed the flight considerably.

Wishes... He drifted. Tess came to the forefront, a poignant diversion. He had coined her "the wish woman" after chance arranged their first uninterrupted lunch chat.

She was an elusive butterfly, vibrant in contrast to the blankness of sterile white lab coats. And she *wished* for things, unselfish things. World peace. Strong, healthy children.

The occluded porthole suddenly cleared. Not a drop of rain. Atop the gargantuan mountain range, a steel and glass mega-structure loomed, its support tubes sprawling outward, poised on the peak like a voracious spider.

The new logo struck Jarod as vulgar in size. Colonial Dynamics Corporation had officially replaced Center for Disease Control. He had yet to find out why...

* * *

Jared braced against the ship's backdraft, wrestling an urge to call it all off. The red beam flashed, and the employee entrance hatch was sliding open.

Tess nudged again. *Had she even acknowledged his leaving?* His final glimpse had revealed her pinched smile, the unnatural stupefied contentment of exhaustion. Her diminished frame was squeezed into Tara's bubble chair, her only response a wordless gentle rocking...

He shoved aside his aversion to airlifts and ducked into one of its circular steel "coffins." The ride commenced with an unsettling vibration. He diverted his tension by rehearsing his plea.

Midway, a sputter, then, a violent shimmying. A pause—and blackness swallowed. His stomach reacted before his brain had a chance to calculate the "fear equation." Partially digested goo shot up his throat.

As he reeled backward, a vacuous *swoosh* caught the capsule in an unseen net, the rebound propelling it upward. Light flooded its reflective interior. Freshly glutted with power, it sped to the top of the shaft...

An empty corridor stretched out before him, echoing stillness like a vault. His initial steps were spongy, but his gait steadied as he plowed forward. Overhead, illumination squares signaled his approach, one by one, and the nape of his neck prickled from the intrusion of "observers"

* * *

Terbrock's greeting was a slight nod, the only indication he'd heard Jarod's footsteps. His profile was highlighted against the window glass, his eyes fixed above the slope of his long thin nose...quite literally looking down on the swarming masses.

"Sir..."

"No need for formality, Jarod." Terbrock's solid bulk swung full circle. "No need for your long journey to recover a *job* no longer needed, either."

"I didn't—"

"Sit. You know I look up at *no one*."

"I'm not here for a job." Jarod hastily seated himself. "I can find out what went wrong. I can backtrack...I *can*." He ripped his hat from his head, feeling the sting from hairs uprooted. "But I'm helpless without the lab!"

"Your tunnel vision is what has handicapped you." Terbrock's pupils widened. "You still don't see the full picture. *Even* now."

Jarod fell silent. *Too much to take in...* Terbrock's uniform bore a curious new emblem. *But the words made no sense.* Jarod's lips moved. "It was meant to restore the ozone layer. Only *that*. Th-the rain...I put out an order to scrap the project. Too risky. My project wasn't ready to be implemented."

"You had no authority to scrap it. See, Jarod? You gave yourself too much credit, and *now* you give yourself too much *blame*. If 'blame' were the accurate term, that is."

"*What?*" Jarod rasped. "What do you call it?"

"Genesis. We christened your 'amplified' project with an appropriate title. Global warming has been vanquished."

"Wait! *We?* You *knew* Barry tampered with...you knew he stole my—"

"Stole? Hardly. The company had purchased the rights, remember? Stipulated in the contract when you were affixed. You were hired on a trial basis, and you proved to be a fine drone. Meticulous in your research. Diligent, *but*...you pretended to ignore the obvious."

Jarod's focus centered on Terbrock's gaudy insignia. *G E*...**Genetic Excellence**. Perspiration beaded his forehead. A mathematician. Yes. Unable to add up simple clues. "You had no right," he hissed. "Violating nature caused this *massacre*."

Terbrock's laugh was forced and brief. "A duty, not a right. You've had it all backwards. This is no *blunder*. The 'Cloud' is self-limiting, timed to dissipate when the task is finished."

A faint, swelling *buzz* permeated the entire complex. Jarod sensed it now. The building vibrated with an invisible force. "The 'Colony'...*tell me*."

"At last you see us." Terbrock's index finger tapped a rhythm attuned with his words. "The Colony has existed, loosely cohesive, throughout decades...*centuries*, if one stretches deductive reasoning. We have metamorphosed as we developed our goal, adjusting our plans to align with nature's plans. That *final* perfection is now in progress. The oblivious or resistant have fallen, their carcasses encumbering all but the most enlightened."

A tranquil smile played at the corners of Terbrock's mouth. "We do regret the loss of an intellect of *your* caliber, to be sure. Alas, it's housed in a swamp of naïveté and delusion. Wasted," he clucked. "But after the present process is complete, the organic sludge will amply fertilize—"

"The *dead*, you mean. *Billions of murdered children*."

"The planet will re-new and cleanse. This past decade's mandated conversion to biodegradable materials in every possible aspect of daily living will all but eliminate a 'clean up' problem."

Beastlike rage took Jarod by surprise, and he lunged. But a blow to the base of his skull brought him and his clenched hand down hard on the desk's glossy surface. He *knew* Terbrock's throat would be forever out of reach, yet he kicked at the fanning black shapes as they draped over and around him.

Jarod's fist made a solitary contact with warm yielding flesh. Attached to its yelp of pain was a sizable price tag. Gloved hands pummeled his spine and ribs as one of the robed thugs yanked him from the desktop by his ankles. His chin struck the floor, the excruciating crunch and searing fire melting his surroundings into a fast-approaching sensory blackout...

There was a brief wave of nausea as Jared was rolled onto his back. Only his eyes retained muscle control. They jiggled. The semi-circle of guards standing over him shared the same unimpassioned face...*exactly* the same face, anchored atop identically clad frames, aligned at equal height. **Detailed duplicates of Terbrock.**

Jarod was semi-aware of his extended moan. He swirled, weightless...sinking into mercy's oblivion.

* * *

It was a hum, comprised of indistinguishable blends of sound bytes from past and present. Intuition told Jarod he still existed. His eyes begged to open, but had forgotten how, his brain at odds with the concept of sensation. Jarod's desire might have been to *stay* in this "place." *If not for the pain—*

The scream was his own, bursting through the muffled cacophony, restoring sound and sight to a hideous clarity. His voice brittled, then broke, clearing space for Tara's wailing and Julian's asthmatic sobs. Tess' eyes widened, exuding fright beyond measure.

Someone wake me, Jarod thought. *Why doesn't mama shake me free of this nightmare?*

He could feel fingers cradling his head. Tess' familiar touch, versus the bludgeoning within. *Yes, he was awake.* The fury of the storm was loosening chunks of ceiling, the powdery *flakes dancing around Tess' matted hair. For a moment, he envisioned a halo.* "My angel," he murmured.

"Daddy, daddy…"

He detected Tara's plaintive, tissue paper voice.

"Did you bring us some food, daddy?"

The perception of his quickening heartbeat manifested only as a rush of blood to his jugular veins. An odd *detached* anguish. He was so very, very thirsty. *And there was water, water…**everywhere**.*

"Tess…I can't move."

It was a desperate *question*, not a statement. She replied by shaking her head. But Jarod knew it meant "yes." He knew he would *never* move his body again. And he wouldn't feel the rise of the flood water…until it reached his neck.

Bird of Prey

Night had passed...

Their gnarled toes encircled gaunt tree limbs picked nearly clean by three consecutive frosts. Bellies engorged with unfortunate rodents, they rotated and puffed, settling into an even-spaced row. The owls killed instinctively, and Berenice wasn't a target. *Yet their presence was a reminder.*

So was the salty taste on her tongue. Biting one's lip to the point of bringing blood was a nasty habit. She couldn't risk squandering concentration, not even *here.* She spat into swelling mounds of multi-hued leaves and trudged on.

No sketching this morning. The light wasn't right. She glanced toward the North Ridge, hastened by cold and the staccato reports of gunfire. Hunters were drawing closer, defying the No Trespassing signs. Their greed was fed by early frost and the resulting loss of natural cover. A ferocious winter had been forecast. *Time to move on...*

She'd vowed to wash the camper before packing up but cut herself slack for having had it rust-proofed in addition to the re-painting. "Details," she lamented, as she mounted the cabin steps.

The door was unlocked. Her stomach convulsed. *Big* detail. She began squeezing the keys into her palm, their scalloped edges punishing her oversight, then hurled them against the wall. To cripple her hand would be the ultimate stupidity.

Summer had been idyllic. As a teen, she might've referred to it as a "spiritual awakening." But the fading of summer currently represented death. Jacob, bright-eyed, eager to start Kindergarten, had sickened and withered...just as leaves were bursting into color, cycling irrevocably into dust. Regardless of how many dollar signs she scribbled, paper checks proved impotent, his descent relentless. As final as autumn decay.

She'd never meant to hurt him.

Her shoulders flinched. She stared at the ringing phone, but procrastinated...until the present, and its urgency, caught up—

"Hello," she said, into the grid of tiny holes.

A disembodied voice from Los Angeles poured into her ear. The woman's air was professional, lavishing praise, just short of gushing. Good breeding would never allow the latter.

Berenice was a product of humble beginnings. It had taken years to unlearn honest surprise and feign a detached confidence. "Very well," she replied. "I'm relocating within a month, so I need to finalize by the end of this week. Do you need to see more slides, or can you make a decision based on those I've already sent? I'd *much* prefer to show the entire collection in one gallery, and... hmm, considering the time involved in sending—"

The commitment interrupted, precisely on cue. Berenice's prowess in select areas left her amazed, as did her inadequacy in others. "N-no," she stammered, "my machine's on the blink. Please fax the contract to my post office box." A deep breath restored her composure. "My pleasure."

She slumped into an armchair facing the open blinds, a recurring thought flooding her. Finally, she met it head on. She *hadn't* meant to hurt Brandon. She'd married him solely as a last ditch effort to save Jacob's life. Jacob's death was sufficient punishment. What kind of monster needed *more*?

The wind picked up. Gray clouds rode the current, blanketing the sunrise. No solar heat today, and the fireplace embers were dying. She re-zipped her jacket. The promise of a California winter would sustain. That, and some overdue luck...

Icy gusts whipped her hair, and the door swung in, knob bruising the wall. She cursed and left it ajar.

As she grappled with shifting logs, her throat tightened. Chopping firewood was out of the question, and money running low. Her supply of both would have to last—

A paroxysm of terror almost released a scream. She didn't move— neither did *he*—but his arms were poised to reach out. "Need help with the wood?" The man's eyes flicked in the direction of the cabin.

"No." She swayed, imperceptibly sliding her foot. His eyes locked with hers, a smile making an appearance. He'd obviously stepped from around the corner of the shed. Her eyes ventured to his shoulder. The strap slung across it held a rifle.

"Um, I'm sort of lost."

Her breath hissed past chattering teeth. "Sort of? Either you know where you are, or you don't."

His expression was sheepish. "I was just passing through."

"You're a long way from the main road."

"I know—do I *ever*." He shrugged, and the rifle skated across his polished orange vest. "Thought I'd do some hunting. Hit a patch of fog that nearly wrecked me. Turned out it was hiding a big rock, and that wrecked my oil pan."

An owl screeched and took flight. The man's gaze darted at the soaring shadow. Berenice shook off an urge to run during the split second his head turned.

"Every drop of oil leaked out. Have to get a tow, if I can remember where I left it. Man, it's cold! Uh, you do have a phone?"

His eyes were wide open. *Round.* But they weren't the glassy, omnipotent globes of a bird of prey...

"Yeah."

* * *

Steam spewed from the spout. Berenice observed his reflection in the stove-hood. The skin atop the bridge of his nose stayed bunched until the shrill whistle was squelched. "Do you smoke?" she asked tersely.

The wide eyes were back. "W-well, no."

"Good." She plucked the kettle with one hand, an extra mug with the other.

"You one of those 'save the environment' folks?"

"Not particularly. Just don't like it." Scalding water devoured his teabag.

"Just kidding. All my jokes fall flat."

"So, what's your *name*? If you have a stroke, I need a clue who to notify."

He blinked. "Um...Jack."

She stopped filling her cup. Her scowl deepened.

"Miles," he finished.

"I have a question for you, Jack Miles."

"Another one?" He stirred his tea and blew ripples across its surface.

She gestured toward his hastily deposited gear. "Are you aware the safety on your rifle is *not* engaged?"

Fingernails flushed red, against the white mug. *Large, interesting hands*, Berenice thought. Strong, but *unweathered*.

"Wish this was bourbon." Jack tossed back a belt and shuddered as if it were. "Been tramping over hills and down ditches, with that barrel brushing the back of my head."

His hand probed the site of the envisioned gaping wound. Locks of hair tumbled forward, and he hooked them back behind each ear. She noted the contradiction of his abundant, just-below-chin-length tresses and the wisps of "crow's feet," pronounced now, as he winced. He cleared his throat, then approached the rifle...

Back turned, he stood for what seemed like forever. Berenice felt the cold floor through the soles of her shoes. A tranquil heaviness anchored her to her chair. She pictured him pointing the rifle, the yellow-blue piercing flash. Maybe it was for the best.

A loud click punctuated Jack's outburst. "Damned safety was stuck!" Neglecting to return his hair to its behind-the-ear position, he settled back into his chair. "Sorry, that was careless. I don't blame a woman living alone for being afraid—"

"What makes you think I'm alone...or afraid?"

Unreadable messages crossed his face. "Assumed, I guess."

"You're not a hunter, Jack."

His mouth re-opened.

"You know *nothing* about rifles."

He puckered into an uneasy snicker. "I'm a beginner."

She laughed, surprising herself. "I don't find it hard to believe you're lost."

He blushed magenta. "I look that stupid?"

"Let's change the subject, but just a little," she hedged. "I saw you admiring my artwork."

"Couldn't help noticing. Awesome." His drink sat idle. "Hmm, *slight* change of subject?"

Nodding, she savored a sip of tea and a pause of suspense. "We were discussing how you look. To be honest, you look far from stupid. To be bold, I find the way you look...*interesting*. Would you like to pose for me?"

His eyebrows shot up. "You're serious? But..." He squinted past the window-glass. "What about the tow truck?"

"Simple. Call back and tell Dave to take it in without interrupting us. He knows me." She paused. "Oh...I didn't even ask if you're in a hurry to get to wherever it is you're going."

"No, no hurry at all. Uh..."

She stretched, reaching for the phone. "Good. I'll call Dave myself."

Jack reeled from his chair. "No problem, just give me that number again."

Under pretense of tidying the kitchen, Berenice eavesdropped, making certain her smile went undetected...

On her return to the living room, she caught him using his flannel shirt to towel off the perspiration he'd left on the phone. "Hey...what kind of posing we talkin' about?"

She'd begun taking stock. *Charcoal or pencil? The 6B Grumbachers had been reduced to nubs over the prolific Summer.* "I want you naked on the bed, of course."

He sputtered, tea trickling down his chin. Dignity forsaken, he dabbed with a shirt cuff.

"Now I'm kidding. Yes, charcoal is perfect for you—and accents with earth-tone chalks." She confirmed the texture of his cheek with the back of her hand, then sampled a swatch of hair between her fingers. "A portrait, Jack. 'Tis a 'head study' I want. Your facial features say things you dare not."

"Wh-what do they say *now*?" His breath tickled her hairline. "You're puttin' me on, right?"

She backed away as he leaned forward. "Sit in the chair next to my easel. Hurry, the light's perfect!"

She heard a tiny groan. Then footsteps, plodding behind...

* * *

The seams of Jack's armor were rusting. After declining Berenice's offer of sherry, he'd reconsidered. His dislike for its taste was conducive to sipping...exactly what she'd intended: a gradual unveiling.

She smirked at the sight of his leg draped over the arm of the chair. Capturing a laxity of his lower lip, she fixed her eyes on the easel, aware his gesture meant *she* had become a subject of study.

"I've never watched an artist before."

"There's a lot to be learned from the art of observation." She blended his chin-line with the edge of a finger and muffled an afterthought. "Profitable, too...sometimes."

"What was that? The *last* part."

She shrugged. "Oh, nothing. I talk to my artwork. Nobody *else* to—" Biting her lip, she ducked from his view. "Can't find the Sepia."

Charging past him, she scattered chalks, paints, and brushes in a flurry of intentional disorder. When she rebounded, Jack's arm shot out, catching her waist. A tug brought her down into his lap.

He wrapped her in a bear-hug. Soft lips trailed her neck. Electrifying...the contrasting sensation of his sandpapery cheek, the intermingling of warm sherry as he exhaled his excitement.

She dodged a kiss. "I barely know you."

"Name's Jack, and life is short." He resumed, on target this time, his hand enveloping the back of her head.

His mouth was regrettably delicious, his tongue transferring musky liquor ambrosia. She clawed his arm half-heartedly. *How easily she could lose herself, just let go.* She grabbed a handful of his hair and pulled. *Hard.*

A yelp accented the squishy loss of suction. As a cliffhanger silence lapsed, his statement of the obvious filled the void.

"That hurt."

"I meant it to," she glowered.

He shook his head. "I'm not especially 'into' that *stuff*." Holds were re-established from new vantage points.

"Jack, that stuff meant *stop*."

"...Stop?" His eyes rolled, wrestling maneuvers stalling. "Something tells me I'd better start apologizing." He looked at his drained glass, but it refused to come to his aid. His smile held dubious remorse. "Sorry, but I'm horny."

"I can tell." She removed herself ungracefully from his lap and scampered to the safety of her easel. His charcoal-rendered eyes smoldered, undressing her there as well. The canvas shook in her grip. Snuffling noises escaped.

"Are you crying?"

She heard his chair scoot. But she was rooted in place, eyelids squeezed shut...

"Berenice?"

He'd pronounced her name for the first time, and its texture swirled around her like a down-filled comforter. His fingers sought out her face—

"That was so damned...*funny*." She choked on a derisive sob.

"Hmm. Distraught, you ain't." His grin fanned her hysteria. Abruptly, he was lost in the portrait. "I look like this?"

His astonishment was sobering. "Yes, you do. Another drink, Jack?"

"If you join me."

* * *

Berenice settled her heels into the hassock. "I don't want to get wasted. Have to go to town after lunch." She eyed what was left of her sandwich. "Sherry makes me ravenous. Fortunately, I don't have to count calories. *Unfortunately*, I'm low on funds."

Jack's brows lifted. "Man, I feel guilty. I insist on helping you stock up. Shame you couldn't make a deal with a gallery in a warm place. Winter in Boulder can be brutal."

She picked at charcoal embedded beneath a fingernail. *Brandon's scoldings about her "grimy" hands making a bad impression on his clients re-emerged.* She snatched her glass and drowned them. "No time to be choosy," she said, looking at Jack's portrait instead of him. "My lease expires in two days. So, Colorado, it is."

She stood, and realized she would miss the odd crunching noises made by the bamboo chair. She was more than a bit woozy. "Oh, and I wasn't hinting about groceries. I'll have plenty to get me there, and an advance waiting. Too bad I'll have to finish your portrait from memory."

"That's my loss…but y'know what?" His smile wandered off-center. "We both drank too much of that bad tasting stuff to be driving to town right away." He swung his shoeless feet from the couch and patted the vacant spot. "C'mere."

"Excuse me?" Her feet were bare, and she had no idea when and why this had come about.

"I told you I'm a physical therapist, remember? Let me take care of your kinks. It's that, or I force grocery money on you."

There was something both child-like and complex about him. Something she wasn't sure she wanted to tap into…

Her neck and shoulders *were* hurting, however. And didn't she need to sit back down and ponder the mystery of her bare feet? "You're right, I'm in no shape to drive." She perched on the edge of the couch.

"Behave this time."

"Yes, ma'am."

His palms circled, warming as they plotted a course. Magnetic. She veered backward, then to the side.

"Nope, not gonna do." He re-positioned his drawn up leg, straddling her, and in the same motion, pulled her in close.

Her mouth flew open, but the high-pitched protest smoothed into a moan. As his thumbs kneaded, her knots abated. "What a wizard. I'll bet you can name your price."

"No." His reply was strained. "I'm a long way from my first million. I'm nearly fifty, and time is...running out."

His legs cradled, allowing his fingers to ransack her psyche and loosen the lock on the trunk stored away in its attic. "Time runs out if it's meant to," she said. "You can't stop it. I tried to, but he died...my Jacob." She caught herself. "Yes, indeed, Jack. Magic hands."

His hands stilled. "Jacob? Who..." The query punctured, then withdrew. "Sorry. I'm sure that's painful, but you *can* tell me."

"He was my baby, my only child. I was forty when he was born. And, yeah, fifty is right around the corner." She suddenly *wanted* to tell him the whole story. "I met his father, Brandon, at my first showing in a prestigious gallery. Sipping champagne with a cultured, wealthy man was flattering. Our dates led to contacts and impressive paychecks...and the chance to fulfill a wish."

The massage resumed and she vented freely. "I'd ignored my maternal instincts. Wanted the perfect love, the perfect father. It didn't happen. I guess I figured *my* time was running out. I got pregnant intentionally, knowing Brandon didn't want children."

She sighed. "I thought he would disappear. Had no idea he was in love with me." A shudder ripped through her. "Love is what he *called* it."

"Hey...we could mix up one fine milk shake with you."

Jack's words were like a finger-snap. Berenice curled into a cocoon, as he bundled her in the quilt from the couch. The alcohol's glow was ambushed by paralyzing cold…

She was a heartbeat away from tumbling over the precipice, onto the downhill slope where the momentum increases—where one watches, but no longer feels. Just the roar of the wind rushing past…

"It burns your cheeks," she murmured, seeing nothing but the opaque backs of her eyelids.

"Must mean you're getting warm again. I thought I might be losin' you."

Jack's voice buzzed against her neck, jerking open her eyes. "Your face is blurry," she pointed out.

"Maybe you should bring your reading glasses to bed. Objects are *much* closer than they appear, baby."

She heard herself laugh. The mystery of her bare feet was compounded, but the cabin's lumpy bed had never felt so luxurious. "I'm toasty now."

"Thought so. Yep, the clothes need to come off. They impair circulation."

"Ah, yes…but I remember a rather confining quilt."

"Quilt?" he asked himself. "Can't recall…"

"The one you replaced with your body."

"Sounds familiar." His lips inspected her eyelids. "Maybe if you described it."

"It was light blue, and—"

"I just thought of a better idea." His mouth covered hers.

For most, kissing was just kissing. For a courageous few, it was an art-form. Jack's tongue slow danced with hers, his lips alternating teases with firm demands. He laced his fingers through her hair and tilted her head back. His tongue anointed her throat, his mouth devouring…

"Is this inborn?" she gasped. "Or did you receive formal instruction?"

"Trial and error. Um hmmm…" He nibbled the buttons on her sweater, probing her breasts with his chin.

She needed no more prompting. She just *needed.*

He summoned both hands to the task of unbuttoning and unzipping. "You wanna wait for me?"

"Are you complaining?"

"No way," he chortled, "and what luck! One of those front-closing thingamajigs." His triumph dwindled. Squinting, he twisted, turned, and pulled...

She brushed his hand aside and squeezed the tiny clasp between two fingertips. Her bra popped open. "Magic."

"I agree." His arms encircled.

Stunned by his tenderness, she felt tears well up. "I don't know if you can understand, but what you're doing has a profound effect on a woman who has nursed a baby. The depth of emotion is...*incredible*."

He paused, and her teeth sank into her lip. Surely she'd destroyed the mood.

His head turned, and he sought out her hand, which had come to rest on his cheek. Interlacing their fingers, he brought her palm to his lips. There, he planted a kiss and lay quietly, his ear pressed against her heart.

Finally, he lifted his head. "I think Jacob's *mother* is incredible."

They made love with no further conversation. It seemed to Berenice that Jack knew intuitively what pleasured her most. They merged with the synchronicity coveted by long-term lovers. Juxtaposed, was the gratuitous spontaneity of 'the first time.' The combination left her weeping and exhilarated.

She nestled in the crook of his arm. "Seriously, I can't remember an experience that compares." A sorrow-less tear balanced on her cheek, a raindrop 'prism' pierced at the mathematically correct angle. In another time, another *place*...she sighed... "perfect" was for fairy tales.

"Maybe appreciation of sex with a special person improves with age, huh?"

Jack's question harbored an odd edge. She turned, watching his profile.

"I... *worship* this little interlude, Berenice. I'm long past fibbing in bed."

If only she could believe—she blinked away her foolishness. The pitiful shrieking of field mice skewered by owl talons echoed in her ears. She tugged at the quilt, betrayed by a rash of goosebumps.

"Cold again?"

Nodding, she presented him with a grateful smile as he re-bundled her. "Jacob used to kick off his blankets in his sleep." Her smile dimmed, and she waited...

A muscle in Jack's cheek twitched. "You were telling me your son had severe asthma, and... things about your ex-husband. At least, the *alcohol* was." He shrugged. "Guess it makes people say more than they plan, huh?"

"What is it you want to know, Jack? I'm gradually remembering what I said. I even remember deciding to change to wool socks..."

His eyes turned toward the ceiling. "I know all I need."

The closure was stinging.

"Uh, your name..."

"What?" Her heart almost stopped.

"I'm curious. Never heard it before." He stroked her arm as if it were a kitten.

Cautiously, she succumbed. "There is a story there. I asked my mother why she named me 'Berenice.' People said it was beautiful— anyway, mom said 'Because of a man I love.' I remember the look on my father's face. I know now it was puzzled amusement, similar to the look on *your* face."

"That'd better not be the end of the story, sweetheart."

"Okay, there's more. In high school, I finally met someone named 'Berenice'...in a story by Poe."

"As in 'Edgar Allan'?"

"Yep."

"Far out."

* * *

Berenice was sober. She inserted the ignition key as the passenger door opened.

"Hey, uh—unexpected delay. Just be a minute. Doesn't take us guys long, y'know?"

She watched Jack trot back up the cabin steps, her stomach taking a dive. As usual, the wind trifled with the unstable lock, and the door re-opened after he disappeared inside.

She exited the driver's seat, readying an excuse in case he suddenly re-appeared. She stopped at the doorframe, straining for a sound.

His muffled voice wafted through the opening... Her body went rigid. He was using the phone.

Hurried sentences ran together, interspersed with breaks in which the tone deepened with emphasis. Although her ears picked out an occasional word, the bulk had the garbled quality of being funneled through a cupped hand. The wind came to her aid once more, with an abrupt lull, just as Jack's clarity peaked.

"Yeah, I'm with her now, and you heard me right, y'dig?"

She returned to the camper with dreamlike swiftness, his words scorching her path. Her scalp soaked with panic. Had she slammed the heavy metallic door? Her kneecap smacked into the steering wheel, and she failed to stifle a cry.

"Hey—what?" Jack slid in beside her.

She steeled herself. "B-bumped my knee." There was an unsteady lapse...

"I'll drive, if you direct me. Okay?"

She forced herself to look at him. "Thanks. I...I think that'll work."

They leaned into the third turn, which she'd indicated in the same manner of the first two...by pointing her finger.

"You're quiet," Jack said. "Bet your knee hurts more than you make out."

Her thoughts careened. If he did anything blatantly suspicious—like a wrong turn—she'd open the door and run...

"Knock knock."

Her head swiveled, the landscape smearing like a watercolor painting.

Jack's smile twisted. "See? My jokes fall flat."

"...Oh no, I just didn't hear you talking. I zoned out."

The engine groaned as he rocked the camper over a clod of hardened mud. "What I said was I wouldn't doubt Dave got himself lost out here looking for my truck."

Their sparse conversation was clumsy with politeness. *Had he caught her eavesdropping on his call?* She gritted her teeth. "Make a right on the blacktop ahead. It leads straight to town."

The road's even surface did little to ease the tension. Snapshots of the day poked at her, out of sequence. The harsh light deepened the creases around Jack's eyes. He wasn't so appealing now...

But a year ago, she'd stopped looking for answers. The test was rigged, so why not enjoy the game? Playing was a choice...with the suicide card tucked into her sleeve.

* * *

Parking was plentiful. Jack grabbed his door handle—

Berenice shook her head. "You don't need to come in. I have more stops to make. Besides, we can get away with not putting money in the meter. Be right back!"

It was overly warm inside the post office. Chafing, she sought out a private corner and skimmed the faxed contract.

After glancing around, she filled in the signature line with 'Mary J. Benton', then skipped to a space reserved for comments. She jotted 'Arriving in Los Angeles one month ahead of schedule. Will be in touch with new contact info.' She finished up and rushed out the door.

A blast of wind iced her perspiring face. She climbed into the camper, finding Jack in an apparent state of relaxation, his neck resting on folded arms.

"Wake-up time. Just want to get some gas...and pay a final visit to a favorite haunt."

* * *

As always, the atmosphere was a full-length velvet cloak that covered her as soon as she crossed the threshold. It was as if the tinkling bells atop the door frame had summoned a nineteenth century butler to exchange it for her coat.

"Spooky place." Jack craned his neck at the rafters. "Why'd they name it 'The Attic Owl'?"

"The owls won't harm you, unless you happen to be a mouse." She lifted both eyebrows. "But beware of the cats."

Jack hunched. "I'm allergic to cats. Bet you can find collector's items, though, if you know what you're looking for."

"Coming here always reminds me of what I'm looking for. What better setting for a used bookstore than a preserved Victorian house? This particular abode has a reputation for being haunted. Believe in ghosts?"

His brow furrowed. "There's not much I rule out...about anything."

"Or anyone?" she shot back. "The poetry room's my sanctuary," she said cheerily, and headed up the staircase. Slowing on the sixth step, she peered over the railing. "Coming?"

His distress was in full naked view. "I think...I want to check out something down here first. I'll catch up.'

"Sounds good." She jogged up the remainder of the stairs, releasing the air from her lungs when she reached the landing. Her mind strayed to the back stairway. The Emergency Exit. She pictured herself running to the camper, driving away...

She sighed. The exit was certain to be equipped with an alarm. She trudged robotically toward the poetry alcove.

Sanctuary lurked inside the attic's mismatched nooks and crannies. Outside the sunlit windowpane, past the balcony laden with flowerpots, the twitter of birds bobbing on limbs could be heard.

She belonged. Yes, she'd visited this house. In her dreams.

The bottom shelves held musty survivors of varied girths, their frayed elegance proof they'd been constructed to last. She sat and drew out a leather hardback. Unable to decipher letters on the worn binding, she searched her pocket for her reading glasses. A gasp rushed from her mouth. Embossed, in gold leaf, was "Berenice: A Tale," by Edgar Allan Poe. Her heart pounded her eardrums as she lifted the cover...

A glow bathed her upturned palms. The inscription was as fresh as if it had been penned that very morning:

For Sarah—

Kindest Regards,

Edgar Poe

Berenice was swept away. Pure coincidence, she told herself. Mere chance her mother's name just happened to be Sarah.

A swirl of vertigo hit. Flowers leapt from the carpet with such ferocity, she threw out a hand to steady herself. Beside the empty slot which had housed the book she now clutched to her chest was a volume she hadn't noticed...or hadn't wanted to: "Flowers of Evil", by Charles Baudelaire.

She shook her head but couldn't banish the 'memory stamp' of Brandon. Compelled, she extracted the book and opened its periwinkle tinted cover. Brandon would salivate. The 1933 edition was complete, with lurid illustrations. She located Brandon's favorite, recoiled and turned away.

Her chin dropped. A third book shouted a stark title: "The Black Cat." Poe's infamous story of a madman who took delight in the murder of his wife...

Jacob was dead. Even Brandon's money couldn't save him. She viewed her baby's lifeless body again, with her mind's eye. What kind of a madman needed more?

Brandon. He would always need more.

A puff of wind on her back forced a look toward the window. Shut tight. Another flutter, a firm nudge, and a *purrr* pounced into her lap. An ebony feline pirouetted twice before settling into his newly claimed throne.

A quote from "The Black Cat" echoed inside her skull: "I had walled the monster up within the tomb!"

With both hands, she cuddled and stroked the cat to his heart's desire. "Some monster."

* * *

As she descended the stairs to the main floor, the tinkling of piano keys drifted past, then ceased. Hearing only the subdued rustlings of shoppers, Berenice glanced backward. The cat, whom she'd seen tracking her on silent footpads, had vanished.

Again, the piano, this time anything but timid. The classical piece was intricately evocative.

No sign of Jack. She would hunt for him after taking care of business at the check-out desk, she decided. She prickled with curiosity about the antique piano she'd assumed was an idle fixture. Did anyone actually play it?

The proprietor lounged in his chair, a half-smile aimed at the figure occupying the piano bench…

Jack! His fingers coaxed rich tones from the mahogany upright. Berenice stacked her books, transfixed.

A conspicuously sour note brought a scream of silence. Jack withdrew from the keys, his fists striking his thighs.

"Now, now," chided the man at the desk. "She just needs a little tuning." He picked up the books and inspected them, his eyes enlarged in the lower half of his bifocals.

Jack was clearly incensed. His white knuckles clutched his knees. Berenice coughed to signal her presence. She and Jack both jerked at the intrusion of a thud from the cash drawer.

Jack failed to conceal his 'wounded animal' eyes.

"Jack, I… had no idea you could play like that." Cold coins dropped into her palm, and she fussed with the bag of books.

The bench scooted. "I'm rusty."

Mumbling, the proprietor disappeared into the storeroom.

Jack's eyes glazed. "I had plans. Concert pianist…" He broke off. "Unbelievable, right? Not the type for 'longhair' stuff."

His laugh dripped sarcasm. "Well, I did manage to grow my hair.

Almost got married, too. She lost interest when I got rejected by Julliard. They all said I'd never amount to anything, so who was I to disappoint 'em? Yep, I've been 'nothing' in more places than I can name."

Berenice struggled to recover her voice. Two jousting entities had taken charge of Jack, one dancing in a circle of fire, the other dragging a self-imposed anvil of brimstone. "You don't just play the piano, you're an artist. Snobby rejections don't make less of you."

"Then I made less of myself." The bench tottered on uneven feet as he jumped up.

She could barely keep up with his strides as he headed for the exit. The bells jingled a melancholy farewell...

He hesitated, then reached for her arm. "I'm sorry."

"I want to drive." She pushed past. Before she could start the engine, he'd hurried around to the passenger side.

A clutch of giggling children burst from a toy store, their mothers swooping into a tight corral. The camper vibrated on ignition. Berenice swung from the curb, exaggerating the arc, and floored the pedal. She reached toward the radio.

Jack caught her sleeve. "We need to talk."

"We do?" She yanked from his grasp and switched on the radio. "Good! Alice in Chains," she said. "Grunge murdered Disco. Justifiable homicide."

As the song ended, she switched off the radio. Streets swam by in silent despair. Her cheeks moistened. "I've always traveled in my mind. It was my way of dealing with situations with no way out. I guess all kids do that. I could feel my illusions, though...see, taste, and touch them. Nobody could remove me, not even me."

She laughed. "I could wander for hours in my artwork visions. Hopefully that 'weakness' has become a 'plus', because survival costs real money. Still, I do paint what suits me. I haven't sold out entirely, eh?"

He touched her arm. "Please...tell me more about Jacob."

She railed against the imposition. "Why?"

"I need to know." He switched on the headlights.

"...I would've died for him, killed for him. I don't expect you to understand." She narrowed her eyes, despising the tricks dusk played.

"Berenice, you have to leave town right away," Jack blurted. "I mean..." His urgency skittered into the shadowed brush. "I've been...I'm delaying you."

She said nothing. Awkward miles unrolled, and the gathering darkness befriended her. She recognized the taste of blood but couldn't spit it out.

Jack was conciliatory. "I may be way off here, but—" He braced against the dash as she turned onto rough road. "This is one thing *need* to say. You're not a fling to me. I thought we could just say goodbye, but I... can't." His voice quavered. "Who am I kidding? You must already have somebody."

"No," she said woodenly. "I'm alone, here and everywhere." The tires muted as they met the driveway. The stillness was colder than autumn's passing. It was as cold as death.

She shrank and pulled away. Jack's empty hand was suspended in the glow from the dash. "What's wrong, Berenice? Why so tense? I just figured you needed comfort." His face was indistinguishable, backlit by the yellow bulb atop the cabin door.

"Let's talk...inside," she said.

* * *

"I have a lot packed." She arranged towels in a cardboard box, her eyes on the one beside it. Jacob's clothes. "Some, I've never unpacked."

Jack sandwiched newspaper-swaddled dishes between towels, then interlocked the box flaps. "I'll take these and load 'em with the rest."

"Wait." She'd blocked his path. "Be extra careful with the one on the right."

"I promise, Berenice." His words held empathy.

Or was it an illusion?

His eyes leveled. "It's time to have that 'talk' when I get back, y'dig?"

Y'dig, y'dig, y'dig—her blood chilled...

She'd calmed by the time she heard the door re-open. "By the way," she said, keeping her back turned. "How about your truck? Dave's open late tonight."

"Oh, forgot to tell you. I called while you were in the post office. Good news—fixed by now. He patched it 'til I get somewhere with no wait on replacement parts. I sure don't want to hang around a week more here...well, you know that."

He'd traveled closer with each sentence. His arms wrapped around her. "I'll call back in the morning. A little more loading up, and we can be ready to leave by noon. I love Colorado. How about letting me tag along? If you get tired of me, you can toss me off a mountain. No pressure. I *mean* that. Deal?"

She detoured the hand edging toward her breast. "You did say you wanted to talk?"

"Uhh...trying to remember."

"I have a surprise." She pumped lightness into her tone. "But first, you have to let go."

"Well, all right." His hands retreated to his pockets as he watched her rummage through the canned-good cabinet.

She held up the prize. Grabbing two glasses, she sauntered to the table.

"Now, wait a minute," he grinned. "This morning you said…"

"I was a bad girl this morning. Didn't mention my stash of Southern Comfort."

"That's worse than bad, m'dear." He uncapped the bottle. Amber liquid gurgled into her glass.

"Whoa! This stuff really loosens my tongue."

"Countin' on that." He poured himself a generous share and headed for the living room.

"I'll be there shortly," she called out. "Soda and ice for me."

"Sissy."

The clock ticked and her heart sped. She slipped into the bedroom and opened a drawer...

Jack looked comfortable stretched out on the sofa. But as she approached, he gave himself away. His face was drawn, his smile manufactured. Placing her drink on the coffee table, she knelt, covering his upper body with her own, and kissed him.

Cool droplets trickled down her shoulder, and his arm lowered across her back. Her lips blazed a trail to his ear. "Your glass is leakin', baby."

"Oh..." His reach fell short, as he strained toward the table.

"Here, let me get some coasters. Things could get...distracting."

"Sure," he said, surrendering his drink.

She matched his promising smile, letting it accompany her to the kitchen. "My, my...nearly half gone. You're mighty thirsty."

Chloral Hydrate tablets dropped from her fingers and plinked into the pool of alcohol. "You don't mind if I add a touch more while I'm out here, do you?"

"Not likely," he laughed.

Two'll do the trick, she thought. The prescription bottle was three-quarters full. Her undealt 'suicide card.' But it had other uses...

He beamed as she handed him the doctored elixir. A gulp brought a watery-eyed wince. "Wow, what a kick. Hey...you never showed me what you bought."

She shrugged. The bag crinkled, and excitement converged with dread as she gave him the first book.

He balanced it on his knee. "Looks like a winner." His eyelashes flickered, and his fuzzy smile made her feel dingy. "Berenice: A Tale," he read out loud. "Amazing."

"Look at the signature on the inside cover." She lowered her eyes, the book on her lap bearing down like an angry fist.

"Don't see one."

"What" Berenice rose, Baudelaire's book tumbling to the floor. "Here, right..." She paled. The inside cover was bare, except for a mildew stain. "It...it must've been some other book."

"That one?"

Flowers of Evil lay at her feet, flung wide open, mauling her with Brandon's favorite, "A Martyr."

Jack set Poe's book on the coffee table and eased onto the floor. He studied the illustration beside Baudelaire's poem. "Gory. A headless woman." Sluggishly, he emptied his glass.

"My ex-husband adores that poem, especially the illustration. The murdered woman's lover simply wanted to insure her fidelity. Look at the way he lifts her severed head by the hair for a farewell kiss. Charming."

The book thumped shut, and Jack added it to the one on the table. "Why do you even want…" His knee wobbled, then went out from under him. "Christ," he muttered. "Start…started t'get up. I…"

Embarrassed laughter filled the gap. He sat, resigned, legs splayed to counterbalance, and mopped his brow.

"Whiskey brings out the fool in us, Jack. Eventually, you either stop being foolish, or it stops you. Wisdom comes with age, correct?"

His eyelids battled him.

"I'll tell you more. When I was a dewy-eyed flower child, safe in my living room, Vietnam was a TV spectator sport."

"Um hmm…it was a trip," Jack slurred. After another aborted attempt to rise, he flopped onto his back. "Listenin'," he assured, one eye mistracking.

"I cried for those poor children, those innocents in the middle…but I really couldn't know what the mothers felt. The terror."

Jack's hand closed loosely around her ankle.

"The soldiers in the trenches," she added. "Pawns."

"Ber-Berenice, I have to tell y-you—"

"Divorces," she interrupted. "Legal, immoral battlegrounds." Scalding teardrops splashed her lap. "Brandon used Jacob as a control—and when his 'tool' died, he didn't shed a tear. All I saw was rage. His hold on me was gone."

She slid from her chair, curling up beside Jack. "Remember the scar?

The one you found here, on my neck. Yes, it was one of many things you questioned me about. So curious, weren't you?"

His lips moved without releasing a sound. His arm rose, and his hand grazed her knee, flailing limply before crashing downward onto his chest.

"I lied," she said. "It wasn't an injury from a car accident. Brandon put it there. With his newest 'tool'—a knife."

Jack's face contorted, but Berenice no longer cared about anything he wanted to tell her. The weight of his body held him harmlessly against the floor until he slipped into unconsciousness...

* * *

There was one reflexive blink. Then, incredulity cast over his eyes.

"Trust me, Jack. The safety is disengaged." Her finger rested inside the semi-circle of the trigger. The barrel pointed at his heart.

His chest lifted slightly—a shallow, willed breath. A word slithered through his pursed lips. "Please..."

She smiled. "My loving husband taught me how to use a rifle. Correction—ex-husband. How sloppy of him to send an amateur after me. You do know Brandon, don't you? Just nod. I know your throat is dry."

He swallowed hard, compounding the difficult act of nodding while lying flat on his back. "Let me explain."

She cocked her head. "Hmm, that means I'd have to continue trying to sort the truth from the lies. Nope, sorry—out of time, out of energy. Been busy during your nap. I'm ready to go."

"You don't have to be afraid—"

"You're telling me? I'm holdin' the gun!" Her laughter quelled when the barrel shimmied. "You didn't call Dave. There's no 'Dave'. I gave you an invented number, and you pretended to use it. I've been playing you."

"It's not what you think. I called Brandon just before we went to town..."

"I know. I followed you and listened."

"...Then you heard me tell him—"

"I heard exactly enough."

"Wh-what? You couldn't have—"

"If you say another word, I'll kill you." Her panting grew strident, fury unleashed in the quivering barrel. "I sh-should've killed you—why didn't I? You came here to kill me."

His head rolled slowly and deliberately from side to side. "No."

"Get up!" She'd spun into a whirlpool of hysteria and cycled back to the surface. "I insist we leave together. Good news, eh?"

He pulled himself up. "He never 'enlightened' me about Jacob. I didn't know. I'm a private detective. He said to find you, that you stole money—"

"Let's go." The rifle stayed trained on his chest. His face was a fuzzy peripheral, his words tuned out. "My guess is he's on his way, to a meeting place you arranged. Around noon, it was? We're early, Jack. Still pretty dark, but it'll be dawn soon."

"No meeting place. Don't you understand? I told him to stay away—"

"Stop stalling. Move!"

He edged toward the door, stopping to pick up his coat. "He knows your present location, but that's all."

"Don't put that coat on—if you don't hurry, I'll—"

"You have to believe me. It didn't take long to realize he conned me, and I told him to back off. But...it's so much worse. That scar—I... give me the rifle, Berenice!"

"No!" Her mind reeled. "You're driving me out of here, and if I see him, *I swear I'll kill you both.* If there's no set-up, there's nothing to worry about, right?"

He sighed, and she let herself look into his eyes, where she could find no malice. But she was so tired, so groggy...

"It's you I'm worried about," he said. "What if he gets the first shot?"

Her reply was brittle. "With a knife? You don't know him like I do. He became Baudelaire's obsessed 'Martyr'. Brandon used sweet words like an eraser...then he cut my throat." She motioned with the barrel.

"Open the door."

It occurred to her to look back just once, as she stepped onto the porch. She'd distill the sanctities of summer and put them in her pocket for safe keeping, for all the autumns ahead. The evergreen hedges were sickly gray brown under the spell of the yellow bulb...always hiding her view of the sunrise from that angle...

An owl's shriek sliced from above. Her hands stung from the skidding of steel and wood, coming up empty. *She ran.*

"Wait—no!"

She bolted away from Jack's voice.

Then came the impact of what felt like a sparsely padded wall. A vise-like clamping of her ribs—

"Miss me, darling?" Brandon's teeth found her earlobe, while a steely icicle licked her throat. The 'Martyr's' blade would complete its task—

Yellow-Orange flashed, as an ear-splitting crack rang out. The slumber-shaken winged creatures vacated the trees, in a collective swoosh. Berenice heard and felt a guttural moan as she plummeted, in still-framed notches, to the ground...pinned beneath the monster.

She lay still, forgetting how to blink, her eyes glued to Jack's silhouette. He lowered the rifle, and with smooth precision, engaged the safety.

She blinked—and he was beside her, dragging away her gore-splattered burden, asking questions she was far too weary to comprehend. *Of course she was all right. She was free...*

"Forgive me, and I'll forgive myself someday, Berenice. I'm no 'beginner'—that was my one good lie," he said bitterly. "I got drafted after Julliard rejected me-—but I volunteered for this tour of duty, didn't I? Believe it or not, I've never killed before—not anybody or anything—not even in 'Nam. Some 'detective'. I resign."

"Shhh...I was right the first time. You're no hunter, Jack."

* * *

Owls (Les Hiboux)
*By Charles Baudelaire

Densely clustered amidst night trees,
Owls line in rows, an evenly spaced frieze.
Like shrouded buddhas, they think;
Unveiling red eyes...they blink.

Stilled by instinctual calm,
Heavily cloaked in darkness balm,
In silent flight, unclouded by light,
Their duty cycle repeats.

This lesson is transparent to the wise;
Reward is most often won by guise
And unperturbed deceit.

But Mankind, wistful—gasps,
Sees rapture at hand...
Then, self punishment demands,
As it eludes a hasty grasp.

Translated from the French by Jane Gwaltney

Good for What Ails Them

He wasn't really a criminal, was he?

What a farce. This whole thing's a farce. Maximum security? Paul laughed out loud, then spun around, startled by the echo off humid bricks. He resisted laughing again. He stood motionless, taking in the scurries and squeaks of bugs and rodents. One over-zealous rat vaulted over his shoe. Stomping them didn't appeal anymore. They weren't the enemy.

The ride had been lacking in creature comforts. Scrunched partially inside a hatch-less wheel well, he'd imagined himself a pinball during extended play. He was sickened from the exhaust by the time Betty opened the trunk and upchucked shortly afterward.

Here, sugar, she'd said. Take a Coke with you. It'll settle your tummy. His hand reamed the pockets of the borrowed coat. The rolled-up bills were still there. Cool. The drained Coke can sailed a good length of freedom before hitting a dumpster. Dogs barked and he ran, giddy with good fortune. Morgue Duty had unexpectedly opened the rusty iron gates at the State Institution for the Criminally Insane. The cadaver had no place to spend his stash now. On the other hand, Betty had 'house payments to make.' Paul slowed to a forced casual pace, reminding himself the worst was yet to come. He drank in the smell of rain…

The cab was exactly where Betty'd said it would be. The diner was closing and the residuals were swept out with the dust. One of them sported a symbol of his trade: a black hat with rigid visor. The man's tap-reinforced work boots clip clopped toward a tired old Buick. A bad paint job had almost obliterated the vehicle's former tour of duty. 'Washburn County Cab' seemed destined as its final assignment.

Paul waved an arm. "I need a cab. Are you busy?"

The man flipped a toothpick into the gutter before swinging open the door to the back seat. "Nope," he said to the murky interior. He turned and faced his client. His eyes were expressionless, but his hand made an expansive gesture. With a shiver, Paul obeyed, sinking into the protesting springs and matted lumps of foam rubber. The heavy steel door slammed. *Claustrophobic.* Like a prison cell. The yellowed dome light came back on as the cabbie got in front. His hat wasn't a snug fit and moths had sampled his greasy jacket.

Paul's attention wandered. The latest *Rustler* magazine centerfold, clad only in stars and stripes, was duct taped to the back of the driver's seat. Her hair was cinnamon colored. *Like Shelly's.*

An upward glance caught the cabbie's gaze in the mirror over the dash. "So where we goin', stranger?" he asked.

Paul composed himself with great effort. "To the bus station in the next town. Belvedere, isn't it, if you head north?"

"Yeah. But it's a long ways. Sure you got the funds? Don't see any luggage. Not even a backpack."

"I guarantee it." Paul pulled some twenties from his pocket and displayed them. "I lost everything. Well, almost. I have enough money, but I'd rather not go into all that. Got ripped off and I'm embarrassed, okay?"

"In that case, make yourself at home and call me Jake." The engine coughed then started up. "Can't remember the last time I got embarrassed."

"Rats," Paul whispered, then laughed.

The cab did a swerve. "What say?"

"Nothing...never mind."

"I just gave you my name, kid. What's yours?"

"Oh. Paul. It's Paul." His knees began to shake.

"Hey, whatcha think of this, Paul? 'Bout to get myself married again. Maybe. I'm probably nuts. My ex was a snobby bitch." He sighed explosively. "Yeah, women are trouble. Better than the alternative though."

"Alternative?"

"Being alone. Can't stand that." The cab barreled down a street that was darker than dark.

"I don't mind being alone now. I killed the woman I loved."

Jake screeched to a halt at the deserted intersection. "What the hell did you just say?" The traffic signal swabbed the windshield with flashes of red. "Let me get a good look at you. Another crash-out from the state institution, I bet."

Paul's scalded eyes narrowed. "No."

Jake swiveled. His hand lunged over the back of his seat and yanked Paul's coat open, buttons flying. "Is this the new get-up for street punks? Hospital PJs?"

Before he could respond, Paul felt the seat knock the breath out of him.

Jake floored the pedal and yelled above the engine's roar. "The decent folks in this town never had a say about buildin' that crazy house here. They wanna get rid of you loonies, but getting rid of a problem doesn't always mean it's gone. You think you're the first wife killer I had in my cab?"

Paul's eyes locked with his tormentor's in the mirror over the dash. He gaped, desperate to speak, to regain control. *He wouldn't go back.*

"Relax, kid. I'm not a judge." The car veered onto a highway ramp. "Just a good citizen doin' the town a favor. One less murderin' psycho's the way they see it."

"I didn't murder her."

"Make up your mind."

Hysteria grabbed Paul and shook the words out. "I didn't murder her. I didn't kill her, but I loved her and she's dead—she's dead because of me." Suddenly he was enraged. "I didn't say she was my wife either—my girlfriend, okay?" he shouted.

Jake grew quiet and gradually matched the posted speed limit. "I'll take my fare, and in advance," he said. "Puttin' my ass on the line here."

Paul's heart thumped. "Do you mean..."

"I'll get you to that bus station, kid. Got a feeling you're guilty of nothin' but feelin' guilty. Like I said, I had a *real* psycho wife killer in this cab before, and he ain't like you or me. He made a big splash in the papers, statewide. His name was Don Taylor. Ring a bell?"

"No."

"Wow, what am I thinkin'? You're way too young to remember. What are you, 'bout nineteen?"

"I'm twenty-four."

"Sorry, old man. Hey, it gets lonesome out here. If you wanna unload, I'll listen this time."

"Yeah, well...her name was Shelley. We were both medical students." Paul's head dropped into his hands. "I-I don't know if I want to talk about it."

"No pressure. I'll turn on the radio if y'want...hmm, a doctor. That's somethin'."

Shelley...why didn't I let you do the driving that night? "Her spine got messed up in a car accident." *I was drunk, and too stupid to admit it.* "She got hooked on painkillers, trying to study, to sleep. Sh-she got to the point of injecting Oxycontin. Crushing and mixing the tabs for injection can be lethal. But she was in so much pain. Confused. So I took charge." Paul's fist clenched. "She didn't have a lot of choices after her prescriptions were cut off. I started stealing whatever I could... 'adjusting' supply records at the hospital. It was there and she needed it. But then I screwed up."

"Yeah? How?"

"I got desperate to break the cycle before we both got caught...or worse. I had a close friend who had all the answers. Said to have the guts to make the 'correct ethical decision.' Do the tough love shit. Make her go to rehab by cutting her off. Well, I did. I thought she was all out, but she wasn't. Oxycontin. She still had a few. She knew the risks of the IV route, but at that point, the way she saw it, she was alone. And that's how I found her. Alone and cold, with the needle still in her arm."

"Hey, that's really rough. Bet your friend felt bad too, y'know?"

"Yep. He sure did. Especially after I held a whole class hostage with a gun in his face. But I'm crazy, remember? It was a toy gun. He pissed his pants because of a toy. I couldn't stop laughing. Not until I woke up in the hospital."

"A toy?" Jake whistled. "The only guy in danger of gettin' killed was you. Christ, that's just plain..."

"Crazy? Not really. Just a simple matter of *ethics*. That's the first lesson at doctor school. First, do no harm: the Hippocratic Oath. Ever heard of it?"

Jake's shoulders tensed. "Well, I feel for you, no kiddin'." He lit a cigarette and puffed for a while. "How 'bout a rest stop? No bus leaves 'til nine in the morning in Belvedere. They won't be looking for you 'til later than that, if they do at all. Once you're over the county line, they won't bother. You can bank on it." He skidded down the Belvedere exit. A roadhouse perched on the side of a steep bluff, beer signs winking.

* * *

"Let's sit here." Jake dragged a chair up to the only table with a view. "I like to see what's goin' on outside and behind me at the same time. *Shit*, I can't see the cab. She looks like a heap, but the engine's cherry. And she's solid. Ain't too many things harder to kill than a Buick." His smile faded. "Wonder what joker took my parking place?" He twisted and scanned the room. "Don't see no strangers. None other than you."

"Yeah? I guess you caught me then."

Jake looked perplexed. And not amused.

"The stolen car I had in my pocket. Had to park it somewhere." Paul's grin was shaky but earned a belly laugh. He appreciated the drafty spot Jake had chosen. His ill-fitting coat was conspicuous but

61

exposing the pajamas underneath could be a one-way ticket back to the loony bin.

"You drink beer, dontcha?"

"Sure."

"Good. Don't mean to preach, but dope makes you a dope. Around here we do just dandy with a couple beers."

Paul mulled over the fact that Washburn County was notorious for meth labs. *Oxycontin's 'Hillbilly Heroin' around here, Jake dude*, he thought. A loud chuckle slipped out.

"Mighty cheerful for a kid in your predicament if you ask me."

"I'm insane."

Jake crooked his finger in the bartender's direction. "That's Alicia, my 'intended'," he said. "The lady behind the bar, not the chippy with the tray."

Alicia finished shining a glass, answering Jake's call with a peculiar half-smile. The stools were empty. After a glance at the clock, she approached the table.

"My fare's just passin' through. Decided to stop and wet our whistles." Jake beamed. "Paul, this is Alicia."

"Good to meet you."

"Uh, same here." Paul was startled by her level gaze. He looked away then back again.

"She's a decent gal. Here, baby. Business is good tonight. Start us on the first round." Jake latched onto her collar and pulled her down to his level, planting a wet kiss while tucking money into her cleavage.

"No, honey. I'm doing fine. Really." She removed his hat and ruffled his hair. Her fingers slipped the money back into his pocket.

After a twenty second stand-off, he switched gears. "Aw, okay. But you just might get an extra big tip," he winked.

When he turned, she snapped upright and shot him in the back with an incensed glare. She wiped his slobbers from her cheek and disappeared into the 'Ladies' room.

Jake emptied his bottle and squinted past Paul, somewhere beyond the filthy window. "I'm lucky to make any money at all. Only one cab company in town, but they roll up the sidewalks at night. Except for the taverns. That's where I get my fares. Lots of good ol' boys would be splattered on the road without my taxi service. Day driver gets the rich church ladies and those hungry housewives goin' shoppin'. Hungry enough to eat you raw, balls an' all, is what he says." He loosened his belt and burped. "Well, shit, we play the cards we're dealt." After Alicia returned to the bar, Jake let loose a wistful sigh. "Yessireee, that's one good woman there. Decent."

A pouty waitress headed their way. On her tray she balanced part of the contents from her overflowing blouse, alongside two beers. "Alicia said she'll bring the next round. Here's your check."

Paul was thirsty. He gulped down half the bottle before he realized it and his stomach expressed its resentment. "Do they have any food here?" The juke box started up, drowning Jake's reply. It jangled Paul's nerves. As Kenny Rogers belted out the last chorus of 'The Gambler,' he chugged his beer.

"What kinda work they have you doing back there, kid? You know, with your education and stuff, I would think they'd—"

"I had morgue duty," Paul said. He recited the job description. "Help undress the deceased for the shrouds. Gather the personal effects for the family, if any." Vivid images of his most recent trip to the morgue raced through his brain. A slideshow. The elderly man's smile was hypnotic, especially in death. "The last guy I took down was a friend," Paul said, his detachment wavering. The old guy had seen the Reaper's approach: *You know those thick soled shoes of mine, boy? They're hollow. My kin's all gone, so when you take me down to the Cold Room, hide those shoes. There's cash in 'em. Tell Betty I trust you...*

Alicia was true to her word, dropping off two more frosty bottles, plus a bonus of nacho chips and cheese. The beer started tasting better and better. Paul's surroundings softened, then Jake's whisper cut through the haze.

"Curious. How'd you bust out?"

Paul bit back an automatic reply. *Damn, almost slipped. Almost betrayed Betty, his angel-in-white. Drugs, Alcohol and Stupid. The Holy Shit Trinity.* "A careless orderly. Long story, man." He flapped his hand and looked away. "You're ruining my buzz."

"Okay, okay."

Everything and everyone in sight was sepia toned. Paul crammed a couple of sticky orange tortilla chips in his mouth and headed for the restroom. It was filthy, pungent with urine. "You have a promising future ahead of you, Paul," he said to the cracked mirror.

He wobbled on the way back. People clinging to chairs and each other took little notice. Their bursts of idiotic laughter sent him flashing back to the institution. Parallel universe. Small wonder the 'decent folks' feared the 'loonies.' He returned to the table and saw Jake messing with what looked like a cardboard sign lying flat in front of him.

What the hell? "That's a chess board," Paul said, flabbergasted.

"How 'bout that? So it is...and I ain't never been defeated. Not that I can find many to play with. The fella I usually massacre's not around tonight. Guess I'm shit outta luck."

"I play. I'm *good* too."

Jake smirked.

"Look, I'm a little nervous for games," Paul said. "I'm wired and tired at the same time. You could say I'm concerned about my future."

Clinks of glass from a nearby table turned both their heads. The waitress, several 'empties' clutched between her fingers and thumbs, eyed them while she cleared debris into a large rubber pan.

Jake polished a tarnished queen with his handkerchief. "Now, Cindy over there, I bet she's a card player. Every time I look at her, I think *poker*."

Cindy abruptly took flight, leaving her work behind.

"Okay, Jake. Changed my mind. You're on." Paul settled in. So did his determination. Defeat wasn't on tonight's agenda…

Two hours later, the roadhouse was nearly deserted. Jake stretched, smug. "Must be like ridin' a bicycle. I think I could go for years without playin' and still beat anybody that comes along. Some things you never forget."

"I'm sleep deprived. Couldn't concentrate." Dominating Paul's peripheral awareness was Alicia. He'd felt her heat throughout the game.

"They rent rooms in the back. I can drum up some more fares while you sleep off bein' a loser and be back bright and early. Just don't go lookin' for consolation with my woman."

Jake's guffaw pushed Paul to the brink. He almost told him Alicia couldn't possibly be his 'woman.' *She's beautiful, you ignorant bastard. Intelligent. That's my Shelley, ten years from now. That cinnamon hair. Soft slim hands.* He could imagine Alicia nude, the smell of her skin. "I need some air first," he said. The knot in his throat was choking him. "I'll be right back, okay?"

"Sure, sure," Jake said. "Gotta go take a piss anyhow."

Paul stumbled out the side exit and tried to orient himself. He wandered until he found the cab, forlorn, at the far end of the lot.

What if Betty was wrong? The toes of his shoes rooted in the crumbling concrete and he swayed, indecisive. An owl hooted above. A chill rattled his teeth as he grabbed the handle. With a loud prolonged creak, the cab door opened. *Just like Betty said it would.* The frigid leather seat was a shock. *I can't do this,* he thought. He was freezing cold, shaking, his eyes darting in all directions.

They're here! He doubled over, his head grazing the steering wheel— and freed the icy bundle of keys from beneath the floor mat. It was easy to tell which one fit. He'd noticed the laminated chess piece dangling from the ignition during the harrowing highway ride. He'd focused on it...alternating between it and soft cinnamon hair.

"Hey! What're y'doin'?"

I can't go back. Paul jammed in the key. Frantic winding. The engine ignited, then paused. It skipped, clattered and died out.

"Hey!"

This time the engine roared, triumphant. The headlights lit up Jake, his jaws working, his legs pumping like pistons.

Paul stomped the pedal. Faces pressed against the inside of the building's picture window. One of them looked like Shelley's. *Ten years from now.* The Buick mauled Jake, dragging him as a starved beast would, then abruptly stopped. A creak echoed and rebounded as Paul pushed open the rusty steel door. Yanking blindly, he disentangled Jake's jacket from the grill. He pulled him by the shoulders into the patch of ground illuminated by the headlights. The sight of blood had never been a problem. "Let me get a good look at you. Don't worry, I'm a doctor, remember? Hmm, neck injury. You can't move from the neck down. Correct?"

"Help me."

"Actually, that's why I'm here, Jake. To help." Paul felt laughter welling up. "Let's see, the way Betty tells it, her sister forgot to mail in the house payment one too many times."

Jake's mouth opened. A gurgle crawled out.

"Betty has an excellent memory. She remembers when you married her sister, Rose. You really don't remember who you are, do you? All that electricity they ran through your brain blew a fuse, dude. You forgot *everything* during your seventeen years in the institution, and the whole county's playing along. You creep 'em out, I guess, after what you did to Rose. Does *dismemberment* ring a bell?"

Paul saw Don Taylor's eyes go wide with recollection just before he rolled him off the edge of the bluff. "You might just say I'm a good citizen doin' decent folks a favor."

* * *

Dawn smelled like diesel. Paul hoisted himself into the seat, next to the burly trucker. "Thanks, man. Been walking for miles."

"You look like you got the bad end of the stick. You okay? Name's Frank."

"I'm Paul. Yeah, I'm fine." He threw back his head and laughed. "Just a little car accident."

He wasn't really a murderer, was he?

Casting Fate

"I'd never picked up a woman in a movie theater. I'd never 'picked up' a woman at all...I wasn't especially adventurous, you see. Mom says I inherited caution from Grandpa Ned."

"I see."

Dr. Holten's canned responses are annoying. But I'd made a deal with myself to give this a try. "I felt sleazy, staring at the back of the beautiful stranger's head," I continue. "Why was she alone in the first place?"

It appears Holten neither knows nor cares. I drift back, replaying those initial tantalizing glimpses of her profile. "I wanted her for myself *exclusively*," I blurt. "The instant I laid eyes on her. I can't explain the intensity. Irrational. It scares me."

Papers rustle. "Did you approach the woman?"

I open my mouth...and bolt from the room.

"Mr. Dunbar? Uh, sir?"

The voice snags me and I turn, aiming my semi-focused eyes in the receptionist's vicinity. "I guess I need to pay?" I'm sheepish. I navigate the plush swamp of carpet tufts, retracing my steps.

"Your session is booked for an hour. You've had twenty minutes." Her chair emits brisk, evenly spaced squeaks as her crossed legs bounce.

I pull out my wallet. "I'm all through." *She's swiveling now. The seat is grinding against its base.*

"Are you sure? I have to bill you for an hour. I'll need your insurance card, please."

"I'm paying 'out of pocket'."

* * *

My heart is heavy and my wallet light as I drive home. I'm scared. I know my landline will be ringing...

It is.

I can't contain my excitement. I need a drink and a cigarette! I don't know which to go for first...

She's whispering sweet "somethings."

"More," I breathe, cupping the mouthpiece. My plea tumbles end over end, splashes into that pool some call a conscience. Mine's stirred murky. But I'm drowning my repressed desires, and this time I'm coming up clean. *Alive.* I was but a floating corpse until—

"No more tonight, darling," she says curtly. "I need rest and so do you. Bye, now."

I moan as the line goes dead. I pour myself a bourbon, not bothering with the ice. I'm the willing kindling for her fire...

But the blaze isn't consuming me. I'm re-animating. No—to be accurate, I was stillborn. I was a stagnant unimaginative child, doomed to bore every creature in this world and beyond...until...finally—I live!

It was her smile that gave me that slap on the bottom. My lungs ballooned and I wanted to cry out my joy, announce my birth to that crowded movie theater. That was when her eyes stabbed an admonishment.

Sobered, I waited out the credits. By this time I was convinced she could read my thoughts.

My patience was rewarded when the lights came on. I stood in the aisle, heart pummeling my chest...

Silently, she slipped her arm through mine.

I smile. A stupefied, meandering smile of bliss. The relationship will be entirely on her terms. I'll woo her like a respectful suitor...

After I mark my place in the journal, I close the sturdy cover and nestle it in the nightstand drawer. Draining my glass further polishes my afterglow. I undress and slip beneath the covers.

A journal. Yes. My former monotonous existence would've withered the pages to brittle yellow as soon as pen touched paper. But now, I've found the love of my life. *Here*, I'll put my rapture into words.

* * *

Birds are crooning so sweetly, I can almost hear Karen Carpenter. Beside me on the seat, in a secret compartment of my briefcase, is the journal.

I'm still humming "Close to You" as I enter the parking garage. The light is perfect at the east end, and the view is...*inspiring*. Funny I never noticed before. Eagerly, I retrieve the journal from its confines.

The Mystery Woman...I don't know what else to call her. It's been two weeks since I escorted her to the theater parking lot. I boldly asked for her phone number. That's when I was treated to her throaty laugh.

"Yours, first," she replied, and I babbled it like marbles rolling from a jar.

"I'll be in touch," she told me, tucking her legs into the driver's seat of a snow-white Volvo. Without reciprocating, she drove away, leaving me feeling foolish...

I was astonished when my phone rang that evening. And each evening thereafter. Her conversation's light, with a magnetic undercurrent of intimacy, painting promises with invisible strokes.

But she blocks her calls. Most maddening of all, she refuses to tell me her name.

I sigh. The clock on the dash tells me it's time to get moving...

Confidence rules my strides. Co-workers' heads pop up as I pass. Some of the women eye me in the provocative manner I used to fantasize about. But they're too late.

"Hey," Al says. "Have you been taking Motivation courses? You're raking in clients we all gave up on." He flashes me a 'thumbs-up' and a shit eating grin.

I feign an amiable bewilderment, then settle in at my desk. He'd like to rub me off the face of the Earth, I'm sure of it. I made him look bad. Might be a good idea to pack the .38 in my briefcase from now on, just as a precaution. I've seen those news stories: *Disgruntled employee goes on rampage...*

Yeah, better safe than sorry. Grandpa Ned used to tell me that.

I return the CEO's call, accepting his offer. I can't wait to share this with my Lady Love. Imagine...training the new recruits. Just a few short weeks ago, I would've blanched at the idea of giving a personal presentation.

My pencil point snaps and graphite pulp insults my desktop like a snuffed cigarette butt.

Gutless. Women've always called the shots. Mom even tells Grandpa Ned what to do and when. His last-ditch rebellion landed him in the nursing home...

After sharpening my pencil, I jot two high priority items in my memo book:

#1 Inform my reluctant Juliet the time for a serious face to face encounter with her Romeo has arrived.

#2 Pay Grandpa Ned an extended visit this weekend.

* * *

I wipe my perspiring palms as the Volvo eases to a stop in my driveway. I don't dare keep her waiting. Concentration slows my feet to a dignified pace. She's teased, beguiled, and eluded. The Saturday afternoon sun is about to steal her cover.

I'm gaping. My hand is a useless appendage, unable to open the car door, because my brain refuses to give instructions.

She smiles.

I gratefully fall into the passenger seat. Her teeth are an astonishing match for the virginal leather-padded interior. They play hide-and-seek with her scarlet lips. "Satisfied, Richard?"

I clear my throat of adolescent squeaks. "At least the daylight rules out 'vampire'."

She sends a chill down my spine by ruffling the curls at the nape of my neck, her fingers doing a suspenseful crawl. "Baby fine," she murmurs.

Her hand returns to the wheel, and she throws the car in reverse, leaving my stomach in the driveway.

"Fine, baby," she coos, exceeding the speed limit all the way to the closest intersection. "I'm in the mood for a sidewalk café." Her abrupt braking at the red light flings strands of silky hair over one eye. She flicks her jet-black tresses back in place with a jerk of her head.

"*Fine...*" I'm mesmerized. She wears her hair in a poker straight, chin length 'bob' reminiscent of the Flapper Era. If I were to guess her age, the number would hover somewhere between sixteen and forty-five...

* * *

I've had three of those drinks with the little umbrellas, and we're halfway through our meal.

"Have you ever been in love, Richard?"

Everybody else calls me 'Dick.' What kind of parents hang a nickname like that on a kid? But *she* makes me feel like Richard the Lion-Hearted instead of Chicken-Shit Dick. "You seem to know all about me already," I balk.

"I want to *hear* you describe it. Have you ever been in love?"

"You mean before *you*?"

She humors me with a nod.

"Once...no, *twice*. I loved my Algebra teacher. She would cover the chalkboard with equations, squiggly symbols that meant nothing when separated from one another. Then she would use them to build powerful, three-dimensional things..."

I blush like the naughty schoolboy I once was. But memories of childish infatuation can't dilute the enduring passion reserved for my ebony-crowned Goddess. "Aw, that was kid stuff."

She's anything but slighted, her proud grin the proof. She signals the waiter and orders chocolate drizzled spumoni.

My chin drops. "That's my favorite. There was an Italian deli on the street where I grew up." I push my unfinished plate to the center of the table. "It seems like a part of you is somehow...*connected* to everything that comes to my mind. Have we met before?" I'm pleading now. "I *have* to know who you are...your *name*."

Her lip twitches, stalling a reply. Somehow I know she aches to tell me. I'd never caught that nuance over the phone.

She flashes those eyes, and it feels like a slap. "Beauty is a gradual unfolding. It's something absolutely ordinary that—well, even your Algebra teacher used suspense as a tool. Unfocused students don't reach their potential."

"I'm not in school!" Defiantly, I throw out the silly straw and drain my drink like a grown man. I look through the bottom of the glass. The clear circle frames her face, shows it crumpling with disappointment. I'm ashamed. Just like when I took my first Algebra test and got a D. *Before* I started paying attention in class...

We're eating spumoni and the silence is all I can taste. I'm mixed up inside. I itch to record all this in the journal. Sort it out.

Her spoon clinks. "I want to visit your Grandpa Ned," she announces. Just like that.

* * *

Antiseptic decay. I breathe through my mouth, but I guess my stomach can smell it. I want to puke—purge my revulsion, so grandpa won't see it.

But he sees. Through those filmy crusted slits, he sees *too much*.

My voice cracks under the weight of forced levity. "Grandpa...I brought you a beautiful woman. Figured you could use a change of scenery, huh?"

His head tilts, then nearly rolls off its stained perch atop the hospital gown. One side of his toothless mouth stretches upward. Combined with his jaundice, the effect is exactly like a half-carved jack o' lantern.

But Grandpa Ned is actually *smiling*, and I'm giddy with amazement.

"Hello, Ned," she says. She collects his bony trembling hand in her own.

She doesn't let go. She pats it lovingly while I give a running commentary of the changes in my life. I *need* to see grandpa emote again. Usually, I'm compelled to get drunk *after* a visit, but those umbrella delights have loosened my tongue in advance.

"If this keeps up," I say, "I can retire early. A tropical island, where the cost of living is minimal.

Suddenly grandpa says something incredibly lucid. "I was a poet. Remember, Richie? I could describe her dancing on clouds."

His expression freezes, his eyes riveted to the glorious creature holding his hand. His chest is rising. Then his body jerks while his chest falls. I wait for it to rise again...

He's perfectly still.

* * *

I'm adamant. I won't get out of the car. But her back seat compromise has *possibilities.*

"You're in shock, Richard. This isn't the time for major decisions."

I'm resting in her arms and her hand soothes my brow, tries to quiet the frenzy. "I want to go like he did, with a smile on my face...with you holding my hand." I take another swig from the silver flask, the emergency bourbon I stash in my briefcase. "But I ain't gonna' be warehoused in one of those 'death holdovers'."

"Talk to me about your *second* love," she interrupts, stringing the words into a pearl necklace. Or a *noose—*

"Forget the psychology crap!" What kind of idiot does she take me for? She beckons, entraps, and shuns me with this endless loop. I should plug my ears. Begone, evil siren!

No... I'm a bigger wimp than Ulysses. "I'm sorry. But don't you understand? It makes *sense.* We'd have enough severance to live for quite a while in Belize. It has to be now. Marry me..."

I've just realized I've never even kissed my nameless lover. *I feel her breath whistle past my earlobe, a gentle breeze as I roll in sweet clover.*

I want to kiss her. My head turns, lips brushing her cheek. "Warm sands. You and me." My description is husky with liquor steeped desire. "I bet I could write a best seller in a paradise like that. Grandpa always said I had a talent...just like him. But he never marketed that poetry, and that's sad. Sad as my 'second love', back in college."

I twist, trying to secure a romantic position. I'm grateful for the spacious seat.

"Sad," she says, very softly.

Dusk is smudging her finely drawn features. I keep losing eye contact, but I cling to the raft of sympathy her lips offer. Her body's eluding me, but I'm on top of her now. *Time to communicate.*

"I almost married Andrea," I whisper against her neck. "She was comfortable, in a 'chicken soup' way." At last—my hand finds an opening in the folds of her blouse. "But I need *more.*"

"No, Richard!" She tugs my wrist and squirms beneath me. "This is wrong."

I stop fondling. "Why?" I'm confused...and scared again.

"I'm not sure. I... I just *know.*" The timbre of her voice is changing, the panic dispersing. The tone deepens and evens out. "I do love you, Richard." She's mechanical now, like an engine on slow idle. "But it can't be the way you want it to be." She stalls out. Cold. "I can't explain."

This can't be happening.

"Richard, it was a mistake to get together. It shouldn't have gone past the phone calls. Let's go back to that."

It's like she's reading a textbook. This can't be happening, and I *can't* go back. "What kind of a weirdo are you?" I shout. A *strange* stranger who gets her kicks casting love spells? Do you use a scalpel and rubber gloves to cut out hearts? How do you keep your hands clean?

Her glare slices the dimness. I cringe at the thought of losing her. Unbearable!

I hear my pitiful apologies drown out the crickets. Then I impose a bargain I intend to enforce. It's only fair. "I'll play your game again, but only for a while. And you have to tell me your name. Say it. *Now.*"

It's like that time when I was a kid. That time I caught a wild rabbit with my bare hands. I can feel the tiny heart hammering the thin membrane, pulsing against my thumbs. Now it's skipping beats...and slowing...slowing to a resigned crawl. "Who are you, Mystery Lady?

Who *are* you?"

"I'm Thalia," she hisses. "Daughter of Zeus...I'm your *Muse*, asshole."

Her eyes roll backward...

* * *

The days and nights are immeasurably long in a six-by-nine-foot cage on Death Row. I've been pondering the existence of a Supreme Being. This is the ultimate "think tank."

Mom's attempts to have me declared insane failed, and I wish she'd just shut up. At least she could talk about something pleasant. Three weeks ago, she brought me a book that says "My Journal," finally released from state's evidence.

The trial was a farce. I don't remember murdering a woman named Carla Perkins. They kept sticking those photos in my face. Dishwater blonde, curly hair...an ordinary person who'd never stand out in a crowd. I'm positive I've never met her.

How did she end up dead, in my driveway? In Thalia's car...

Thalia. My Mystery Woman's name. She's still missing, and no one will look for her. Dear God, I hope she's safe. Why did she refuse to marry me? It helps to read the journal and make new entries. I'm close to filling in the blanks—

"Dick?"

I look up. I hadn't noticed so many creases in Mom's face until just now.

"Won't you stop reading and listen?" she asks tearfully. "The visit's nearly over, and I'm lonesome, with your grandma and grandpa both gone now."

I groan. She's tripping down memory lane again. What the Hell, I'll open my ears this time. Nobody else gives a damn about me.

"Grandpa Ned used to say your grandma inspired him, kept him going. He sure went downhill when she died. The nursing home. His mind was gone. He did nothing but ramble about her 'pretty black hair.' Oh, and about the way they danced the Charleston together when they were young."

Mom pauses. "Truth is, your grandma never *ever* had black hair. Why would he—oh, I remember. He said she was *possessed* by some Greek Goddess who taught him to write poetry. Imagine that! He called her that same odd name you use when…oh honey, I'm sorry. I don't want to get you started again."

I jump to my feet.

Mom's blathering is fading as the guard nudges me down the hallway. By the time the cell door clangs shut, beads of sweat extrude from every pore.

Impossible!

I spend long moments suspended in a daze. Then, I open the journal.

I can think of absolutely nothing to write.

Solemnly, I close the book. There'll be plenty of time to finish my thoughts on the matter, I tell myself. I'll yearn for Thalia's return and that island of warm sands…

And just like everybody else in Death's Holdover…I wait for the phone to ring.

Expectations

The craving had originated in Jillian's brain, lying dormant, sharing space with her lightning-strike lusts for chocolate.

Pete caught her smile and did a double take. She saw entire sentences string together and disintegrate before he could tack on question marks.

His fingernails humored the spot on the back of his neck. The spot that pretended to itch when he was puzzled. "…What?" he asked.

"I didn't say anything." She laced her shoes so fast, her hands were a blur. "I was just thinking about my run. Seven miles yesterday. I'm sure I can do eight today."

* * *

That evening Jillian terrified Pete in the bedroom again. His perspiration and her tears merged like tributaries, raged like the legendary Falls of Niagara. She ended as explosively as ever. He spent himself and braced as she bounded off the bed and streaked from the room.

Wool blankets. Certainly not an encouragement to snuggle or linger. He fished his robe from the carpet and smothered his chills with flannel. But he *itched*.

Curiosity drew him to the doorway. "I wish you would treat *me* like that."

Jillian continued tending her latest passion on the counter next to the stove. Her face was buried in lush foliage, and her body still glistened with heat. "You're jealous of a plant?"

The cut was so icy he shivered again. Her fingers, usually engaged in a mechanical buzz of activity, stroked budding offshoots with suspenseful deliberation. *Tenderness...*

She plucked a tissue and dabbed her eyes, then pressed it to her face. The turbulence oozing from her pores was absorbed. Her cares fluttered into the trash. "Want a snack before bed?" She extracted a wicked carving knife from the cutting block. "Your nutrition is just as important as mine."

The smile he'd been stifling won out. "I've had all the dessert I can handle, thank you." He watched her dice apples, sprinkle them liberally with ginger and cinnamon, drizzle honey overtop, and gorge.

"No chocolate?"

She wrinkled her nose. "I've had all the *endorphins* I can handle, thank you."

A frown furrowed his brow. If he didn't voice concern, she'd eat nothing but raw fruit and vegetables for days at a time. But he bit his tongue as she crunched and slurped. The Speech was eminent. The one in which she extolled the virtues of select varieties of 'pommes' and dismissed others as 'tasteless cellular rubbish.'

The Speech wound to a close with Jillian's delicate burp. Pete's cool palm came to rest on her belly, reminding her she was nude. "I guess I'll take my shower now," she said.

Pete's hand refused to budge. "Any news for me?"

She jerked away. "I have news for *us*. I was assigned a new project."

His swallow was audible. "Does this mean a less demanding schedule? Time off for—"

"I'm not pregnant."

He flinched. His hand fell to his side. "Well, we didn't give it enough time yet...or rather, *I* haven't. Can't help it." His nails drummed the counter. "So—the project. Exciting?"

A nod.

"That's all? C'mon, tell me some little detail. Anything at all. I'm your husband, the future father of our child."

"Sorry." She felt a strong pinch of regret. "I wish I could tell you."

He motioned with splayed fingers. "Never mind. It's only *me* you're talking to. Don't betray your precious code. Whatever 'breakthrough' your team is about to unleash will save the world again. The salmon won't have to exert themselves swimming upstream. You've discovered how to teleport them, right?"

"Ah, *spawning*," she sneered. "I'll get right to the point. I can't get pregnant. The DNA suture failed. I can't carry our baby and we both have to accept it."

Pete sat, his mouth dry.

Jillian sighed and began checking the needs of her collection of greenery. "I'm sorry to blurt it out like that." She coaxed a wayward vine out of harm's way, dimmed the lights, and composed herself. "We *can* be happy, Pete. You'll see."

All was quiet. She turned to find he'd gone...

After a leisurely shower, she slipped beneath the blanket. His breaths were deep and evenly spaced. Minutes later, she succumbed as well.

The clock was programmed to wake her in exactly sixteen hours.

* * *

Eight hours had passed when Pete's alarm signal shook him from oblivion. Before rising, he let his eyes wander from Jillian's face. They outlined the slopes and valleys of her neck and shoulders. The shallow movements of her diaphragm were puzzling, as was her recent switch to extended sleep. And the *cravings*...how could she not be pregnant?

He forged through the jungle in the kitchen, his eyes stinging from the onslaught of intense color. After turning off several sunlamps, he gathered breakfast.

Two Mealtabs went down with coffee. Rivulets of red streaked the chopping block and a hefty portion of raw beef filled his bowl. As he chewed, he relished the advantage of starting the day without Jillian. *I hear them shrieking,* she would wail, her palms clamped over her ears.

"Shrieking," Pete said to himself. "Cows." He shook his head and cleaned dribbled blood from his chin. Before leaving the house, he re-lit the sunlamps.

* * *

Roused from blank slumber, Jillian stretched. Strong bitter coffee finished the job. She munched carrots as she dressed, then reviewed a co-worker's audiofile as she headed toward the door.

Abruptly, she came to a stop. A frown dispersed as soon as she'd recalibrated the ultraviolet saturation in the lamps. Her illicit greenhouse would thrive, despite Pete's carelessness...

* * *

From all indications, the updated transit system was flawless. The new Chute navigated blind passes with minimal effort. Shoe soles absorbed the slight vibration, the only detectable sign of motion. Jillian mutely acknowledged eye contact from fellow passengers. Pleasant conversation jangled against claustrophobic gibbering.

"Mama, where did the windows go?" a young boy implored. He rose on tiptoes and peered into a ventilation slit.

"Sit," his mother reprimanded. "There's nothing to see until we get to work anyway."

The boy's wide eyes made Jillian's heart thump. Exactly when and why had 'child's play' become an anachronism? She recalled the satisfaction in sneaking off to invent her own toys. And she recalled the *loneliness*...

The vacuum lock sealed Jillian in, and the chaos *out*. Her office was a sheltered womb, ruled by her own pulse. Here, she envisioned fertile fields springing from barren landscapes. The child in her mind viewed picturesque scenes through "travel-windows" instead of history books—

"Maintenance."

The voice was a friendly tap on the shoulder. "Come in, Maddy."

The door obliged, admitting a stout figure swathed in white. "So this is where you went off to. Permanent transfer this time?"

"Yes, indeed." Jillian replied. She stepped aside while the room was sanitized.

Maddy removed a cloth from her uniform pocket and hand-polished a large mirror. "That's what it comes down to. Finding your 'place.' I was a Tech in my youth, you know. I'm happier now."

"I'm glad you were my egg donor, Maddy."

Both women were taken aback.

Jillian flushed. "I... have a habit of shocking people lately. Including *myself.* I hope this isn't an intrusion—"

"The project was double-blind."

"Double-blind was a hyphenated joke to those of us who hacked past it." Jillian struggled to read Maddy's emotions as she continued. "Some of us needed to be more than an unromantic encounter between sperm and ovum in a Petri dish. We needed *names* on our test tubes. I've always felt...*something* around you, a connection—I don't know." She averted her eyes.

Maddy sighed.

Jillian turned and staged a familiar confrontation. Their gazes merged—as they had countless times—in the mirror, a duplicate of which covered one entire wall of every nursery and office in the Complex.

As always, Maddy's smile coaxed the same from Jillian. But for the first time, she embraced her daughter. Their faces aligned, their reflection a vibrant contrast to the synthetic sterility surrounding them.

The moment was perfection. "The only differences I see are a few excess pounds and some wrinkles," Maddy said.

Awe had stolen Jillian's voice. She marveled at the sensation of being cradled by "one's own flesh and blood." *This is what it feels like to be a child.* She wanted to tell Maddy her wrinkles were anything but a manifestation of defeat. Her mother's skin personified the woman underneath...relaxed, accepting of passage and change.

A ripple of sensations teased. "I grew up surrounded by mirrors," Jillian mumbled. "I always had the feeling there were other people...a *world* inside them somewhere." Suddenly, Maddy's body heat was stifling. "Silly me, thinking I was doing all the watching," Jillian said, shrugging free of her mother's arms. "I've graduated from the Nursery Lab—*and* the two-way mirrors." On impulse, Jillian covered her reflected face with a perspiring palm, then withdrew it, seared by guilt. "I'm sorry."

"Just a smudge," Maddy said. A swipe from her cloth restored Jillian's image. "That isn't you anyway. You are here. *Here,*" she repeated, pulling off her glove. Her bare hand cleaned tears from Jillian's cheeks.

"...Am I?"

* * *

Where is 'here?' Jillian's question meandered through her thoughts after Maddy's departure. It stayed, in spite of Pete's chatter. She cut him off. "I'd rather not go past the 'baby factory', today. Let's just get lunch. I'm behind schedule." She darted toward the Chute without looking back.

Pete caught up as she finished entering her ID data. "Well, thanks for waiting."

She smiled inwardly, relishing his breathlessness.

A synthesized voice demanded attention: "Exiting Progeny International. Destination?"

"Terra-Park East," Jillian stated.

Pete provided his own data and took the seat Jillian had saved for him by stretching her legs across it. He deposited her feet discreetly on the floor.

On the other side of the aisle, a skinny old man's lascivious stare made Pete sweat. Bony fingers clutched his knees as he leaned forward. "How many children have you, huh?"

"That's not your concern," Pete said through gritted teeth.

"Oh, you have them hidden away, do you?" Amusement wadded the craggy features, brows nearly swallowing his eyes. "I sire only the sturdiest. Good stock. I donate the *natural* way, that's why. I'm the best there is. I can lay your woman down but once and she'll give you a son."

"Shut your ugly face or I'll have you taken away," Pete snarled.

Laughter followed as Pete nudged Jillian toward the far end of the seating section. "Young studs with no seeds!" came a hoarse bellow. "You know it all, do you?"

Jillian covered Pete's Communicator screen with her hand. "He's harmless. Don't report him."

"He's an errant from Geri-Care, I'd wager on it. Shouldn't be running around loose.:

"It's not forbidden to be old and healthy."

"It's forbidden to solicit sperm." Pete fell silent for a moment then closed off his Communicator. "He's lying, anyway."

"Fine," Jillian said, relieved to hear Terra-Park East announced. They scuttled out the treaded ramp. "I'm starved. The Oasis looks fairly private." Her lunch pack was heavy with apples. "Meet you there."

Pete watched her disappear into the crowd...

Included in Jillian's earliest memories was the lure of plants. She bit into a magenta apple, her teeth skimming the core, and re-lived the first time she dared venture a taste. Safe beneath her bunk, she'd licked juices from her small fingers and vowed to steal just one apple a day. Surely a single forbidden fruit would escape notice. *Endangered species...penalty...the warnings had only fed her guilty pleasures—*

"Jillian, must you be so blatant?" Pete hovered over a gathering of children.

She returned his scowl and addressed her uninvited audience. "Go wash your bloody faces, you little predators!"

Their collective trance broke. Most dispersed, stumbling and jeering, but one of the youngest lagged behind. He gaped, smearing snot with the back of his fist. A sibling corrected the ill manners with a smack from a raw leg of lamb before tugging him along.

"Here," Pete said. After handing Jillian a dark block of chocolate, he scooped apple cores from the table and threw them as far as he could.

Raucous honks from migrating geese swelled above. Widespread activity skipped a beat, then people scattered. The fowl dipped low, some shearing the tree-tops, others entangling themselves.

Jillian resisted the impulse to cover her eyes. "Poor confused creatures."

"They look delicious." Pete smiled and patted his stomach. "The vendors had jellied calf liver. Went down so easily, I ate it on the way. Cheer up. No stains, see? Oh, spoke too soon." He cleared a knot of dried blood from his long wispy hair by combing through with his fingers. "From breakfast," he said, tucking the results into his work cap. "I just don't know, Jillian. Why all the compassion for silly geese and pure snake venom for children?"

She began packing up to leave. "So you really think you know how I feel about them? You *don't*."

"I don't know if you have emotions at all. I thought so when we met—obviously. You cried when I told you I work in the Meat Factory."

"I grew up talking to lab animals, you know. And plants—"

"You sure are selective about which 'friends' you eat."

She stood. "We'd better get back to work. We can argue while we travel."

Pete joined her but sulked in silence. Jillian made use of the time to observe, absorb, and calculate. Her job was a constant travel companion. Others like her wove in and out of the controlled chaos. To differentiate them from the masses was the easiest of her assigned tasks.

She and Pete side-stepped a writhing mob of children who grinned with mischief as they flung bloody leftovers at one another. "I suppose lab children are the fortunate ones," Jillian said. "But we're all *someone's* experiment."

Pete's mind was elsewhere. He sparred playfully with the children then sent them flying with a display of beastly roars. The excitement pumped color into his complexion. Jillian didn't object when he hooked his arm through hers. She chose the long route back to the Chute.

She continued to observe, calculate, exchange imperceptible nods with colleagues. The heat from Pete's body was an unexpected diversion. Desire was a nettlesome torch, such a perplexing and pleasant tool—

"Over here." A yank brought Pete with her, past the Access Forbidden sign. They descended the steep hill, Pete's protests spliced with choppy breaths as the air fogged with rain forest humidity.

Macaws swooped. "Uh oh, nesting area." Jillian pulled Pete into a patch of towering broadleaf plantain and tore at his clothing.

"Surveillance can see everything we're doing."

"I don't mind." Jillian laughed briefly. "Neither do *they*."

"You're not totally immune to laws."

"C'mon, open up, Pete."

He sighed as she slipped the wafer-thin lozenge under his tongue. In seconds, a tide of nausea washed over him. Gradually, the tingling made him forget it. "Maybe you *are* immune." An explosion of pure lust shortly thereafter enabled him to satisfy Jillian's every need…

Pete's fuzzy smile hung on as they scaled the hill and threaded back into the bustle. He stalled, admiring a new ad board.

"Hurry," Jillian said. "There'll be no scenery left if those ads get any larger."

"There's still hope for us—for a baby."

The boards agreed. Cuddly round infants illustrated brazen banners that screamed: DONATE SPERM! SURVIVAL IS IN YOUR HANDS.

"Our jobs await," Jillian reminded.

"You want children. I know you do, even if you pretend—"

"Exiting Terra-Park East. Destination?"

"Progeny International, sector 119, gate 7." Jillian entered data for herself and Pete. "There's no time to debate," she said. She joined harried passengers, not caring if Pete caught up.

But he did. The angle of his jaw confirmed his agenda: a debate. "I *see* how you look at babies when you let down your guard."

She was cornered. "They're a curiosity. I feel…drawn. But detached. My kind was engineered for perfection. Perfection precludes irrational emotion."

He opened his mouth—

"Wait, what if I *can't* love a child, Pete? If reproduction were a true survival instinct I would have it. Another interesting fact: same-sex marriages among Natural Borns are producing the most children."

"Well, yeah. By adopting the gender mixes and mutants nobody else wants."

"Through adoption *and* insemination."

"You're lying!"

"Fine. Have it *your* way. I'm a liar and part of the 'grand plot' to destroy 'normal' human perpetuity."

Pete was clearly incensed. "If you had it your way, we'd all be monsters—*worms*—fucking ourselves."

Jillian was remotely aware that all surrounding conversation had ceased. "Dual sexing is a choice, lest you forget, one of many alternatives—*solutions*, actually, if society would accept them. But don't worry. 'Normalcy' will reign as long as we still have a few good men around. And we do. *Very* few."

Pete shot her a look. "By the way..." His words pierced like meat tenderizing spikes. "My sister Natalie is still unmarried. Afraid she'd turn you down twice?"

Jillian bit her lip. Then she let out her wrath. "Said by a man who disposed of his first-born. It was a *baby* you tore from your ex-wife's arms. Shall I tell you what your sacrifice to the 'common good' was subjected to?

A hand on Jillian's shoulder put her face to face with a pregnant woman's rage. "He had no choice, you cruel bitch—*none* of us do. And... don't you *dare* say they suffer. Try spreading your legs instead of propaganda!"

Pete deflected a blow. "She's *my* problem, and this is our stop. Please excuse us."

All within range had snapped out of spectator mode, mauling one another with pent-up frustration. For the first time in her life, Jillian reacted to the scent of a fearful mob. She stopped in the doorway. "Does this world need more human beings?" she shouted. "Why don't we boycott suffering? Why don't we all just *stop reproducing*?"

She fought Pete's attempts to dislodge her until the sorrow in his eyes overwhelmed. Together, they exited the sea of uniforms, the path down the Chute ramp plunging them into another.

Domes inside of domes. People gazed through the glass, admiring exactly what they were meant to see: a replenishing Outside, progressing on schedule, courtesy of Eco-Graphic Imaging.

Jillian knew what *really* existed Outside. The fragile eco-system had morphed into an auto-immune disease. *Mother Nature had eaten*

Herself alive.

* * *

The cravings would *not* be postponed. Jillian left her office early, unable to concentrate on anything but her insatiable thirst for running...and for sex. Confusing. Few lab-born males were able to complete the sex act. Even fewer females derived any pleasure from it whatsoever.

Yes, she was restless. At least she'd managed to make a long overdue decision today. She would discontinue the search for her sperm donor. Her *father*. The term had no meaning. Why not keep it that way?

Her pace was swift, but she took in the sights and sounds of the International Complex. The well-oiled machine in which the population had placed its faith gleamed with promise, unemployment non-existent. First-born offspring comprised the mandatory cogs—substitutes for animal subjects in research and clinical studies—the last-ditch effort to ensure human survival. Thus, the supply of food animals would be maintained.

For the Good of All. The slogan was plastered everywhere, especially in the Adoption and Sperm Donation Center, where aging Natural-Born males formed queues. Grandchildren fulfilling the field trip requirement for their Human Reproduction courses were often in tow. As she passed, Jillian's ears caught the slew of obscene propositions aimed her way. Even those disguised in foreign tongues were easily deciphered.

"Grandfather, don't!"

Jillian forced herself to look. A pre-pubescent girl hugged an old man's arm, pleading, "Your country's gone, don't you remember? You have to speak One Language now." She buried her face in his uniform sleeve. "Please...I don't want them to take you away—you'll *die*."

A little girl's intuition, Jillian thought. Somehow the child sensed the fate of ill-fitting cogs and dissidents. No courts, no prisons. 'Stress Units' provided permanent treatment: exile, *outside* the domes.

Jillian mounted an escalator. Up, she traveled, and away...

At the Terra-Park South entrance, she broke into a run, the oxygen glut competing with her own nagging voice: 'hypocrite.' Night crew zombies streamed in the opposite direction. Spindly limbs and bloated bellies. Pallid faces. *Ironic*, considering their steady diet of blood and protein.

She shook her hair from her cap and let the wind have it. Her uniform licensed unconventional behavior. As a girl, her cartwheels on sandy beaches had raised few eyebrows. She transferred that exhilaration from past to present, evicting the anchor of dread slowing her feet.

The effect was as fickle as those grains of sand. Her free-flowing playgrounds had been seduced into extinction, hardened into massive circular prisons of glass. She shrugged off a paroxysm of anger and started up an inclined trail.

Left behind was the swarm of fools. Jillian gulped moist earthy fragrances and climbed upward, letting her knees and hips absorb the impact. But she wasn't *entirely* alone. Natalie was still in her head…taunting…accusing—

"Out!" Jillian screamed, scrubbing her scalp with clenched fists.

Footfalls. All was quiet inside Jillian's head now. Beside her was Natalie, their steps in tandem. Their fingertips brushed. "I love you," Jillian said.

Natalie lengthened her strides, allowing a side view only.

Jillian could barely keep up. "I should have told you."

Natalie's face turned.

"But I…" Jillian caught her hand and held it. "Your brother—I *have* to do what I'm doing." Natalie's fingers whipped free. "For the good of all," Natalie said, sunny as daisies and acrid as laboratory vapors. " When will you tell the poor 'cattle' the planet is *not* regenerating outside the domes?" She laughed as she sped out of sight…

Regret plagued Jillian's descent toward the home she and Pete reluctantly shared. This night would mark the final phase of her plan.

* * *

As Jillian's 20th hour of sleep approached, Pete was on the verge of summoning Medical Emergency Assist. At the 16th hour her alarm signal had been ignored. Her skin paled with time's passing. Was he imagining the tinge of blue?

Just as he reached for his Communicator, she stirred. Her misty green eyes brought him to a standstill. "You should be at work," she said.

"I was worried. You made sounds in your sleep, like you were in pain."

She was famished, and so chilled, she fantasized her bones had frozen. "I do love you, Pete..."

"What? I can barely hear—"

"Just warm me...with chocolate—and with *you*."

He rifled through his pockets. "How 'bout a compromise? Chocolate Mealtabs."

She smiled demurely.

He ripped the packets and pushed two tablets past her lips, his heart pounding. "You're not well. You should have meat."

"Then give it to me." Her arms slithered around him and he pitched forward, into bed.

Her tongue was gritty with Mealtabs, and warm—a shock—in contrast to the cool texture of her skin. To his surprise, he needed no Virilozenge.

Soon, perspiration was sprinkling her. Pete felt tireless...immortal. He was re-generating, like the natural world *Outside*. The dysfunctional paradise inside the domes was a shriveling pacifier. *Their children would play in authentic sunshine, tanning their skins—*

Jillian's laughter-rattled sobs broke into his reverie. She flooded him with tears, then slipped from his embrace.

"Stay this time," he begged.

She staggered to the doorway. "Don't follow. I need a few minutes alone."

"You're ill." He scrambled from the bed, panicked by an odd noise. At the entrance to the kitchen, he stopped, addled.

The plant. Top-heavy, it had fallen to the floor. So had Jillian. "Stay away," she said, entwining in the foliage. "Just stand there and *listen* to me. We can't create life without passion. An essence is missing. Maybe I'm proof."

Pete wanted to move. Instead, he listened.

"Splicing DNA from human newborns with plants is insanity! I didn't have the suture. I had a project all my own...*no one* knew about it. DNA from sweat and tears. Yours and mine. Our life-blood rain has incredible powers." She unraveled a mesh of leaves, exposing a round solid 'fruit.' Methodically, she detached it from large-diameter vines, each spurting a green fluid. Then she rose and wrapped herself and her charge in a blanket. "I've never really *lived*, but maybe I'm about to be born."

"Wh—what is that?"

Jillian doubled over with an exquisite pain. "Our baby," she gasped, collapsing into a soft chair. Her legs closed spasmodically around the ripening 'fruit.'

Disbelieving, Pete watched the loathsome thing inch up her thighs and disappear beneath the blanket—

His spell broke and he lunged, but the gooey bulbous mass evaded his fingers. He grabbed again, sickening as it writhed against the material.

"No!" Jillian shrieked. Her eyes latched onto Pete's and stilled him. "Let go," she said gently. The bulge oozed from Pete's grasp, tendrils undulating, and Jillian's belly inflated.

The room swam. Pete was spinning, tunneling...a surge of euphoria greeted him as he lost consciousness.

* * *

He awoke, convinced he'd emerged from a hideous nightmare.

Jillian. Her smile was a radiant invitation. Never had she looked so beautiful, her hair glowing as if she were bathed in sunlight—

The lamps. Every lamp in the room was powered to the maximum. The heat was almost unbearable—

The bundle. Pete jumped to his feet and stumbled, one knee hitting the floor. He rebounded, playing back their numbing conversation, the plant—the monstrous...

The bundle. Jillian's arms were a cradle for a swaddled shape. Pete's tongue choked him. He knelt beside her, lost in her smile. A *mother's* smile. He remembered the comfort of his mother's lap—

Jillian drew back the blanket. Tiny arms and legs squirmed. Perfect fingers and toes, a plump round body—of pale olive tint—and a *cabbage* where a head should be.

Not a cabbage, logic informed him.

Jillian's loving hands resumed their task, peeling layer after layer of interlocking sheaths. Underneath was smooth, olive-green skin. In the center of the baby's face was a flap. An eyelid.

Jillian's smile beckoned.

Pete obeyed, massaging with a fingertip, instinctively gentle.

The lid flew open. Miniature eyeballs revolved in all directions, like immature peas in a pod. From the precisely formed rose-bud mouth came a sound like a mosquito hovering just outside Pete's ear. The sound of a parasite seeking a host.

Revulsion. Then, an empty space of amazement. Pete felt—*drawn...*

Overhead, the ceiling's reflective surface transmitted unobstructed data to a remote location. Olive-hued limbs quivered with rapture. The team leader cleared his vocalization orifices with his finger-buds. "Another Progeny international breakthrough," he announced. "My progeny has done well. Far better than she believes."

Officially dismissed, a dying ember coasted in the center of Earth's orbital path, no longer the giver and observer of life. Soon it would be reduced to an impacted cinder.

The sun was a blinded eye.

Dead On

"Mousy Brown." Dana grimaced. "I never gave it a thought until lately. This has to change. I'm coming into the daylight now."

The stylist puckered her lips as she shuffled a rainbow-hued bundle of hair swatches. "Maybe a transfusion is what you need. Ah, here's a little Bride of Dracula number that'll set off your skin."

Dana's composure dissolved when the sample was nestled against her cheek. Her grey-green eyes became glimmering emeralds mounted on alabaster. Celtic Goddesses began weaving magic and mayhem on looms of bright copper...

"Hmm? What'd I tell you? You're a closet redhead."

"Do it—yes!" Dana exclaimed. "It's perfect."

She completed her day of illicit shopping, re-constructing her exterior. Her final acquisitions, a rust brown leather jacket and hand-embroidered lavender silk shirt best reflected the mysterious stirrings of her "insides."

She frowned. *Gas*, Michael had said, before returning to his laptop display of stock market hieroglyphics. It'd be an icy day in Hades before she confided the stirrings of her insides to *him* again.

Safely home, Dana ignored the ringing phone. She salivated over her purchases and prepared an exotic dinner-for-one. A full stomach led to a solid two hours transfixed in front of the mirror. Eventually, the necessity of sleep lured her to bed.

* * *

She woke, ravenous. But not for food. Her fingers clambered up the base of the lamp and pounced on the switch—*click!*

Flooded with light, the notebook and pen on the bedside table were barely allowed a blink and a yawn. Dana spilled the contents of her freshly broken dream, panting from the rush to transcribe each subtle nuance before the inevitable fade-out.

Finally, chilled by her soaked sheets, she abandoned the bed, notebook in hand. Wrapped in a blanket, she curled in an overstuffed chair to review her spontaneous outpourings.

Her eyes widened as they glided over the scribbled lines. It was as if she'd plucked a volume from a shelf in the personal library of the Marquis de Sade. Ghoulish visions had bruised her psyche like an over-excited lover. She'd vented her wrath at his trespasses onto snowy paper, now heavily tracked with bloody mind-prints...

Confusion lurked nearby, grinning at her burden of secrets. She could feel its cadaverous fingers tickle her scalp. "*Fiction*," she stressed.

She stumbled back to bed, her eyelids fighting to stay open, trained on the sanctity of the lamp. The image split into two as she yielded to dreamless slumber.

* * *

"Are you *insane*?" Michael's anger was louder than he'd intended—crass, amid the polite murmurs and clinks of fine crystal. He dampened his tone, but his emotions raged on. "You're turning down a syndicated column for-for...horror is a *mongrel* genre. A joke."

"Tell that to Edgar Allan Poe!" Dana shot back.

His pupils shrank to the size of steely pinpricks. "Well, well. Case in point. Had I lived during his time, he'd get the same advice from me, minus the expensive French wine. He was a kick-ass journalist. Dead at age forty. Pecked to death by a creepy redundant birdy—"

A dousing with expensive French wine ended Michael's rant. Dana returned her emptied glass to the table, then stood and draped her serviette over his sputtering face.

As she passed the waiter, she tucked a fifty-dollar bill into his cummerbund. "Drinks are on *me*." She smirked. "Although my escort may scarcely agree."

Michael dabbed at his sodden pride and silenced the tittering fools around him with a razor-honed stare. Trouble was on the way. A major rift. *She was expecting far too much from him.*

* * *

Dana was frenzied by the time she got her front door unlocked. She sprinted to the bedroom and seized her 'special pen' in a passionate embrace, vowing never to leave the house without it again. It had insured her lucky strike of publication successes from the very first time she'd set it to paper. The series of self-help articles had established her name. Now, the pen was braving new territory.

The story she'd leeched from her dream the night before continued. She was a mere bystander, an instrument of its will. For the first time in her life, the path to fulfillment was in sight. Ten pages later, she studied the results while blotting beads of perspiration from her forehead.

A shadow loomed from over her shoulder, and she spun full circle. "Michael!" Papers fluttered to the carpet.

"I didn't even have to use my key." He glowered. "You left the front door wide open." They stood face to face, *poised*. Michael's eyes flickered—

Simultaneously, they dove to the floor, Dana withdrawing from the tussle to avoid having her manuscript ripped to shreds. She folded her arms and watched his mechanical mind digest her budding masterpiece...

"Stereotypical, formulaic spookfest." His voice echoed the hollow coldness of a coin return receptacle. "You'll make a fool out of yourself if you market this. You've already made a fool out of *me*, of course. I pulled the strings that got you off that free-lancer's ledge."

"I didn't ask you to. You knew I didn't want to be chained to a magazine column. The deadlines for the ditzy articles are tough enough, but they more than pay my bills. I'm satisfied with that, and I'm finally free to... *experiment*."

Michael felt a sting. "Teen-agers experiment. They also rebel." He grasped Dana with his eyes and straightened his wine-stained collar while he seated himself on the edge of the dresser. "I had the courtesy not to embarrass *you* in public but aren't you chronologically past membership as a Goth…or whatever category your new look fits."

"I wasn't seeking a category. Maybe I look the way I just happen to *feel* like looking?" She severed eye contact and pulled her writings from his hand, depositing them in the nightstand drawer.

"Categories, indeed," she added. "My fiction is more suspenseful than horrific—and I feel a sense of…*power*. Do you really think I'm going to confine myself to monotonous drivel like this?" She flung open a glossy issue of "Executive Savvy." In her most annoying nasal drone, she read the bold-face heading beneath her photograph and bio. "Practical fashion and hair care for the woman who means business."

Michael popped a stick of gum in his mouth and wadded the wrapper. "Well, let me pitch you a new idea for an article. Kind of a genre blend, with no big risk of selling yourself out. Here's the title. 'Sadistic tortures for the terminally bored.' There you go. I'm sure I can find a market. So, enjoy. Write your 'powerful' suspense. I have enough income to support us both when we get married."

Dana felt a valve go *pop*. "For your information, Famous Publisher Guy, this is only *one* of my stories. I've been writing steadily for weeks…starting around the time your paranoia surfaced. When I finish one more, I'll have an even dozen, which is the title of the collection. Blackwell-Walsh has already paid me an advance. They've even mapped out a book signing tour."

Michael had nearly lost his gum. He gazed solemnly at his hands. "Could you ease the pressure just a little? Maybe.. I could accept some of this if…" His sigh immersed all traces of arrogance in a well of self-pity. "Sorry I can't keep up, Dana. Sorry I don't excite you anymore."

She backed up, knees buckling, and sank onto her bed. "God, Michael…you're so moody lately. And there's something else." She noted the diffused tension in his slumped shoulders. His shallow breathing. "It's almost *frightening*. I don't understand this 'pressure' you talk about."

"You *wouldn't*, would you?" Half-heartedly, he picked lint from his sleeves. A dull throb in several fingertips reminded him he'd bitten the nails to the quick. "I've never been prone to depression. At least not until I fell in love with you."

Dana grew desperate to avoid another spin into his circular conversations. "You keep saying that" she blurted. "It makes no sense, so I'm tuning it out until we find a way to start communicating again."

She rose and approached hesitantly. "That sure doesn't mean I'm giving up." Her voice muffled as her lips pressed against the side of his neck. "Does it feel like I'm giving up? Hmm?"

His left arm found her lower back. "By the way…why did you switch to purple ink?" His hand scampered, spider-like, up her spine. "I gave you a 24-caret antique fountain pen." His fingers gathered a thick knot of hair and tightened, tilting her head backward. "It didn't provide enough inspiration until you filled it with purple ink?" He slid from the dresser and stood, right arm encircling—pulling her in close.

"Michael, I don't like what you're doing."

"You *used* to."

"It was *playful*, not painful. *This* isn't the same—"

"Neither are *you*. You made that pen your weapon."

"Let go of my hair. That *hurts*."

"It hurts because you're moving."

"I'm *trying* to move because it hurts!"

He was stony-faced. "Try being perfectly still and see what happens."

It was still a game. A mighty serious one, all of a sudden. She relented, taking a deep breath and holding it, focusing beyond the pain.

The vice-grip uncoiled.

"See? Told you it wouldn't hurt." His words were soft, scolding, his logic irrefutable...to *him*.

She cringed as he wrapped her in a gentle two-armed hug. "If you say so."

"Just stating a *fact*."

Dana wanted to lash out with a string of obscenities. She wanted to double her fists and hit him with every ounce of her strength. Instead, she remained motionless. Baffled.

His touch became intimate.

"I... I'm really tired." She wondered if her voice was audible. It seemed trapped, attempting to beat its way out of a place she couldn't name. *Ludicrous*, she thought. A writer... running out of words. She fended off an impulse to laugh. "I just realized we haven't had dinner!"

Her exclamation stopped Michael *cold*.

"N-no wonder..." she stammered. That's why I'm so tired."

He released her. "Um-hmm. Tired of *me*."

She teetered off balance as he turned on his heel. By the time she recovered her wits, the front door had slammed. Seconds afterward, his car was revving. Her stomach twisted, chasing her hunger as the engine's roar receded into the distance.

What her naïve heart had shrugged off, her brain would tolerate no longer. She was angry. She was angry at *Michael... angrier at herself*. If a miracle failed to intervene, their relationship was destined to end. She'd been submerging her tears in the watery graves of her stories...

Calming, she returned to her nightstand, caressing the maligned pen with a fond eye. *Harmless*, she reminded herself. At least she was channeling her frustrations in a healthy direction.

Anyway, it sure kept her out of bars.

* * *

Michael killed the engine. "Prather's Tavern and Eatery, here I come."

Gravel crunched beneath his strides. Rusty hinges protested as he neared the squat brick building, and a trio of juiced locals tumbled out the door. Alternately, they helped upright one another, oblivious to Michael's disdain.

He swerved and trotted up two steps, plunging into a barrage of tacky blinking neon and raucous merry making. He made his way past the jukebox, to the far end of the bar, settling on a stool flanked by a grove of drowsy patrons.

The bartender approached, a hulking rough-around-the-edges guy, whose swagger shouted authority. "What can I get you?" His stare grazed Michael's shoulder, scoping out the dim perimeters of the establishment.

"Bourbon. *Straight.*"

A shot glass thunked against sturdy wood, and the soothing gurgle of bottled amnesia yanked Michael's wallet from his pocket. He downed the booze, motioning for a re-fill with a twenty-dollar bill.

Shortly after gulping the second shot, he indulged an urge to strike up a conversation with its supplier. "Women," he said.

The reply was a nod.

"I'll do anything for her. She knows it. Maybe that's the problem."

"Hold that thought. Be back in a sec'." The bartender strode a few yards and shook a snoozing customer. "Your ol' lady just came in, Floyd!" he bellowed. "Settle your shit *at home* tonight, hear me?"

Michael resumed his tale as his drink was re-filled for the third time, sluggishly trading it for another crisp green bill. "She's the only one I ever felt like sharing *everything* with...hey, is this your place? I mean, are you Prather?"

"Yeah."

"Well, let me introduce myself: Big-Shot editor and publisher. Michael Leeson. Heard of me?"

Prather blinked, once. "Sure, pal. Who hasn't?" He turned his head briefly to check on Floyd's predicament. "I don't do much readin'...but, yeah."

"I lied to her," Michael confessed. "Her fiction's pure genius. A slow squeeze to the jugular." He lifted his glass, meditating on the glittery reflections clinging like sequins glued along the rim. "Uh huh, that's what I'd put on the dust jacket. Something like... 'without spilling a drop of blood, she eviscerates the reader'." His hand jerked en route to his mouth, leaving behind a splash of bourbon. His gut rumbled.

A shallow basket of cellophane-wrapped beer nuts appeared. "On the house," Prather grunted. "Better slow yourself down. I don't take kindly to cleanin' up puke."

"Sure thing, man. Got it under control. Y'know, *all* my involvements have been with writers. But none of those women could get below my surface." He yanked and twisted, but the sealed bag refused to give up its contents. "It's so cliché, but... I've never met anyone like Dana."

He flinched. Hearing her name, even uttered from his own lips, was a sobering slap. The cellophane ripped, pelting him with an explosion of nuts. "Aw, damn it." He jumped from the wobbly stool. "I bet you hear this shit all the time, anyway. Here, sorry 'bout the mess," he added, tossing another twenty on the bar.

Prather eyeballed him until he'd completed an unsteady exit, then spat into a towel and erased the dribblings from watered-down whisky. "So long, fuckin' loony toon."

A cool breeze hit Michael's moist face, fanning his resolve to vanquish sentimental intrusions before they could infiltrate his core. His foot mistreated the gas pedal, spraying Prather's gravel in all directions. Fishtailing, he skidded onto smooth pavement.

Women had always used him as a stepladder. They used his name and reputation. Dana was using him. She was using him *up*.

He was aware of an ache, subtly etching the boozy haze. Yes. She'd used him up. She'd gone far beyond the others, and he was at a loss to explain it. But the ugly truth jutted through his mental fog: he'd do anything for her, *even still...*
Anything but share her.

The tires screamed as he deviated sharply, crossing all four lanes. Narrowly missing a decayed road-side phone booth, he hit the brakes just short of plowing into the dense thicket behind it. He vetoed the notion of backing up. One blown tire and no spare in the trunk left only one option. Phone in hand, he jogged up the incline...

* * *

Dana let go of the towel. It unwound from her wet hair, sailing lop-sided to the floor like an injured butterfly. The phone number was

Michael's, but that voice just couldn't be his. She tapped the speakerphone icon and re-played the voicemail.

It *was* Michael, no doubt about it. The speaker emitted a single muffled word:

Whore.

The microwave dinged but failed to snap Dana from her trance. Dinner was left to grow cold, and she ignored her dripping hair as she penned the opening paragraph of her twelfth story.

* * *

Days blurred into one another. Dana couldn't quite date the point in time when concern for Michael's profound sadness had abandoned her. His explosive outbursts and accusations of infidelity were no longer a source of dread. Initially, she'd been perplexed by the insidious wash of *excitement* experienced after just such a session. Still, there wasn't much chance to analyze, even if she cared to. Her final story deadline was drawing near.

Her ringtone's plaintive whine cut into Billie Holliday's drifting lullaby. Michael, again. She pressed "answer" but didn't make a sound. Tapping the speakerphone, she waited…

"Billie Holliday used to make you cry."

"I remember," Dana responded. "I asked you to get up and stop the CD player that one time...when..."

"When we were making love," Michael finished.

"I don't need to cry anymore. Shouldn't that make you happy *too*?"

"You'd think so, wouldn't you?"

His absence of sarcasm surprised them both.

Michael tried to clear the lump from his throat. "Sometimes I wish I could cry the way you used to. I envied your tears. You cried just as hard when you were happy as when you were sad. *Dana*...I understand it all now, I don't know how, but it's like I'm with you. *Inside.*"

She took of sip of lukewarm coffee, anticipating a long and productive night…

"Maybe I'm having hallucinations," he said, "but I think there's something we're both meant to see. I can *feel* this, can't you? We're so close."

"There's only a veil between us, Michael. Nothing more."

His last defense crumbled. "I'm taking the afternoon off tomorrow. Let's drive out to the cabin and talk about this. *Please*."

"I'll be ready." She smiled.

* * *

They savored the nectar of the sun's warmth. It seemed few words were needed during the long drive. Silent seeds had been planted, the tender offshoots yearning to blossom. Michael reached for Dana's hand as they strolled. "It was early Spring the first time we came here. Identical weather."

She nodded, watching the wind tousle his hair. Lacy tree bough shadows swabbed his face with newly budded dots. *A dark, crawling veil...*

"What should I do about the nightmares?" he asked her.

She shrugged. "Give them to *me*. And stop reading my stories."

"What's happening to me?" He wanted to wring the answer from her entrapped hand. She subtly attempted to wrench it free, and he could feel his panic rising. "Who's the man in all your stories? The one who *always* appears. He changes forms—"

"*Fiction*. Let go of your obsessions and let go of my hand!"

Michael was ashen. "I'm sorry."

"Maybe this wasn't such a good idea." Dana yanked away and walked fast, back toward the cabin. Firm footfalls crackled twigs behind her, their distance holding steady. She was out of breath and unnerved when she reached the porch. "I've had enough!" She turned, backing Michael up with sheer will. "*Enough*," she repeated. She retrieved her notebook from the top step and plucked the pen from her pocket. "The ending's clear now. Don't interfere."

Michael shook his head. "I can't believe this. You're...*writing*? I'm giving this all I have."

"Shhh, I'm almost finished."

"Dana, please don't write tonight. Listen to me just this once," he pleaded. "Let's go to a movie. Something light, not morbid—"

"Shut up. I can't hear my Muse. Damn it…oh, *damn!*" she wailed. "The pen's run dry." Wild eyed, she scribbled invisible circles, then slammed the pen beside her. "Two more lines." She began to weep…

Michael's anguish conceded to a balm of blankness. "I love you," he said. He sat, gathering Dana in his arms. "But you bled me dry, just like…" Her head sought the comfort of his shoulder as his fingers closed on the pen.

It wasn't a choice. Michael plunged the wicked gold tip into her neck until it pierced the jugular. "They say dedicated writers have ink in their veins."

Dana screamed just once…as he pulled the pen *out*. A warm crimson fountain showered them, slowing to a gurgling stream. Her terror merged with heightened *expectancy* as she pulled the slippery pen from his hand. "Two sentences." She slid down his chest, groaning as she siphoned blood into the gilded barrel. Sprawling across her notebook, she ended her finest piece of work.

She rolled onto her back, her eyes glazed, her voice a raspy whisper. "Isn't it obvious now? You've done *far too much* for me, really…but my publisher is waiting." She managed a faint smile. "One more kindness, Michael?"

Her jaw slackened, and he stared, until her pupils dilated. From her notebook, scarlet words jumped out against a purple and white contrast. He leaned in and squinted:

She expected far too much from her Muse. And she got it.

Michael's laughter swirled inside his head. When the cold shock evaporated, sobs broke through, scalding the irony in a hot bath of tears…

* * *

Dana's body arced gracefully on descent. Sunlight caught her hair, transforming it into a flaming torch. It was extinguished by the rushing currents…

Ancient wood creaked as Michael navigated the bridge. He turned onto the rock littered dirt road that would eventually lead him to the interstate.

No woman had ever made him cry. As far as he could recall, no one or *nothing* had. Tomorrow, he'd type Dana's manuscript. He'd place it in a nice clean envelope and mail it to her publisher...

He nodded, then his lips moved. "It's the *least* I can do."

Court Case

"Mr. Taskovski?" Judge Ratliff put on his glasses.

"Yes, your honor." His smile was as tight-lipped as his briefcase. "Here's the file." Taskovski's shin jostled the table leg in his eagerness to forward the report to the clerk.

She swooped in and clipped it from his grasp, then thumbed through the crisp dot matrix sheets. "Eight months!" she barked. "This year's painting season is ending, yet Mrs. Vail *still* has not seen fit to finish the trim on her second story windows."

The judge yawned and waved her aside. "Mrs. Vail," he called out, without looking up.

Taskovski squirmed with delight.

"She's a 'no-show', sir," the clerk stated.

"*Oh*?" Judge Ratliff gnawed his bottom lip and peered overtop his glasses.

A hush suspended over the courtroom, as the shuffling of defendants came to a collective halt.

"Warrant. *Next* case."

* * *

Taskovski practically floated to the parking garage. *Nothing like a productive day to lift a man's spirits.* As he inserted his car key, an electric-charged tingle pitter-pattered up his arm. Quizzically, he wriggled his shoulders and rotated his neck. *Maybe a pinched nerve...*

Nothing would dull his sword of victory, he vowed. A raise and promotion were within sight. He rewarded himself with The

Boardwalk's famous filet mignon, blood rare, before heading for home...

His foot bore into the pedal, as the isolated section of upscale architecture receded and the decay of public housing took its place. Shrill bickering and the racket of squalor swarmed inside the structures, spilling into the street.

He rolled up his window, glancing at the neat row of two-story brick flats standing proud and intact amidst the siege. Mrs. Vail's flat was dark. The absence of a functioning porch light was conspicuous.

It wasn't his concern, he reminded himself. Being blind didn't prevent her from checking the status of the bulb. Simple. All she had to do was use her hands to detect the warmth, or lack of it. The fact was, she had it easy. She was retired and unencumbered, with a guaranteed income from Social Security.

He, on the other hand, held a job. Building inspection was grueling work, and he didn't manufacture excuses in order to shirk his duty. *Mrs. Vail's* duty was to maintain her property or give it up. The state amply provided for 'invalids.' Hell, they used *his* taxes to do it...

A black Labrador gave Taskovski's hand a cautious slurp as he entered his house.

"Get out of the way, Smokey, you damned mutt! I'm calling Sheila tomorrow. She made a chump out of me, then hit me with divorce papers. But this is the new, *improved* me. She's had long enough to get settled, so she's coming to get *you*, fella'. Can't find an apartment where she can have a pet, eh? Well, that's what the City Pound is for."

Smokey's ears drooped, and he retreated, tail tucked between his legs.

Taskovski stood in the middle of the living room, still wired, too restless for TV. Maybe he should've passed on that second cup of coffee. One thing was certain. He had over-eaten. He loosened his belt and turned on the ceiling light.

No wonder his arms were itching furiously. A peculiar crawling sensation had manifested in the form of a fine rash, and it was spreading. *Hmm, tainted food?* He jotted a hasty memo. He'd personally see to it The Boardwalk underwent a rigorous kitchen inspection. No doubt they'd ferret out an unsanitary illegal immigrant cook or two.

He rubbed his temples. The fullness in his head was comparable to an impending hangover, but he hadn't imbibed. Disgusted, he popped a couple of pills and snatched the phone.

Normally, the last thing he desired at the end of a workday was conversation. But he needed to share his pent-up emotions with a colleague. *A bit of gloating wouldn't hurt either...*

"Mac? Hey, how's it goin'?"

"...*Taskovski?* Goin' alright, I guess. Uh... what can I do for you?"

"It's more like the other way around, I'd say. Just wanted to let you know all your good advice is paying off. Yep. Without somebody like *you* to break me in, I mighta' folded and gone back to selling cars." He paused to light a cigarette. "But word's come down that *I'm* about to move *up.*"

"Yeah, I heard. *Supervisor's* what I heard. *Shhh*, keep it under your hat." Mac's conspiratorial whisper was shunted by a guffaw. "Congrats, man! *Knew* you could do it. Like I said, a thick skin and a thick skull, but don't forget your hard hat."

"You bet," Taskovski said smugly. He kicked off his shoes. "Damn. Spent all day sittin' in court. I hate that. My feet feel swollen—"

"That reminds me," Mac broke in. "Remember the computer punk who thought he'd get away with doing his own wiring? Had him in court yesterday. Got to admit he did a primo job. *Better* than code— but that ain't the point."

Taskovski grinned. "No permits, eh? The fines'll hit his pocketbook...and *fatten* ours."

"He'll be praying to get off that easy! It's a two-family flat, and the wiring was already fucked downstairs when he bought the place. Says his grandparents live there, so he needed to fix it for 'em right away."

"Uh oh. Wait'll he finds out he has to hire contractors for a multiunit."

Mac roared. "The dumbshit! I'd like to see his face when they tell him he's gonna' *pay* to watch 'em yank out his work and put it back all over again...and at *minimum* code standards, of course."

Taskovski felt a twinge in his gut. *Heartburn.* A belch gave no relief. "I guess he'll use 'poor grandma and grandpa' as a hardship excuse."

"Sure. Tried it with me already. Something about ol' grandpa's stroke and bone marrow cancer. Ah, but I don't budge an inch. No guilt. Y'let people get under your skin, they'll *own* you. Hey, I hate to cut this short, but the wife's yelling to use my phone." Mac's voice lowered. "Dropped hers in the toilet again. But she can yak on mine all night for all I care. Better than havin' her raggin' at *me*, y'know?"

"Sure do. Later, pal."

A fogbank of melancholy swallowed him, and he stretched out on the couch to brood. There'd been too many major life changes in close succession, he reasoned. That's what was wrong. Even changes for the *better* stressed both body and mind. He'd turn in early tonight...

The bed appeared anything *but* inviting. Exhaustion forced him beneath the covers, but anxiety kept his eyes open wide. Reluctantly, he switched off the lamp.

He lay tense and aching, watching the luminous green hands on the clock travel slowly from one number to the next. Finally, he acknowledged sensations never before experienced: a fear of being alone, plus an outright terror at the thought of falling asleep.

Eventually he succumbed, dozing and waking fitfully...entangled in a solitary cycling nightmare. His dreamscape projector held him captive to a replay of his last face-to-face encounter with Mrs. Vail...

"I'm all alone, Mr. Taskovski. My husband's illness and death took every penny of our savings, and my monthly check is so small."

He scribbled designs on his clipboard. Anything to avoid her creepy blank eyeballs. "I've heard all this before. Ask for help. That's what relatives and neighbors are for."

"B-but...I've told you I have no relatives. All dead. I do what I can,

but it takes time. The neighbors help sometimes. I can't see who to trust, though. The young ones, even the smallest children play tricks on me, you know? They tear down my fences. Throw rocks at my windows. At night I hear gunfire...somewhere, out there." Her voice trailed off...

Taskovski looked up, but his reply stalled out. Something was different about her eyes. Bathed by sunlight, their opaque glaze was silvery...reflective.

"When my husband and I were younger, when I still had my sight, I had beautiful flowers here next to the porch."

Her trembling hand clutched Taskovski's arm. "I remember the fragrance," she whispered. "I can still see them, if I try." Suddenly, her grip tightened. "I will see flowers again," she said fiercely." You'll help me!"

Repulsed, he shook free of her bony fingers and rushed to his car.

His bedroom popped into sharp focus. Rays of early dawn were filtering through the blinds.

The door creaked, as Smokey nosed it open. His tail rose, hesitated, then began to wag. Tilting his head, he sniffed his master's scent. Something was *different* about the figure sitting on the edge of the bed. Especially, the gentle warmth in the gaze...

Taskovski stroked Smokey's soft fur. "Sorry, boy. Bad night. I need to sleep a little more before breakfast." He fell into slumber as soon as his head met the pillow...

* * *

He woke abruptly. *Noise.* A pounding sound. He rubbed his eyes. The pounding was impossible to ignore, yet he was groggy, *confused.* Who could be at the door in the middle of the night?

The room was black. He swung his arm at empty space, baffled. The lamp was nowhere to be found. Careening from the bed, Taskovski stumbled toward the racket, his panic rising. Oaths spewed from his lips on impact with a solid wall. He sprawled across the floor, his brain writhing to provide an explanation.

The sickening crunch of mangled wood solved the riddle. The front doorframe was splitting from its hinges. He squinted, then reflexively rolled into a ball. Intruders were invading his home!

Footsteps thudded in his direction and came to an abrupt stop. He grimaced, sensing the presence of at least two people towering above him. The panting from their exertions iced his veins.

"Mrs. Vail...*Mrs. Vail*, are you alright?"

"Maybe she hit her head," another voice chipped in. "I'll call EMS. Do you see any blood?"

Taskovski recoiled, as hands prodded his neck and shoulders. "Who *are* you?" he yelled hoarsely. "What do you want?"

"She's conscious. Try to stay calm, Mrs. Vail. We're police officers. I-I'm sorry to have to tell you this, but we have a warrant for your arrest, and—"

"What the fuck are you talking about?" Taskovski sputtered. "*Mrs. Vail?* Why do you keep saying that?" He struggled and blinked frantically. "I can't *see*, God damn it! *Why can't I see?*"

"This is a shame, man." The officer let out a long sigh. "I *hate* puttin' handcuffs on a blind old woman."

The battle was brief. Taskovski barely recognized his own shrill scream, as he felt the cold steel enclose his wrists.

You Snooze, You Lose

7:16 AM: the ritual. Kyle could neither escape nor explain it. Sleep would evade…

"Damn!" He could hear Skip Tate firing up that monster truck.

Concentrating harder, he surveyed the room. The throw-rug lay unbuckled, centered between dresser and bed. Pillows were fluffed. He sighed, then drained his teacup of bitter Skullcap, ready to perform the final act. Succumbing fostered guilt but refusing left him open to nightmares. *Or worse.* Studies revealed the effects of long-term sleep deprivation: hallucinations, paranoia…

He did the deed.

Kyle's face contorted. Tate's heap of junk had died, and its resuscitation was violating the dawn. He envisioned the blue-gray smoke wafting into the cab to seek revenge on Tate's lungs. *Soothing…*

Kyle's fists unclenched as the truck roared out of the apartment complex exit. He'd yet to even lay eyes on the son of a bitch! One month prior, he'd awakened to the clamor of a moving van. The all-day racket continued long into the night.

He *hated* Tate. This he acknowledged as he drew back the bedspread. Indeed, he *loved* watching Tate's wife Melinda prance across the parking lot enroute to her morning jog. The corners of his mouth crinkled as he drifted off…

* * *

"Don't you think you should answer the phone?" Melinda purred.

The ringing was *infuriating*.

Kyle snorted awake as his dream went *pop*, hand grasping air. It curled into a fist and dropped onto the alarm button.

The apartment was black as pitch, but he maneuvered with the finesse of a man born blind. He flipped the bathroom light switch and started the shower. Laughter amplified within the steamy echo chamber. "You're a real *killer*, y'know?" The shout bounced off his reflection as it dissolved into the fog...

He yanked his shoelaces into knots. *Better wait and call Claudia from work*. The deadbolt rammed into its sheath.

Dusk had thrown a blanket of shade over the parking lot, but halogen streetlights glittered in Tate's bumper. The outline of a sticker titillated. Kyle loped across the blacktop...close enough to make out the words: *Fuck The World. I Wanna Get Off!*

"Figures." Within seconds he'd unlocked his jeep, refreshing his disdain for the word 'Cherokee.' Determined to afford bigots no fodder, he'd never owned a pickup truck. But wasn't the jeep an equal sell-out?

The engine hummed. As he dropped his gaze, hair cascaded, and he groped for the elastic band in his pocket. He *sensed* her approach and lifted his head. She was inanimate in the headlights' beam.

Incredible...Melinda had the submissive, liquid eyes of a doe.

He'd yearned for this moment. Sunlight had flaunted her lithe, powerful legs, skin as smooth as stretched deer-hide.

Headlights showcased eyes illuminated by tears.

He jerked the door open as she turned. "Melinda!"

She did a half-pirouette.

Kyle found *himself* caught in the spotlight.

She found her voice. "You're the neighbor who brought our mail yesterday morning..." Shielded by the sanctity of darkness, the heat from her flushed face closed the distance between them. "I looked out the peephole just as you walked away."

"No point in disturbing postal workers...why are you crying?"

He heard her breath catch. As he stepped closer his shadow spoked, betraying her cover. She was exposed in the headlights again.

Her lips denied anything serious. Her eyes darted to her apartment...

* * *

Her scent tantalized. Musky, addling as smoke from an opium pipe. Those emerald eyes—

The steering wheel groaned under Kyle's grip. Melinda's jeweled eyes, tarnished by fear of that bastard! He swung into Employee Parking.

He'd overheard Tate, been jolted from slumber by the one-sided attacks outside his fortressed bedroom. The jeep's door slammed. He was certain he had Tate pinpointed. Typical redneck, with musclebound arms, undersized flannel shirt, pendulous beer belly peeking out front and half his ass 'wavin' the flag.' Greasy hair tucked into a ball-cap graffitied with obscenities...and lastly, a pair of big stompin' boots. And Skip! Skipper? A *dog's* name—

"Jesus!" Sam exhaled a strand of oaths as his hand slid off his holster.

Kyle's eyelashes flickered.

"Sh-shit... never see you comin'. Somebody busted in 'cross the street. *Killed* the guard. Christ, didn't y'hear?"

"Nope. Looks like you're gonna' blow me away one of these nights if I don't learn to whistle." Kyle raised a handful of keys, giving them a lusty shake.

The twitch beneath Sam's eye responded before *he* did. "Aw...dunno' how t'figger you. *Christ...*"

The pneumatic hinge hissed, the steel door pushing out Sam. Kyle sized up tonight's workload.

"Fat-assed pigs." The 'crime scene' featured a popcorn fight. His foot transformed a nest of popcorn into airborne projectiles. He yanked a banner off his shoe, then sat to peel tape adhering to the sole.

Glaring at the rolled strip of taffeta, he unfurled it across his lap: HAPPY...OVER...THE...HILL...DAY!

Viciously, he wadded it...*thwack*! It skimmed the edge of a trash can, plummeting into a bag of Micro-Pop. A fireworks display poofed, then sprinkled the carpet like spent artillery.

Kyle's jaw dropped. He laughed until tears squeezed from his eyes. Then he slouched, head dropping into his hands.

A tear doused the tip of a finger...he examined it antiseptically. Months back, he'd shed more tears in twenty-four hours than in all the days of his life...and none, since.

A phone came into focus. Claudia would be waiting for his call.

* * *

The vacuum cleaner snuffed the remnants of stilted conversation. Actress, Claudia was not...

The hose coiled and snaked, slurping the day's 'leavings.' He kicked the OFF lever, and silence enveloped. Like a friend's handshake...*if* he could label any living soul as such.

"Any *human* soul," he amended. Cece's nose probed. He ran both hands through her silvery layers of fur.

The overnight janitorial job met his needs. No one to answer to, no one to talk to but himself...and Cece. The biggest advantage was being able to sneak her inside. They were a *team*. "The perfect couple!"

She'd rolled onto her back, offering her belly. Obediently, he scratched her pleasure spots. Cece was content, her eyes narrowing into slits, her paws crisscrossing her chest.

Kyle winced, remembering how her bony body had cowered on first meeting. Months of gentle persistence were required to heal the terror and scarring from metal cages. Fortunately, the Takers' attempts to profit from inter-breeding wolves with German Shepherds backfired. Puppy mill disassembled, Cece would live out her days in peace.

Cece's eyelids unrolled. An amber hue warmed her irises, her docile side taking over. She would die for Kyle, if need be, employing the prowess of her wolf ancestors to shred his enemies in her steel-trap jaws.

For now, she regarded him through the eyes of a German Shepherd. He sensed her confusion during *other* times. Neither dog nor wolf, she didn't quite belong in either world.

Kyle understood too well...

The term 'Native American' tumbled end over end. So did *genocide*. The sterile gauze of political correctness would never heal the wounds.

Cece was snoozing. Kyle tiptoed throughout the cubicles. There was voyeuristic intrigue in sifting among workers' belongings. Sweaters bearing traces of perfume draped secretary chairs. Comfy shoes were stashed beneath desks, and preschoolers' scribblings thumbtacked at eye level. Scraps of home-lives...

Kyle noted the time on the buzzing monstrosity on the wall. No wonder his stomach was growling.

* * *

In the breakroom, he corralled a sandwich and TV remote.

A face filled the screen, mouthing bleeps of rage. Kyle propped his feet up. 'Low-life cretins.' The pimply kid's nose ring bounced as he spewed accusations at his petulant gum-snapping counterpart...

A commercial intervened. Pensive, Kyle observed the sleeping city through partially opened blinds. Rain sprinkled the window, turning passing cars' headlights into sparkly specters.

His mind strayed to his gun cabinet.

A TV voice encroached. New guests were introduced. The woman sat, tears coursing down her cheeks. A semi-literate oaf shook his fist. He was 'tradin' the old broad in on a new model.'

Tate! This slob was his *clone*. Tate would break Melinda, use her up—Kyle jabbed OFF, and the screen extinguished, with a gluttonous *pop*...

Melinda and the shivery delight of their meeting kept him company throughout the remainder of his shift.

She dominated his dreams, even that compartment of consciousness that held him limb-locked, paralyzed by impending slumber. The hypnogogic state had been a misery since childhood, rendering him captive witness to night terrors, mocking his attempts to rouse himself. Now he welcomed it with open arms...*filled with Melinda.*

His hands warmed as he returned to the storeroom. The compact space hummed with the hot water heater's rhythmic gurgling. If

Melinda were here right now…

He smiled wryly. Claudia would turn up her nose at the greasy concrete floor. And the idea of having sex standing up, propped against the shimmying water heater—*horrors!*

Reverie dissipated, he tossed scavengings into a bag: expensive equipment, cast off instead of repaired. He had no qualms about lugging it home. There was virtue in 'stealing' what others misused.

Cece crouched on her haunches next to the exit. There she stayed, until Kyle assured himself Sam was at the far end of the lot. A signal, and she bounded forth, flashing into the rear of the jeep.

The compactor gobbled as fast as Kyle could feed it. He entertained the thought of Tate's truck mangling inside its jaws—and the screams' metallic echoes…

* * *

A tangerine glow swelled the horizon. Tires swished, birds twittered, conducive to pleasant rumination or the total lack of it. Kyle's mind stretched in the expanse. Even the sight of Tate's truck couldn't deter his bliss. He strode into the apartment, Cece at his heels.

Opening the windows, he peeled off his clothing and stepped into a brisk shower…

Sunshine had yet to scorch the rooftop. Kyle allowed a breeze to exhilarate his wet skin before tying a towel around his waist.

Through fluttering curtains, he caught glimpses of Melinda's apartment. Her drapes were discreetly drawn.

He sank into mama's velvet couch cushions. Her record player was within reach, a vinyl disk suspended above the turntable. Time to lift its burden of dust and let it spin freely. He no longer feared being swept away on the wings of Hendrix' Stratocaster. *He would join mama…*

His heart pounded as he raised the dust cover. The record was immaculate. He sighed, the sound mixing into the rustle from her sleeve. *His heartbeat quieted with her touch…*

Her hand upon his shoulder had numbed his pain one afternoon long ago, when he'd returned from school to find her sitting in the kitchen...a note on the table. Daddy was gone. He'd driven away, to another wife, another family. Kyle would always hate pick-up trucks—even more, the smell of stale beer.

'Electric Ladyland' elicited a shiver. He smiled, as tears flowed at last...

A tapping noise broke in, growing insistent—he bolted upright. Seconds passed. Then...*knocking*. He stared at the door.

It was his policy to ignore visitors. But his hand was turning the knob.

Melinda.

Holy shit, she was beautiful. What was she holding in her hand?

"I...um, this is..."

"An envelope," Kyle finished.

She seemed elated. "Yes!"

Curiously, he could make no eye contact. He took the envelope, the brush of her fingers clearing his tongue of all but an automatic, "Uh...thanks."

He felt a draft.

The wind gust snatched Melinda's hair, and it fluttered wildly as she wrangled it away from her face. "Your mail! Left in my box..." She blushed.

Suddenly, Kyle knew why. The letter hit the floor instead of his slipping towel. He'd caught it and hastily re-wrapped. "I'll pick up the later, *letter*." An eternity passed. "*Letter*, I mean...*later*, uh..." He shook his head, unable to wrench his eyes from her shoes. "Yeah, what can I say?"

Then came eye contact. "Fate's playing tricks on us?"

He laughed. "I think *so*." It was only right to offer her a cold drink at this point.

* * *

Melinda was more than he'd even imagined. Their tastes in music, art, and literature were parallel. Thus, the timing was perfect. "Are you ready to tell me what *really* made you cry last night?"

In an instant, she lost animation—*freeze-framed in headlights*—as before. She jumped to her feet. "That's none of your business."

He caught her hand. "I just thought…"

"*Assumed* what? Let go, Kyle."

He wanted to keep her hand…

She had closed the door behind her.

Alone. Drowsiness took claim. Not the siren song of a nap, but the leaden anchor lifted only by the full repertoire of sleep cycles—that circadian journey averting the cliff-fall into madness…

He blinked. He'd sleepwalked into mama's room. If only he could curl up in her bed and drift away. Maybe *Melinda* would drift away…and there'd be no score to settle with Tate.

Mama's room was as she'd left it, her departure as graceful as her everyday existence. He'd enclosed one frail hand in two of his own as her pulse ebbed…

But he couldn't part with her. Turning from her bed, he *searched*. The bookcase beckoned.

A volume stood out from the rest. He smiled. How many times had he fought sleep, begging mama to read one more chapter from Alice in Wonderland?

The pages were yellowed. Mama's cherished flea market find. Her voice still highlighted each word as his eyes glided…

He yawned. One hand slid the book into its niche as the other saluted two posters. Yes, Jimi Hendrix would've been proud to share space with an American Indian Movement activist.

Leonard Peltier's eyes glinted.

* * *

The alarm jostled Kyle from his favorite dream. Three years had passed since he'd last experienced it. He dawdled amid its freshness, dissecting each detail.

The dream was the embodiment of waking control. He could voluntarily interrupt, then return to sleep, continuing where he'd left off. In this twilight world, he inhabited a life-form midpoint between man and beast. In joyful pursuit, he would run through ageless forests, bare feet leathered, reflexes diamond-honed, bounding from cavernous ledges to gnarled tree boughs...

He grinned, almost emitting a ferocious growl.

Then, he remembered. Claudia.

"Fuck." He stumbled out of bed.

* * *

Claudia fastened her seatbelt, scowling. Kyle played with the thought of finding her hopelessly ensnared, begging him to free her. He would stall, studying her without expression. Her pulse would quicken, and a flush ripen her cheeks—

"Kyle!"

"Huh?"

She was glaring, in a *puzzled* way. "I asked where we're going."

What a contradiction. Stiff, but sedate. Irritated as hell...

"What's funny?"

"Sorry, Claudia, just haven't been gettin' enough sleep. Movies make me drowsy."

"Just the ones I pick."

"I liked the movie," Kyle soothed. "Oh yeah, got a surprise. Somewhere we've never been before..."

* * *

"It's the only place left with traditional curb service. Came here when I was a kid."

Claudia gawked as a teenager-on-wheels approached.

Kyle's nostalgia dimmed. "Rollerblades?"

"Yeah." The girl's ponytail dipped as she checked out her feet. "You ready t'order?"

"Uhh...they used to wear those regular skates, the old-fashioned kind." He cleared his throat. "Still have poodle skirts and cashmere sweaters, I see."

"Hah, yeah. They force us to wear this funny shit. I feel like a frickin' moron."

Kyle swallowed hard. "Two chili dogs, no onions, and two medium root beers."

He watched the skirt's appliqués flounce to the order-window. What had become of the scratchy Fifties tunes blasting from the P.A. system? "I don't get it," he muttered to the back of Claudia's head.

The response was a snuffle.

"Claudia?"

"You sure don't."

* * *

"Careful. It's hot!"

"...Oh—thanks." The carhop's sultry twang had startled him. And the *wink*. She couldn't be more than seventeen. Kyle's smile was time-delayed by obligatory guilt. He reached for an object on the tray, refusing to allow himself to enjoy the view this time as she skated off. "Ow! Son of a—"

"She told you it was hot," Claudia huffed.

"I guess it's worth it. You're *talking* to me." He sucked his singed finger, then offered it. "Here, taste…best chili in town."

She shook her head.

He plunged the throbbing digit into his root beer. "You know how to hurt a guy." No point in fretting. She would talk when she was ready. He perched her chilidog on the glove compartment lid and nestled her root beer into the drink holder. "There you go, Ilse," he said softly.

Her expression stabbed him. "I... haven't called you Ilse in a long time."

She receded into a shadow.

Kyle knew how far he dared venture. German by birth, adoption had stripped Claudia of the identity bestowed by her natural mother. *But she was truly Ilse*...if only he could convince her.

The radio helped fill an awkward pocket of silence. What luck! KMGG was launching into Focus Fifties Hour. "Strange, eh?" Kyle mused. "This place is in a time warp...but nothing survives intact."

"Hmm..." Claudia emerged, halfway.

"You're pouting."

"I'm not."

"You're not eating."

"It's too hot."

He shifted. *If she would just direct that icy stare at that steaming chilidog...*

"What's funny?"

"Nothin'." He blew the heat off a forkful of chili.

"The windshield's dirty," she said. "A bird must've bombed it."

"I'll get my revenge next hunting season."

A flurry of motion resulted in a shriek. Kyle battled the emergency with napkins and water, but the toppled chilidog had defiled Claudia's linen skirt.

"Stop it—just...*stop!*" she yelled.

He felt the sting of a slap.

"Wh-why?" she stuttered. "Why did you bring me here? You know I'm on a diet."

"Diet? You don't need—"

"*You're* deciding for me? You want me to be fat, don't you? So no other man—"

"Now, wait!"

The sodden thud of napkins hitting aluminum snipped her tirade. *The shadow tugged, eclipsing all but her eyes...*

"We've known each other since we were kids, Claudia. You *know* me—better than anyone, except..." His hand tippled his cheek, re-tracing the poker-hot 'brand' of fingerprints. "You slapped me before, once. Remember?"

A nod.

The windshield. He considered turning on the wipers, squirting it with fluid. Just wash the crap away. All of it. "How many times since, do you reckon you *felt* like slapping me?"

He heard a hollow laugh—then recognized it as his own, surprised it had squeezed past the lump in his throat. "Dozens...*hundreds?*"

Her eyes betrayed her. And her *scent*. People's bodies revealed secrets, especially their eyes. Liquid remorse, naïve innocence, tawdry sleaze. *Claudia reeked with ennui.*

"Were we meant only to be friends?" He'd finally said it. Rapid fire images were zinging through his head. He wanted to be sorry. He *wasn't*.

Claudia exploded—as raw as it was *in* her to be.

Coldly, he watched her unravel. She simply had no passion…

* * *

Claudia's plaintive whine still ricocheted off the jeep's interior: *I'll never be what you want me to be.*

Their relationship had ended with a death rattle. Kyle felt nothing.

Headlights—he recoiled at his pin dot pupils in the rear-view mirror. A vehicle sped around, painting stripes of rubber. An insult of exhaust stung Kyle's nostrils…mixed with a *familiar* scent. His foot bore down.

Miraculously, the truck executed a hairpin turn, hurtling onto the ramp. The stoplight's red reflection swabbed Kyle's windshield as he clung doggedly to the bumper. There, Tate's *sticker* taunted.

They merged as one entity, into highway traffic. Kyle followed until the swarm diminished and inky darkness overtook. He held steady, turning off his headlights and dropping back.

A twinge of regret seeped through. *Damned shame about Claudia…* The herd had to be thinned, but she'd never see that. So illogical about his hunting. But life and death was a system of checks and balances. How could he explain what he felt in his gut when he spotted his quarry? The excitement in knowing his presence was unperceived…

He smiled. The truck was slowing. When it veered onto the exit, he closed the gap like liquid graphite. His horn blared—

After herding the truck into a field, he switched on his headlights. It came to a stop, engine sputtering. Kyle thrust his arm beneath the seat as he popped open the door.

"Get the fuck outta there, Tate!" The rifle barrel rested cozily on the window frame.

The target twitched, eyes squinting into his mirror. "Wh-who are you?"

"Where'd your 'eat shit' voice go, big man? The one you use to wish Melinda a nice day."

Tate moved. The steering wheel was wearing his hat, his head wedged underneath. "Is that a-a *gun?*"

Kyle roared with laughter. "A cowboy hat. It's a fuckin' *cowboy!* Yes ma'am, Mr. Custer, but she'd druther you call her a rifle. She resents the misnomer. By the way, y'all comin' out t'dance?"

A bullet sheared off the mirror, the cacophony of its discharge and Tate's shrill yelp echoing through the cornfield.

"Don't kill me! G-God, are you insane? What do you want?"

A harsh *"caw"* blended into a menacing rumble of thunder...

"Your mirror fell off...Skip." Kyle shrugged. "But what can I say? You went'n bought a Ford. Cool bumper sticker, though. Out of the truck. *Now!*"

The sobbing occupant spilled to the ground, onto his knees...

Kyle's stomach fluttered, re-experiencing horror mixed with exhilaration... *like that day of cliff climbing, when the branch detached from the crag and he dropped, still clutching as he tumbled. Then—the pulse pounding in his ears as he dangled over a gaping precipice, another branch jutting through his pierced jacket—*

He erupted in gales of laughter, and his rehearsed speech crumbled. "No wonder you need that power over Melinda."

Tate's thin-lipped mouth bargained. "My wallet—take it! I'll be good to Melinda, I *swear.*" His glasses clouded, and his owl-eyes peered overtop. The stiff business suit was too large for his puny frame. "My watch." His tie jerked, Adam's apple bobbing like a yo-yo. "It's expensive."

"Shut up!" Kyle shouted. "You still don't get it, do you?" He was no longer amused. "Stand right there..."

* * *

Kyle lit candles...and *paced.* Sleep was out of the question.

He backtracked, jamming square blocks into square holes, round into round. Around and around, full circle. Yes, his uncertainty had begun with Claudia, and there it would end.

The knot on the back of his neck tightened. No, it was *Tate*! Claudia had begun to emerge—and he'd waited so long—his fist pounded the kitchen counter.

He'd *owed* her his patience.

Her slap in the schoolyard that chilly morning was deserved. His new neighbor had entrusted him with her secret. Cementing a bond, they'd shared the summer fending off mosquitoes from his porch swing. One night their lips met...*then, school started.*

He'd seethed as Claudia cultivated friends, the boys ogling the precocious eighth-grade girls. Undersized boys...with oversized feet and hands.

Kyle hung back, smug in his role as 'redskin savage,' although no one dared taunt him anymore. The last to sneer 'Geronimo' would forever wear scars from the concrete playground.

Pride eventually sealed his debt to Claudia...

Humidity chafed like a wool blanket. Perspiration oozed. The candles usurped oxygen and vibrato rolls of thunder mocked. He shook his head, lacing his fingers across his skull to counteract the building pressure. Unbearable. He considered shaving his head.

Mama had cut her hair during a traditional period of bereavement, ending the dance of its feathery ends brushing the backs of her knees...

A slam and the patter of rain on asphalt converged in a sensory clash as Kyle bolted from his apartment.

Cece's growl tickled his spine.

"Kyle—"

The sound of his name was strangely foreign. He gripped a steel handle, mentally squeezing off a shot, and spun around—

"Oh!" Melinda's eyes were huge.

"Back!" Cece skidded to a stop when Kyle raised his hand, reversing into the jeep.

Melinda's knees visibly buckled. "Wh-what?" Her head swiveled, rag-doll fashion.

Kyle ignored the pain the door handle's edge had creased into his skin and evened his breaths. He shut the door. "Whatever's wrong, I can make it go away."

The snuffing of the dome light had brought blackness, except for mushy gray flickers volleying through the clouds. *But he didn't even have to squint...*

"...The outage." She sighed. "Too hot to sleep. I was on my doorstep, dozing. Do you have an extra flashlight?"

"I was about to go for a ride, outside the city, where it's cool...any reason you shouldn't come along?"

* * *

"I'm not dressed for an outing." Melinda wriggled her toes in front of the A/C vent.

Kyle grinned. *Ahh...spontaneity.* Her fear scent diminished with each turn of the odometer. He needed no further proof. She was 'The One.'

"3:30 a.m. I'm sleep deprived and giddy." She basked in the lime-green illumination from the dash. "Next stop: Insanity."

"Hmmm, yeah...just saw the sign go past." Kyle swung onto the highway, switched off the A/C, and popped the ceiling hatch. His voice floated above the rush of air. "Sleep's a *bitch*, ain't it? Oops—sorry."

The high beams delineated a long snake of open road. "Sorry for what?" She drew up her legs and folded them...sitting on one heel, hugging a knee.

"The 'B' word. I was taught respect" He noted her mute surprise. "I haven't been sleeping well." Kyle went on. "The lines, they sometimes...*blur*." A self-conscious smirk appeared as his eyes returned to the road. "As long as those *painted* lines stay clear, we're okay."

Miles zipped by, Melinda the first to break the silence. "I rarely see an empty highway. You were right. It's cool. I can smell the rain...uh oh, here it comes!"

It fell like a curtain, pelting them with mammoth drops. Jagged blue streaks split the sky, and by the time the hatch snapped shut, Melinda's laughter had given way to hiccups.

Kyle guffawed. "Ever try the 'breathing into a paper bag' method? Or I could try scarin' you."

"This always happens when I laugh too mu—*oh!*"

"Well, I'm turning on this exit. Need a safe place 'til this blows over."

He navigated the narrow side road, startled by a *significance*. Abruptly, he jerked into a driveway. "Auto-pilot," he said, killing the engine.

"Huh?" Melinda craned her neck.

"Nothin'. Rough ride, eh?"

She broke into a wide grin. "Just what the doctor ordered. About time I took my own advice."

"So you advise people to chase tornados?" Cece nuzzled the side of his neck. He patted her head, then gave her an admonishing push...

"Hey, my hiccups are gone." Melinda pressed her face to the window. "I can't see a thing!" Her head turned. "Did I tell you I'm a doctor?"

Hail drummed the roof and played a lively game of ping pong across the windshield. "*Doctor*?"

"Psychologist."

"I don't think I'd forget *that*." His mind outlined a small building, like dot-to-dot drawing. He crossed the creaky threshold. "So, you probe people's minds? Tell 'em why they do those things they do?"

"If only I had that gift...no, I advise clients, assess options."

"*Clients*? Thought the term was 'patients'."

"Personally, I reserve that term for psychotics...ehh, beyond my expertise. I refer that category to someone qualified."

"Mmm. Good idea." His toes were cramping. He tried stretching his legs. A knee rammed the dash. "But...sounds *risky*. I mean, is there a tactful way to say 'Hey, you're fuckin' nuts—oh...sorry." *Damn, his knee was throbbing...and Melinda's skin had the delicate finish of the china figurines on mama's dresser—*

"Kyle, stop apologizing! I'm not made of fine china."

He did a double take.

"I can't recall the last time a man took back his 'naughty' words." She severed the thread before he could reply. "Look, the rain slowed. I still have no idea where we are. Hope you do."

"I know this place inside and out. Each blade of grass. The exact position the sun takes on the horizon when the red winged blackbirds sing their first notes...and *nothing* keeps the crows out of the cornfields."

"...I've heard that about crows."

Kyle drifted. *Moist yellow cornsilk between his fingers. The sun parching his scalp. Microscopic scissor jaws of red ants. Sweet juice from tender corn kernels exploding on his tongue...* "Even gunfire," he said glumly. "The crows come back."

"So do memories. The disturbing ones...is that what we're talking about, Kyle?"

"I was still hoping you'd confide in *me*." Turning, he settled his elbow on top of his seat and placed his hand on Melinda's headrest. *Her hair had the texture of moist cornsilk...*

"Funny," he said. "We talked so long in my living room, but never mentioned our ages. You out past curfew?"

"Not at thirty-three." Her hand found his...but didn't reprimand.

"How 'bout that? We're the same age. I have *another* surprise. I'm a 'Sanitation Engineer'."

He could detect no reaction. "You use a shampoo with chamomile, don't you?"

She tensed. "Y-yes."

"As I was about to say, I didn't finish college...been thinking, though. I made some changes recently. Might go back. Got a knack for computers. Techie stuff."

"Yes, that's a good plan." Her voice crimped. "My...husband is a Systems Analyst."

"You don't wear any rings. Pretty amethyst earrings, by the way."

"Wow, you must have eyes like an eagle. It's obvious how you can tell I have no rings on the hand you're inspecting, but it's too dark to…well, you're amazing…and *direct*."

He grimaced. "Directness can be cruel. I once got slapped when I called a German girl a fraud for concealing her birth-name. It was in a schoolyard. Her so-called friends dumped her, began calling her 'Nazi'. I was a hypocrite. 'Kyle' isn't *my* real name. I'm Oglala Sioux, grew up on Pine Ridge Reservation. My mother named me 'Blind eyes see'."

"Blind?"

"The doctor thought so. The hospital insisted on a birth certificate with a 'Christian' name. 'Kyle' means *blind* in Celtic. *Victory*, in Latin…anyway, mama knew I could see. A re-examination pronounced me 'sighted.' But enough about my eyes, Melinda. Yours told a story when we met. The tears tell me why you run. They're there again."

"I'm not cry—"

"Yes, you are." His hand stroked her cheek, thumb gathering the evidence.

The *shocker* came when her hand found *his* cheek, sliding further, through his hair, until it wrapped around the back of his head. She pulled, her mouth crashing into his…

His 'urgent' question disappeared, and his hands couldn't decide where they were needed most. He groaned as one found an exquisitely formed bare breast. He groaned again—*loud*.

"Mmm…what?" She'd managed to wrestle his shirt halfway off—

"Damn, that hurts!" The location of the emergency brake was distressing. Melinda's head jerked, colliding with his nose. "This isn't working," he whimpered.

"The rain's stopped, baby." Fingernails raked his back. "Plenty of room *outside*…" Her door opened. "Coming? Believe me, you *will*." She yanked her shirt over her head, and the dome light bathed her breasts.

His mouth opened, just one second before her wadded shirt hit his face…

It was no contest, even if she hadn't lost her footing. Kyle caught her in mid-fall, and having casually dispensed of his own shirt, tumbled and pinned her to the ground.

His hands regained purpose, stripping the remainder of her clothing. Her protracted moans and choppy gasps became the roadmap for his siege...

Finally, grabbing his hair, she paused the delirious torture. "What are you waiting for?" She groped at his waistband.

"Not here," he said, scooping her into his arms. He carried her through the blackness. *There was one rightful place to consummate their union. The act would banish his accumulated guilts and restore the balm of untroubled sleep.*

His thick soles snapped twigs and mashed rocks into the muddy path. Melinda's arms tightened at the yipping of wolves. "You're safe," he assured. "I'll carry you back, too. Don't want you to cut your feet."

"But where—"

"We're here."

A spray of raindrops christened them as he lowered her onto a plush grassy mound. He savored the aroma of damp earth wicking moisture through a sieve of foliage.

"Those animals," Melinda whispered.

"Wolves. Harmless...Cece is half wolf, and she'll love you as much as I do." He unzipped his pants.

"Cece?"

Melinda's skills put fantasy to shame, and with the co-joining of their essences came flight from Kyle's netherworld...

He felt the tips of Cece's mischievous claws skim his back. Her tongue flicked his cheek, her melodic whine tweaking the quiet. Playfully, he pushed at her muzzle. She began digging.

"It's Woodstock," Melinda announced. "Mud and rain...and I hear music!" A hint of melancholy softened her zeal. "Dawn is breaking through the clouds..."

"I'll get a 'day job.' My face is what you'll see each time you open your eyes in the morning." He placed his palm beside her left breast. Her heartbeat quickened.

"...Kyle, I..." The corners of her mouth twitched, in a losing effort to preserve a smile.

He watched the blood course from chamber to chamber, the thin walls shuddering as her heart pumped. Beautiful on the inside. So rare... "Cece set us both free." He patted the ground adjacent to Melinda's body. Then he repeated the ritual on the opposite side.

"What do you mean?"

Cradling her head, he stretched out on top of her again. "Cece is here...underneath us."

Melinda stiffened—

He rolled, pulling Melinda onto her stomach. "I'll show you her name."

Propped on his elbows, he yanked and tossed aside handfuls of weeds. Daylight threaded through the trees, casting lacy patterns-in-motion across his shoulders. A translucent beam lit the spot where he busied his hands. Melinda inched closer...

She gasped. "A gravestone!"

"Stay...*please*. She won't hurt you."

"Wh-who is Cece? She's buried here?"

"Yeah, this is a wolf sanctuary. She...was a German Shepherd-wolf hybrid. Mama and I were volunteers. Cece was rescued in a 'puppy mill' raid. My closest ally, *always*...mama's too."

Mama had pitied Claudia, but Melinda would've pleased her. He watched her crawl forward again, this time to trace Cece's graceful inscription with a fingertip.

"I've been a selfish son. I have to let go."

Tears had etched muddy trails, transforming Melinda's face into a charcoal portrait. "I got this feeling yesterday. Your mother..."

"Passed on, yes. About a year ago." His eyes became scopes, penetrating the dense forest. *Experience reminded him he could scale the fence surrounding the enclosure in less than a minute.*

"Lupus...Latin, for 'wolf.' She literally gave her life to them." A sigh sealed his anguish. "The place was re-named, in mama's honor. It's 'The Raven Corbin Sanctuary' now."

He continued. "Since she died, I... have a *ritual*, several things I do before I can sleep. One I save for last. I can't fall asleep, unless...*unless I kiss her photograph*." It was as if he were rotating a brightly colored balloon in his hands, testing its buoyancy. Suddenly, a thunderclap implosion—"I've never told *anyone*."

So much to tell. Later, Melinda would hear about that night, three years of eternity ago...when dad showed up to re-claim his Raven. Drunken cursing. Fists bashing the door—Cece's lunge at his throat.

A wolf's precision, a jugular tapped. Blood coagulating in her silvery tipped fur. Kyle could still smell the discharge from the cop's gun...

"Oh, Kyle...we all have compulsions. Even in sleep, the psyche must have order...*control*." She shook her head. "Mirrors and photographs. Contradictory symbolism. Have you ever stared into a mirror so long, your image disappears? I've shattered that slick, polished mirror of mine. Long overdue," she added. "Been ages since I stayed up all night. College 'pajama parties' come to mind. Secrets crumbled by dawn."

"I have the advantage here," Kyle gloated. "I'm *always* up past dawn—and your 'pajamas' are somewhere between here and the jeep...while I manage to keep my pants within reach."

"Except when you answer your door!"

"Fresh out of the shower does *not* count."

She made a face and collapsed. "I hope you meant it when you promised to carry me back. I'm wasted..."

"Can't move a muscle, huh?"

"...I don't believe this." She smiled, as he planted kisses along her shoulder.

"Nothin' like having the advantage," he whispered into her ear...

* * *

It was a churlish enigma. Fresh from the shower, Melinda lay naked on Kyle's beige sheets. He chortled, convinced nothing quieter than a jet

131

take-off could awaken her...and he anticipated her surprise in waking to find her hair arranged in two prim braids! After lowering the thermostat, he covered her with a light blanket.

The sight of mama's face immobilized him.

First came the usual sear of anxiety...then he perceived a 180-degree turn, followed by a Great Quiet. He closed his hands around her cowl-shell photo frame.

His bare feet padded into mama's room, to the bookcase. Sunlight slit the curtains, welding the window to the top shelf...setting the incense burner aglow. Mama's portrait was a perfect fit.

How wrong he'd been to capture her soul with the camera lens as she lay in death's repose. The curse of insomnia and garish visions had begun that night. The kiss had allowed mama a temporary passage into the Afterworld as he slept, *fitfully*...fearing if sleep were prolonged, she might not return.

Cruelty for *both*—finally ending—as ashes plummeted to the base of the frame.

* * *

Melinda's muffled sobs opened Kyle's eyes, his arms clutching her cold pillow. The phone cord led him to the hallway.

She cringed as he opened the bedroom door, eyes apologetic. *Her braids were undone...*He snatched the phone from her hand—

"Skip? Ah, thought so. Do we need to talk?" Kyle smiled, replacing the receiver. "He said he smelled something burning."

Melinda's jaw clenched, then unlocked, releasing an incomplete series of phrases with all the makings of a linguistic car crash. She began again. "I know you mean well, Kyle, but isn't this the *last* thing I need?" She tugged at the hem of his borrowed tee shirt.

"It's the last thing you'll *ever* need. You realized that last night. I'll take care of you—"

"T-take? You're presuming again! Confusing the issues—"

"I'm not one of your patients—um, *clients*."

"And I'm not one of yours!"

"No problem, then."

She crossed her arms, then undid the gesture. "We're supposed to have a... talk? Like this? Ridiculous. You're naked."

"Take off my shirt and we're on even ground," he laughed. "The ground...muddy, wasn't it? Let's talk about *Skipper*."

Melinda paled.

Kyle caught the scent of her rage. "I'm *sorry*. I was wrong to assume."

Her backstep faltered.

"Let's get dressed. Let's *talk*, Melinda..."

* * *

The phone would ring. If not today, surely tomorrow...

The story was big, and newscasters shook their heads while directing queries to on-the-scene reporters. Kyle had diverted Melinda's attention so far. Not difficult, considering the choices to be made, the options to be assessed. *She'd be driving home now...*

Late-breaking details unfolded. The next of kin had been notified, so they could now divulge the identity of the victim...

Kyle flinched. "*Ilse!* Her name was Ilse!"

They garbled on, with 'shocking' revelations about the 'grisly' discovery. No forced entry. The victim had died of blood loss, her throat ripped open by an animal, initially assumed to be a large dog. Sketchy reports from the coroner's office hinted at something far more sinister. The incisor wounds were characteristic of a different variety of canine. *A wolf.*

Kyle lunged for the remote control.

Melinda looked over her shoulder, then shut the door in a hurry. Her eyes questioned.

"I... dropped the remote." He got to his feet. "So used to living by myself, I don't expect the door to open. Uh, how'd work go?"

Her silence was alarming. He took her in his arms. "I know it all feels upside down, your first day back." He kissed her temple. "I'm calling in sick."

"No..."

"Did Tate bother you? You did_have his calls forwarded to your lawyer, didn't you?" He was content to be her protector—like Cece had been, for mama...*and for him*.

Melinda relented. Kyle made the call, and the night was free to erase her doubts. He closed out the world and they made love...

As Melinda slept, he sipped tea and read 'Alice in Wonderland.' She would know about Claudia when the time was right. But only what she was *meant* to know.

* * *

The call came not more than one hour after Melinda left for work.

"Yes, that's my name. What's this about?" Kyle pursed his lips, anticipating the moment he would interrupt...

"Claudia? No...no! She *can't* be!"

* * *

A badge was displayed. "You look like you haven't slept a wink," the lieutenant commented.

"I work nights. Graveyard." Kyle rubbed his puffy eyes. "Have a seat and get to the stuff you wouldn't talk about on the phone. You...you said she'd been killed by...a wolf? What the fuck—"

"That's *part* of it. There's an even stranger element."

"What's stranger than a wolf coming into the city to hunt down a woman? Wolves don't attack people. They run from 'em."

"We figure it must've attacked on command, been trained. An animal didn't wrap a bumper sticker around her throat after tearing it open—"

"What...this is a *joke*?"

"I wish. I've seen a shitload of weird crimes, but this is in a class of its own. If...*when* we find the owner of that sticker, we've got that killer nailed. A real *stupid* bastard. It says 'Fuck the world. I wanna get off'. I can just picture that type, can't you? Shame we have a major glitch..."

Kyle braced.

"Very little mess. Damned tidy psycho. No prints so far, except the woman's, and what's sure to be yours. On the TV remote, things like that...*expected*, seein' that you two were dating. Her family's suspicious, but that's to be expected, too. So, I'll stay in touch. Your input's vital." The lieutenant headed for the door. "Don't sweat it, though, pal. Nothin' to lose sleep over."

* * *

"Dinner's ready, Melinda. Then...there's something I have to tell you."

"Tell me now, Kyle. You're upset." She touched his cheek. "See? I know you so well, already. I'm *so* glad your Cece brought us together. I love you, baby."

His arms surrounded her.

Yes, they'd always be a team, he and Cece. The perfect couple.

A Slight Hitch

The wind tenderly lifted Gerry's hair, pulling her back into childhood's arms. Her stomach fluttered and embraced the bliss. Freedom and security held hands…

A jolt widened her eyes:

WICKIT'S AMUSEMENTS

The sign was neglected. From her vantage point, she could see freckles of flaking paint and burnt-out bulbs.

"Amusing, huh?"

Gerry gasped. "Where did you come from?"

Her stomach hurtled into treetops as the Ferris wheel seat descended. Beside her was a short, ugly man. He grinned.

"Who are you?" she yelled, her voice warbling through ground level laughter and wonky music. She gripped the rail. Her hair whipped across her face as they sailed backward, then up again.

"I'm your personal demon, baby. What's your pleasure?"

When her hair blew clear of her eyes, the words on his tee shirt ambushed:

YOUR WILDEST DREAM

"Shit, I hallucinate in clichés. By the way, Mr. Hell Warmed-Over, I don't like you."

"You're not supposed to. But after you get to know me…"

"Forget it. You stink of garlic and cheap cigars."

He swung his stubby legs like a joyful child and crossed them. "Maybe you take stuff too serious. Got to just let go sometimes."

"Well, I'm here for that very reason. To unwind. Obviously, you're here to ruin it for me." The ride slowed, quieting her grateful stomach. "Are you a *random* philosopher," she snorted, "or something even worse?"

His brow crinkled. "Worse? Clue me in, baby."

"*Paid* philosophers—you know—marriage counselors, psychotherapists, and the like."

"Nah, never done that. People share their secrets with me willingly. They get intimate and I return the favor for free. 'Course I gotta eat. I'm a Jack O' Lantern of All Trades, y'might say. I even sell shoes on the side."

They jerked to a stop. "Good, I'm next," she said, watching the seat below release its occupants onto the rubber treaded ramp. She felt her unwelcome guest's eyes caress her shoes.

Her violated toes reacted with a painful cramp. *The shoe store.* She'd never forget that repugnant troll at the cash register. *His yellow-toothed leer, hairy wrestler arms—*

The mammoth machine's gears disengaged and wheeled the next-in-line to the ramp, the ferocious racket ending Gerry's ordeal. Without looking back, she ran for the exit as fast as her maximum support joggers allowed. "By the way," she called out to no one in particular. "My husband's a clown."

* * *

That troll again. The greasy little weasel. "I have a confession, Geraldine. I'm in love."

"Go away," Gerry said. "I'm counting to ten." She shut her eyes…

"Ten!" Her eyes opened as a warm shot of air parted her bangs. The odor of garlic made her retch. She struggled to lift her head from the pillow, her throat aching in the hollow spot a scream should've filled. Inches away, Duane's face wore its usual expression of seamless slumber. In addition, it sported full clown make-up, except for what was smeared on the linens.

Enraged, she puckered and emptied her lungs right between his eyes before rolling out of bed. Tatters of guilt ate at her. She stood, back turned, listening to him mumble about spiders while he rifled through the bedding.

"I felt one with lead boots tromping on my forehead, Gerry. Right *here*."

She glared. "Apparently, he got stuck in the greasepaint."

"Another spoiled-brat birthday party gig. I was too tired to even wash, just conked out. But what can I say? Entertainment's in my blood." A frown exaggerated the droop of his drawn-on sadness. "I ate nothing but pizza yesterday. The little shits wouldn't even give me any ice cream and cake, 'cept for what they threw at me. Har-dee-har-har." He belched. "Demon seeds, all of 'em." A puzzling smile exposed a set of perfect white teeth. "That reminds me. When will the stork bring us a bundle of our own? I'm hungry."

Her shoulders slumped and she sought out a chair. "Duane, I see less and less of you. All these dead-end temporary jobs. Was having a family a joke from the beginning?"

"Joke? Hell, no—never a joke. We need a baby. Family equals stability." He unclamped his suspenders and his pants fell.

"You don't see the dysfunction? The house is in shambles. What happened to our 'I'll-clean-up-while-you're-at-work-and-vice-versa' deal?" Her eyes rolled. "Wait a minute, I'm interacting with a costume. It used to be fun, in a kinky way—and hey, no problem. You're hiding in there now. You need the kind of help I can't give you."

"You're the one who needs help, Gerry. Two sessions with the marriage counselor and you bow out."

"I'm supposed to sit there and watch you do your act? You would've charmed the pants off the therapist by the third session. Maybe you have. The fact that she didn't object to counseling a woman and a caricature with big red Bozo shoes makes her as weird as you are."

"Jealousy and paranoia won't save our marriage. Get a grip."

"Okay, if you insist." She yanked the glittery red ball from the middle of his face, giving his nose a vicious twist. "I want a divorce, Duane. I'm sorry. At least I *think* I'm sorry. No, I'm *not*. You lie to me constantly."

"My nose—give me back my nose!" he squealed.

"See? You won't have a sane discussion. I'm serious, and you just stand there making stupid noises…" Gerry trailed off, her eyes riveted to Duane's hands. They cupped the center of his face. Red liquid trickled from between his fingers. His painted eyes reflected horror.

Suddenly, she was terrified to look at the rubber ball or his face. "Stop it! This isn't funny anymore." She threw the clammy thing at him and ran to the bathroom. Behind the locked door, she sobbed into a towel until she stopped hyperventilating. Then she took a shower…

Anxiety took hold again as she rummaged through her bedroom closet for clean clothing. She found her purse upside down where it had fallen from the dresser. Her eye caught a glint from a half open drawer and she stared, disbelieving. *A gun…*

Duane languished beside the kitchen table, nose intact and un-bloodied, sipping a cup of coffee. His free hand played 'catch' with the rubber ball. The tails of his bedraggled fancy-dress coat dangled over his polka-dot boxers. "Your mom called." He sat, stretched his long bare legs and propped them on the opposite chair. "Said to tell you 'Happy Birthday.' Also, she wants you to leave me, Gerry."

"She didn't tell you that."

"You mean this isn't your birthday?"

Anger and confusion collided. "No—what? I don't even know. Will you stop talking nonsense? It's addling." She shoved heaps of overdue bills and junk mail from countertops, searching for the calendar recently ripped from the wall. An envelope addressed to Duane intercepted. It was riddled with holes, as if stabbed repeatedly by a pen. "This is from the clown college. What's it about?"

"It's of no importance whatsoever."

"Then you won't mind if I attempt to read it."

"Amuse yourself, Gerry. Today's your day."

She yanked out the sheet of paper. "It says 'Reason for Dismissal.' Duane, what did you do?"

"They didn't like what they found in the background check."

"What did they find?"

"Nothing."

After a huge sigh, she continued to read in silence:

Reason for Dismissal:

Your reports presented a problem. The necessary psychological evaluations reveal vulnerabilities and behavioral predispositions that preclude the advisability of a career in clowning. In short, staff and instructors feel you take your studies too seriously.

As per your contract, you are entitled to a pro-rated refund, which you will receive by check within thirty days.

PS: please turn in your nose, as it is official copyrighted property of this establishment.

She waved the document in his face. "The staff is funnier than you are. But I guess this tells me all I need to know about your 'diploma' in there on the wall. It's a phony designed and laser-printed by a phony. I was naïve when I was a kid. I thought all that stuff at the circus and carnivals was for real—"

"It's called 'magic.' If it has a name, can it not be real?" Duane's voice boomed. "Ladies and gentlemen, children of all ages!"

"Exactly. I need to grow up now. I'm going to Wickit's carnival. I'm sure you know it's in town again. There's a mystery begging to be solved."

Duane appeared genuinely aghast. "Why do you want to go back to that place...after what *happened* there?"

Her encounter with the ridiculous creature in the Ferris wheel seat flashed through her mind. "How did you know? You're *following* me now?"

"Don't leave me, Gerry. I'd be lost without you." Tears rolled down his slick purple cheeks.

An attack of regret left her speechless.

"I mean it. I'd be lost." He snatched a horn from the waistband of his boxers and honked it. "I'd go back to selling shoes."

A rubber chicken peeked from his oversized coat pocket. Gerry grabbed it by the scrawny neck and used it to knock Duane's top-hat off the table. "The magic is gone," she announced, and stomped out the front door.

* * *

The back roads were muddy from sporadic cloudbursts. Gerry vetoed her impulse to confide in her mother. Instead, she clutched her phone and called Duane's friend.

"Ben, I'm not sure why I'm calling. I guess because you've been pals with Duane since way back. He's not close to anybody else, as far as I know."

"Gerry? What's going on? You okay?"

"Duane's acting weird, *really* weird. I'm worried about him." Silence hung like dusty draperies. "Hello?" she said. "Are you still there?"

Ben made throat-clearing noises. "Gerry, I'm much more worried about *you*."

"Oh, he's not dangerous. He's scared of his own shadow, you know that. It's...he's just so depressed." She zoned out, alarmed that Ben had gone silent again. The time and date display on her phone floated on the periphery.

Today was her birthday! She breezed through a stop sign and narrowly missed a row of sawhorses bordering the parking area. Dazed, she pulled into a spot and re-charged her phone.

Oppressive heat had never hampered the carnival's attendance. Wickit's annually planted itself in remote, rustic surroundings. Advertisements were scant, but folks stampeded in droves. Gerry left her car and blended into the throng of merrymakers. It occurred that as far back as she could remember, she'd never caught sight of anyone from town. "Odd," she muttered.

The magnetic aroma of cotton candy obliterated her jitters. Drifting past the booths, she took comfort in the pops, pings, hoots, and hollers from the shooting gallery, balloon dart game, and milk jug ring-toss. At the first concession stand a beady-eyed old man with large ears handed her a freshly spun cotton candy before she'd even opened her mouth. He hummed something unrecognizable and dropped her coins into his pocket.

She cringed when he scratched the peeling sunburnt bald spot on top of his head. "It's my birthday," she told him, backing up. "I'm regressing."

The uneaten cotton candy went *thump* in a trash container along the teeming midway. The Funhouse loomed. A mechanically animated hobo projected gales of mirth at the entrance. As she approached, his salutations altered. "Abandon all hope!" boomed out. He cocked his filthy straw hat and bowed.

Laughter tinkled beside her. A young child clapped her chubby hands. Gerry turned her head, anticipating a set of close-by parents. She blinked. The midway was deserted.

The little girl appeared enamored of the mirror next to the hobo. "Are you lost?" Gerry asked. She stepped behind her and peered into the mirror.

Their reflections bent and twisted like two ends of an over-enthusiastic taffy pull. The only response was more laughter and hand clapping. *Hmm, maybe too young to speak.* "Sweetie, let's find your parents," Gerry said, placing her hand on the small head.

The 'little girl' toppled to the gravel, face up. "Happy birthday, Mrs. Clown," spewed from immobile lips framing a grimace of ice-pick teeth. Gerry let out a shriek. Feral eyes jiggled inside lacquered eye sockets. Arms projecting from the mummy-case body resumed clapping. Gerry ran.

She was out of breath when she reached the Ferris wheel. Before she could dissuade herself, she stepped in line. It was time to prove or disprove the existence of a self-proclaimed demon.

The sky was a clear and calming blue. A handsome youth with cornflower-colored eyes bore a stinging resemblance to Duane. Awkward and polite, he secured the safety bar then shuffled back to his chair. Clanging levers sounded out and the giant wheel groaned into action. *So much like Duane, when they first met at Wickit's Carnival, six years ago.* Her gaze lingered, as the object of her affection shrunk smaller and smaller.

Her phone's Swan Lake ringtone dispersed the reverie. "Hello?" She hunched, a finger in one ear, to decipher the meanderings of a frantic caller. "Ben called you? Well, yes, I did tell him I'm divorcing Duane, Mom."

Her mother's panic rose, high-volume. "Please come home with me and your dad, Gerry. You need help to get you through this trauma!"

"Through *what*?" Overhead was a cauldron of churning grey clouds. "Another storm's coming, I think. The sound's breaking up. Did you say—"

"Trauma, baby."

Her heart skipped as her head turned. "Should I be shocked, Duane? Logical explanation: you jumped in while my attention was elsewhere. You're agile, if nothing else. Also, out of uniform. Imagine that! Jeans and a tee shirt. You almost look human." She sighed, and ambivalence seized her. Exhaustion etched his unpainted face. "Yeah, divorce is traumatic," she said, as gently as she could manage.

"There's more to it than that. Look in your purse."

She humored him, violent gusts of wind complicating her efforts. "Why did I bring—I don't use this purse anymore. Not since..." Her tongue stilled when she brought out a newspaper clipping encased in a plastic sleeve:

Man Falls to His Death from Ferris Wheel

A 29-year-old Cooper County resident fell from a Ferris wheel car Saturday afternoon and was pronounced dead on the scene. He was identified by his wife as Duane B. Wickit, great-grandson of the creator of the traveling carnival, "Wickit's Amusements," where the incident occurred.

Preliminary investigation revealed a probable suicide.

"There's another souvenir in there. Look at the dates real close, sweet meat." A metal file materialized. He used it to smooth a chipped thumbnail, then picked his teeth with it.

Her fingers dove behind the clipping, pulling out a raggedly torn second, much of the text missing.

Body of Suicide Victim Disappears from Morgue

She shuddered as she focused on dated page headers. *Everything* fell into place, with the subtle persuasion of a de-railing locomotive.

"Yeah, sweet meat, I took the leap on your birthday. One year ago. It was inconsiderate of me to ruin it, don't you think? But I really didn't mean to hurt you...much."

The change in Duane's voice whirled her around, just as the giant wheel came to a halt—at the very top of its cycle.

"Ha ha, made y'look," the smelly little guy sneered. His 'Got Guilt?' tee shirt was the bruising punchline. He lunged. The seat rocked, a toy at the mercy of twisting treetops. Bolts of lightning, thunder, and rain drowned her cries as the barbed-wire hair on his arms raked her skin.

She felt her ribs cleave. Her heart squirmed inside his hand until it fluttered intermittently...a netted bird, succumbing... "No," she whispered, losing her grip on the bar. The seat tipped at an extreme angle. She heard an abrasive cackle.

"Aw, you're dyin' to get rid of me, huh, Geraldine?" She screamed as his arm withdrew from her chest. He yanked her backward, righting the seat. "Don't fret, I'll never let you go— lucky for you—it's a long way down. Who else would marry me? I ain't good lookin', but you know I can change for *you*. See?"

His eyes. Coronas of flame dissolved, revealing irises of cornflower blue. A tornado siren hem-stitched the carnival's cheery pipe organ madness as Duane took form. Without a word, he draped his legs over the bar and propelled upward before arching into a graceful dive...

No lightning, no rain. Gerry watched, detached, the lights splashing red on the ambulance below. The siren ceased and EMS workers loaded a sheet-covered stretcher at a leisurely pace. The Ferris wheel yawned, began turning, until her seat dropped to eye level with the scene. Her clothes were dry, not even a blood stain. No big surprise.

Mr. Personal Demon was back at the controls, butt-ugly and unrepentant. She braced for a confrontation as the grimy hands unlocked the safety bar, but his blank eyes made no contact. He motioned nonchalantly with his cigar. "Watch your step on the ramp, ma'am."

Gerry's head swiveled when her feet met loose gravel. The ambulance and hysterical onlookers had vanished. The cigar puffing, pizza-eating *changeling* remained. Now it had a name. It no longer mattered where it had come from. What mattered was 'he' planned to stick around.

The next seat swung down and emptied. He aimed his rotten yellow grin at a startled brunette and pointed his cigar at her shoes. "Hey, I like your stilettos and striped socks! Yeah, my ex had a stick up her ass, know what I mean? Sensible shoes, boring—hey, watch your step on the ramp, honey."

Gerry felt a blast of rage...then an astonishingly pleasant tingle, ending at her toes. She looked at her feet. *Ruby slippers.* Her heels tapped together three times, as she reached into her purse. Giggling like a schoolgirl she aimed the gun at his buttocks...

Experience is the Best Teacher

It wasn't working...

Jessy scowled at her reflection. The 'frown lines' deepened. 'Worry lines' began to appear. She looked away and applied the brake so fast, her head jerked. "*Ow*," she moaned, rubbing her neck. It crackled, the vertebrae reluctantly aligning. She pushed her sunglasses back in place.

"Hey, babe." His Corvette rumbled, deep pitched and sexy. Just like his voice.

Her fingertips tapped the steering wheel as she waited out the red light.

"Got somethin' for you. Over *here*."

It would be foolish to look. She knew better. But *maybe*...she glanced his way, just as the light turned green.

He pointed at his crotch.

"Aw, grow up!" she yelled. Her tires grabbed the pavement, and she lost him at the next corner.

By the time she'd slowed enough to pull over, her heart was hammering. She dabbed perspiration from her face and throat, tugged at the neckline of her blouse, and used the material as a fan to cool her chest. *Was this some kind of joke? Get rid of the PMS, and hot flashes take its place?* She rifled through her backpack for her phone...

"Oh, I thought you were out, mom. Was just going to leave a message. I can only come by and get my stuff. I'm almost to the driveway now. See you in a minute, okay? Bye.”

She winced. Mom was standing in the front doorway. She parked, slightly askew, and bolted toward the house, head down.

“Jessy, I just don't understand.”

“Let's talk inside,” she said, brushing past. *Ahh, the lights were mercifully dimmed.* She walked briskly to her room...

The suitcase was filling, and Jessy had so far managed to keep her back turned. “It's just *time*, that's all. Living on campus prepared me for that next step.”

“But, what's the hurry? It's what your *father* said about being inexperienced and immature, isn't it? You know he didn't mean it the way it sounded. This isn't necessary,” mom dithered.

Forgetting, Jessy spun around. “It's not just Dad. Derek called me an infantile brat when he cancelled the marriage... and I don't feel respected *anywhere*. Friends *and* strangers treat me like some sort of object. A *thing*, not an adult—”

“Did Derek hit you?” Mom advanced, and Jessy recoiled, shielding her sunglasses. *Remembering.*

“Do you have a black eye under those glasses?” mom demanded.

“What? No, of course not. Derek...well, he's a *vegetarian*, for cryin' out loud.” The packing resumed. “I've been a little weepy, that's all. So my eyes are puffy. Sensitive to light.”

“You taking drugs?”

“*No!*”

“Jessy, this is your home. You didn't need to rent a room. It's as if you're hiding from us...and you must do a *lot* of crying. Your voice is deep and husky. A mother *notices* these things.”

Jessy sighed and closed the suitcase. “It won't be long. I have to see this through. I'll keep in touch, and we'll get together before classes start again.”

Mom was beginning to snuffle as they made their way to the front door. Jessy relented and gave her a quick hug. “This may be the best decision I've ever made. Trust me, mom.”

Mom choked on a sob. "Jessy…you've put on a bit of padding around the middle."

Jessy's eyes rolled, and she exited, shaking her head and patting her pocket for the keys…

"Oh, my *God!* Could you be pregnant?"

Jessy stiffened, then hurled herself into the front seat. "Cafeteria food!" she shouted out the window. The tires squealed, and she was *free*.

* * *

Her first stop loomed. She pulled into the drug store parking lot, deep in thought. Yes. She could recall the exact moment she had started to hate her voluptuous figure. *Eighth Grade*…Billy Crawford's low whistle. *Nice tits*, he'd said. How her face had burned…

She held the dangling price tag off her nose. A blink brought the sample eye chart into focus. She double checked the numbered empty space on the rack. +1.75 *Intermediate*. She snatched off the glasses and looked for the matching numbers on the temple. Finding only a blur, she growled and plucked a second pair from the rack, using it to read the numbers on the first.

Satisfied, she gathered her purchases and deposited them on the pharmacy counter. She leaned forward, peering expectantly into vacant air.

A nearby clattering progressed to the unmistakable sounds of spilled and rolling pills. After a momentary scuffling, an enthused young man swaggered up to the cash register. "And what'll it be, today?" he beamed.

"Um, do you have any of those herbal supplement things for…" She cleared her throat. "Hot flashes. You know…uh, for—"

"So your mother's got you doin' her shopping, eh?" He winked. "Yeah, we carry several brands. They don't do *my* mom any good, though. 'Bitchy' ain't the word for it."

"Pardon me?" Jessy feared she would hyperventilate. A sudden flush of warmth was a major nuisance, but the overwhelming surge of rabid *lust* was just plain terrifying. "Check me out, please. I'm in a hurry!"

The machine whirred and pinged. "I'm checkin' you out, alright," the pharmacist laughed. "Oh, *sorry.* Bad joke." *His eyes devoured her...*

* * *

She was flustered, almost desperate. The key turned, at last. She darted inside and closed out the world.

This wasn't making sense. She sank into the welcoming recliner. *She was changing, at a dizzying pace...had matured at least twenty-five years since midnight.* "*Some* enlightenment. People are *still* treating me like an empty-headed bimbo." *Surely she was entitled to a refund. She'd take that con artist to court.* Her shoulders hunched. "Yeah right, Jessy." She picked up the remote. "Talk about airheads. What judge would believe *this?*"

The late afternoon talk shows were spinning their webs. Her attention span waned on the subject of juvenile prison reform. She flipped to the next channel, and her jaw dropped. The topic was "Mid-Life Madness: The Multi Orgasmic Woman." A pack of paunchy ex-husbands expressed outrage at being abandoned in favor of "young studs."

Jessy leapt from her chair and paced, but the room was too compact to dilute her cravings. She needed chocolate, and she needed sex. She needed them now. The phone gave her a 'come hither' look. The next thing she knew, she had called Derek.

"Yes, you heard me right," she emphasized. "I realize what you said is true. *All* of it, especially about sex. There wasn't enough, and I was too inhibited. I need—I mean *we* need less talking and more sex. *Sure,* I want to see you! Let me give you directions here...oh, and Derek? Bring me a one-pound box of chocolate truffles, okay?"

The adrenaline rush made her feel downright frisky. After converting the futon frame to bed status, she donned the silk robe Derek had bought her. Her dash to the bathroom delivered a jolt of reality. She froze in front of the mirror, comb in hand, and stared in horror at the silver streaking her hair like a road map...

* * *

The door opened, barely more than a crack.

"Jessy? Wow, it's dark in—*hey!*"

Jessy yanked Derek through the widened crack. She slammed the door, grabbed his shoulders, and turned him to face it.

"What the—"

"Shut up, Derek. You're *mine*, now," she whispered, slipping a blindfold over his eyes. "Give me that candy and behave, or I'll have to hurt you."

"*...Damn*," he shivered.

"No cussin' without permission." Shredding the wrapper, she ripped it from the package and dove in. She proceeded to ravish the truffles and Derek simultaneously, shoving both him and the empty box back into the hall approximately one hour later…

"Run along, baby," she said, setting her alarm clock. "I'm refreshingly free of the need to discuss marriage plans. You keep banging on my door, and a guy with a badge'll escort you home."

Derek's pitiful whimpering persisted. "I love you more than ever. I want to give you babies and grow old with you, Jessy."

Wonder and joy threaded her veins, nearly stilling her heart. She ran into the bathroom and flipped the wall switch, flooding the interior with light. The mirror registered her anguish, then her determination. *She had to know...*

"Come back in, Derek. When I turn on the lamp, take a good look. But first, listen carefully. I need to ask you some questions. Your answers are vital."

He took her in his arms, but she gently pushed him away. "First of all, would it *matter* if I can't have babies?"

His instant reply was startling. "Of course not, honey. You're *more* than enough."

She fumbled in semi darkness, until her fingers found the lamp's pull-chain. "Am I?" she asked. She sat and bathed her face in the Tiffany's glow. "I've grown up a *lot* since I last saw you, haven't I? I'm on my way to growing old already."

"You're beautiful. How could you ever be anything *but?*" He ran his hands through her hair...

The details about yesterday's events could wait.

* * *

Pain inched up Jessy's spine and sent satellite signals throughout her body. She rolled stiffly onto her side, groaning aloud with the effort.

Derek stirred, but didn't awaken. A sunbeam highlighted his nakedness, skipping and playing across his firmly defined contours. Jessy's misery receded as her eyes fixed on his abundant hair tickling the pillowcase. As always, jet black stubble awaited his morning shave. Out of habit, she reached, anticipating the nubby delight against her fingertips—

Her scream was hoarse, her shock equaling *nothing* yet experienced during her lifetime. Her *short* lifetime.

"Huh?" Derek's eyes flew open, and he jerked upright.

"Don't look at me," Jessy ordered. She pitched forward and scrambled to the bathroom, slamming the door behind her.

Her hands were misshapen claws, and their shriveled crepe-like covering extended to include the rest of her. *The skin of a woman of eighty.* The room spun as she raised her face to the mirror...

* * *

She could tell she was in Derek's arms again, but even after several blinks, he remained fuzzy. The futon frame creaked.

"Jessy! Should I take you to an emergency room?"

"No... *please.* There's nothing they can do. Only *Ulalume* can help me. Take me to her. Not sure I can drive...I think I'm getting cataracts."

"Who? *Cataracts?* Don't be silly. Now, I *know* you hit your head."

"Don't you want to know how I got like this? So *old* and sick and ugly..." She began to weep. "How can you stand to look at me?"

Derek shrugged. "You don't look any different."

"Why are you being so cruel? At least be *honest* with me. "I'm only twenty-one, and I'm bent like a pretzel—"

He cut her off with his laughter. "Age is a state of mind, Jessy. I know that's a cliché, but...well, you've *always* been pre-occupied with your looks. So pre-occupied, you can't see I'm *not*. That's what our split was about. Your lack of trust. If you were grossly disfigured tomorrow, you'd still be the person I've shared my dreams with, the one who never stops looking for answers. You'd still be *you*."

She cringed in agony, as he gave her an encouraging squeeze. "You just need to convince *yourself*."

Rapture. Her sniffling stopped. "Maybe my latest search for answers has done just that. Oh, how I love you, Derek."

"Yes!" he exalted. Let's make love all day." He clasped her body to his, in a frenzy of passion.

"*What*?" she gasped. "Are you kidding? I can barely *move*."

Derek made a sour face and rolled off her. "So...*still* withholding sex every time we have a silly argument."

"Argument? Don't you get it? I have to get to Ulalume! My hair's gray, and I'll probably be bald by—"

"*Hello*? You discovered a gray hair? Is *that* what all this is about? I thought you'd wised up, but *no*—melodramatic, as ever." He had put on his pants and was slipping his T-shirt over his head. "Speaking of which, first thing in the morning, you scare the crap out of me with some God-awful shrieking. What a way to wake up. Was that some kinda' *re-birthing* shit? The marriage is off. *Again*!"

If only she could muster the energy to throw him out properly. She pointed a crooked finger at the door. "Go," she croaked.

* * *

Jessy squinted at the windshield, worming her way through traffic. *People in a hurry.*

An elderly woman pulled up beside her. "Brand new driver?" she asked, sweetly. "Don't let the horns get to you." Giving a 'thumbs up,' she sailed on by...

Ulalume's Antique Shop awaited. Jessy located the parking lot she knew to be closest, a one block walk. Her hands trembling, she tried repeatedly to lock up the car, but the keyhole eluded. She bent, her lower back throbbing, and searched with her fingertips.

"Hey...nice ass."

The voice was close-by. She halfway straightened, leaning against the car for support, and turned.

The young man whistled, almost inaudibly. "Nice tits, too," he added as he drove away.

Jessy sighed, then wheezed. "My God, it's true. Men'll screw *anything*." She hobbled off...

* * *

Ulalume appeared exactly as before, materializing before Jessy's eyes...in the plush velvet wing-back chair. "You return to Ulalume, as I knew you would." She bowed her head, slightly. "But, then...I am The Seer."

"Well, I'm *not*," Jessy snarled. "And I'm not ready to be one of your antiques, either. Wisdom—*bah*! You know what I learned? People lie, that's what. I already *knew* that."

Dingy gray smoke spindled from the ancient hag's 'porthole' of a mouth. She leered, like a toothless Jack O' Lantern. "I could have told you that."

"Sure, sure. But I'm young and naïve. I *was*, rather. This sucks! Give me back my youth. I feel like shit, and it's not worth it. 'Pretty and dumb' will do me just fine."

Ulalume leisurely shuffled cards, stopping intermittently to upright several across her lap. "The deck was stacked, and so are *you*." She presented Jessy with a lewd wink. "You are beginning to see the former, but the latter will remain visible only to others."

Her audience's eyes widened.

"Allow me to make it clearer, Jessica. Your aging process is seen and felt solely by *you*. The rest of humankind still perceives you as a beautiful and rather gullible twenty-one-year-old. Oh—with *one* exception. Your mother. Mothers *notice* things." Her craggy eyebrows lifted. "But, *no*. She won't treat you as an adult, *ever*."

A tide of emotions engulfed Jessy, relief on the forefront, and she staggered...giddy. An onslaught of delirious laughter left her breathless. "Wow, this has been an awesome experience. I *do* have insight. Thank you, thank you, *thank you*! Knowing what I know now, I can go back and do it right. This is the *wisdom* you promised." She scooted an intricately carved oak chair up close to Ulalume and lowered herself into it. "Okay, I'm ready. Reverse the process."

A flaming corona outlined Ulalume's bulbous head, and sulfur yellow etched her fire-coal orbs. Jessy drew back as an alchemic explosion showered her with sparks, but she was held fast to her seat by anticipation.

Suddenly, all was quiet. Ulalume's coarse features had melted away, and in their place flashed a succession of images.

"It's *me*," Jessy murmured, transfixed. It was as if home movies from consecutive stages of her life had been spliced together for convenient viewing.

With an audible *pop*, Ulalume re-appeared. "You wish to go back and do it right, yes? I'm afraid you were right the first time. You were as wise as you will *ever* be when you came to my shop the first time, *and* the second. As you said, *people lie...*"

She gathered Jessy's hand in her own and gave it a maternal pat. "The process is irreversible."

The Peaceful Place

Janine strained at an awkward angle, too entranced to open the car door.

The house she'd seen in her dreams. From the second floor, she'd be treated to a spectacular view each dawn. Slender fingers of sunlight would tickle the tree-tops awake. As a child, the image had translated literally, raising her head from her pillow as 'fingers' played across her scalp.

She cleansed her lungs with deep drinks of honeysuckle. "At last, we *meet.*"

The sweet essence lingered on her tongue as the sun journeyed its transitional arc. When the cicadas began their chorus, she started the engine and drove back to her cramped apartment.

Sunsets had always been a fascination. Recently, they'd become a horror.

* * *

"Is this wise?" Andy's fingers curled tersely around his cup. His eyes were soft.

"I'm buying that house," Janine repeated. There were other things she'd intended to say. The words were gone. So were the fears.

After Andy left for work, she rummaged through drawers until she found a needle and thread. She sat in the light from the kitchen window, smoothing imaginary wrinkles from his shirt. The call to the real estate agent was postponed until she'd secured a loose button...

* * *

Andy clutched his phone and squinted as sun rays stabbed beneath the visor. "I know. She usually only drives before dawn, when the streets are empty." He listened, then sighed. "Maybe she won't be so restless if we move to that big house." He turned in the drug store parking lot. "Thanks. See you in about half an hour."

His path led straight to the pharmacy, where he purchased a box of gleaming hypodermic needles.

* * *

Janine ambled across the vast front lawn, as courageous as a toddler.

"I thought I'd married a city dweller," Andy grumbled, as she spilled into his lap. "C'mon—my back's sore. One week of hauling furniture up Mount Nosebleed equals one week of rest."

The ancient porch swing creaked from the weight of the two of them. Janine was silent, her arms clasped around him. He detected a tremor.

"What is it? You're shaking."

"You know that antique mirror in the upstairs hallway?"

"Yeah."

"This morning, before you got up, I looked at my reflection..."

"And?"

"My eyes were yellow."

His neck muscles jumped as he swallowed. "Don't worry about it," he said. "Probably just a trick of the sunlight."

She kissed his cheek and got up. "I'm starving!" The paper bag at his feet bulged with temptations. "You didn't forget pickles on my tuna salad, did you?" She had it unwrapped before he could answer. "Perfect."

"Well, of course."

Lunch was finished in contemplation of cloud shapes passing overhead. Abruptly, Janine abandoned the swing. "I want to explore the gardener's cottage in the back. Coming?"

Andy groaned. "The wiring's messed up, remember? Electricity's unhooked."

She flourished a wide-eyed flashlight. "That's why *these* were invented.”

Weeds obscured the cottage path. “I see the purpose in giving a gardener his own house.” Andy wiped sweat from his brow. “I can handle the front, but we’ll have to hire somebody for *this*.” The rusty hinged door resisted, so he braced himself against the jamb—

Her hand on his arm interrupted. She stared at his weary face. *She was changed from the inside, poisoned and hideous.* “You’re always here when I need you,” she said, her voice thinning. “And... I need you so much. They say that’s bad.”

“They?”

“They say a woman shouldn’t *need* anybody.”

“Why should somebody named ‘they’ do our thinking? Screw ’em. What I'm doing is supporting you in *your* decisions.”

“And that could land you in jail!”

“That’s *my* decision.” He yanked open the door.

A swirl of dust poofed from the interior, into the contrasting shaft of light.

Janine hesitated. *The thought of stepping into darkness...* “I’m not sure this is the right time, after all. I ate too much. I’m queasy.”

Andy took the flashlight from her hand. “Okay by me. I’m not into ‘adventure’ in this heat, but I’d better take another look at that fuse box. Just be a minute.”

The humidity was stifling.

“Janine?”

She drew back, and her vision zoomed in on the motionless carpet of wildflowers. “I’m all right, Andy. Go ahead.” After a pause, she heard his shoes mount the step and shuffle into the cottage.

She watched her shadow shift as she pulled the ribbon from the braid looped over her shoulder.

The shadow vanished. She looked up, her gaze swallowed by a fast-moving bank of charcoal clouds. A clatter sounded from behind. Andy shouted. She spun to the ground.

Eyes. Huge yellow eyes, framed by blackness. The creature’s eyes were inches from her own. She covered her face. Icy fingers drummed her arms and legs. She felt her body uprighted, scooped from the tangle of weeds…

"Open your eyes!"

The voice was Andy's. She blinked to confirm it, the wind whipping her rain-soaked hair around both of them. Her screams burbled into laughter. Marbles of hail bounced off Andy's head. Allowing the fury of the elements to flail her against him, she kissed his astonished mouth.

They tumbled into a bed of violets, rocked by peals of thunder, tearing at clothing adhered to skin...

Outdone by Janine and Andy's frenzy, the storm retreated. They lay, entwined, amidst a potpourri of bruised flowers. "Sweeter than a hundred chocolate bars," she said, nibbling his earlobe.

"Quit, that tickles." He laughed. "Forget all my complaining about the back yard, y'hear?"

Events wound in reverse, and she stiffened. "Something scared me." She glanced left and right, into the distance. "Just before the rain came, I heard you yell."

"Yeah! What *was* that? It jumped out, and I dropped the damned flashlight. *Possums* sure don't move that fast. Glowing eyes, that's all I saw."

"Me, too." She gathered her clothing. Luminous 'snakes' hung from dingy clouds, the muggy atmosphere returning. "Just another trick of the sunlight?" Without dressing, she whirled and headed toward the house.

Andy caught up, his clothing bunched in his hands. He didn't speak until they reached the back porch. "Are you moody or *what*?" Panting, he flung open the door. "It was probably just a stray—"

A slinky black shape zipped past them, disappearing into the house.

"*Cat*," he finished, agape.

* * *

They were worn ragged. A week had gone by. Seven days of systematic hunting, from attic to cellar.

Andy wrinkled his nose. "You'd think we'd find him because of the *smell*. Did he drag a litter box in with him?"

At times, jokes broke the tension. Not this time. Janine snatched a butter knife from the table, and without rising from her chair, hurled it into the sink. "You're just...leaving?"

"I can't take any more time off. I'll bet that cat slipped back out the door days ago. My vacation's over. I'll get fired."

"Breakfast is over, too." She motioned toward the door.

He straightened his tie. "I guess that means no kiss."

"We're not Blondie and Dagwood," she said.

He knelt beside her. Wrapping his arms around her waist, he used her lap as a pillow. "How 'bout Romeo and Juliet?"

"Bonnie and Clyde," she corrected, mussing his hair...

She laced her fingers as she watched him drive away. Anger boiled at the intrusion of their uninvited 'guest.' The vagrant was laying waste to her paradise...*and her plans*. "Here, kitty," she called, between clenched teeth.

She halted at the stairwell. An empty cat food can. She'd placed an opened, full one there just before making breakfast.

"Out of my house!" Outrage sliced the stillness, rattled hardwood floors, and bounced off vaulted ceilings.

Her ears buzzed. She slumped to the bottom step. Folding her arms, she hugged herself and rocked until her heartbeat steadied. Then, she circled back to the stairwell.

After a few firm thuds from the heel of her hand, the corner panel yielded. Behind it, the air was cool, an appropriate hiding place for musky treasure. She rolled and lit a joint, replacing the panel as she held in her first hit.

The quandary of the feral feline withdrew, a notch for each drag, the 'mellow' reaching saturation point midway through the Grateful Dead's "Box of Rain." She luxuriated in the center of the living room floor, surrounded by unpacked cardboard boxes. "Thank you, God, for whomever invented music."

As the album ended, she was back on her feet, twirling in slow motion. Face upturned, she chanted a poem, a childhood gift from her father, written "With Janine in Mind."

> "She dances in the rain,
> drenched with jewels...
> From Darkness, comes Light.
> Raindrop-prisms."

Rain. Cleansing, like tears. She marveled at the resilience of varnished wood as she made her way upstairs. *Dark clouds.* It had stormed the day her father died. She'd felt the barometer plunge. Then, the headache—

The mirror.

She hurried by—

She'd seen something.

Her head swiveled. The bedroom door looked like a dart board punctured by splinters of sunlight. Fractioned rainbows chased around the edges of the mirror frame, spraying the wall behind it. She took three steps backward and a half-turn. Now, she faced her full-length reflection straight on.

Circling her ankles, was the cat...but he was the color of Summer. Goldenrod yellow.

Janine's eyes were a placid blue.

* * *

Andy fumbled with his sunglasses, cursing the glare, and spoke into his phone. "No, there's no phone at the house," he lied. "Use *this* number. My cell phone. So when will you know?"

His eyes watered. "All right...thanks."

His mind had been on Janine instead of clients. Good thing he'd allowed for a possible two-hour commute, he reminded himself. On a trouble-free day, with no accidents, an hour would suffice. *Trouble-free day...*

He sped to the exit ramp. The rest of the drive would be cool and shady. He'd breathe in the inevitability of nature's plan, fold his wife in his arms, and drown in her hair.

He took the front steps two at a time. But as the screen door closed, his sharp intake of breath was all he heard. The *quiet* was a sinister bank of fog. Music had been his welcome home since the day they were married, even if Janine was nowhere in sight.

Panic crawled from beneath his sticky collar as doorway after doorway opened into empty space. Their sparse supply of furniture rattled about like loose teeth…

"Janine!" he yelled, from the back porch. Then, he spotted her…in the grass, *rolling*.

A sprint closed the distance, but his heels dug in when he stopped. He stood, gaping, over two forms caught in freeze-frame on the ground.

Two sets of eyes met his, then flickered with amusement.

Relief shook him free.

The cat resumed his frolic, tangling in auburn tresses, swiping at Janine's lashes with soft paws.

"It looks like he had plans of his own," Andy said. "Crazy cat."

"Not so crazy." She pacified the critter with rhythmic scratches behind his ears. His yellow eyes narrowed as a sunlit breeze rippled his jet-black coat.

Janine extended a hand, pulling Andy down beside her. "Did I tell you about the cat I had when I was a kid?"

He shook his head.

"Daddy brought home a yellow Tabby. I named her Topaz. She was sun-shiny."

Andy's reply was a whisper. "So are you."

She squeezed his hand, but the action was spasmodic, like the battle raging between her head and heart. "Sometimes I get so tired of it. Besides the obvious…do you know what grieves me?" She looked past him. "Losing my sense of humor."

A bee hovered close. She spat at it. "When my father died there was nothing left to laugh about. His corny jokes, the little magic tricks…*gone*. The 'death watch' was excruciating. The only peace I remember was when we watched sunsets together."

Andy could think of nothing to say. *Nothing.*

"You have the most incredible gold-specked eyes, Andy. Who was it that called them 'windows of the soul'?"

"Du Bartas started all that. Don't think I ever met him though." He crossed his eyes.

She reacted with a cuff to his cheek. The startled cat hissed and streaked into the lilac bushes.

Andy matched her, kiss for kiss, abandoning concern for his grass-stained shirt.

"Why didn't I meet you a long time ago?" she asked.

"Maybe I didn't deserve you."

He started to turn his head, but she caught it in her hands. "You make me laugh. You make me happy."

Salty tears sprinkled his face, his open mouth. The thirst was unquenchable...

Dinner was a picnic on the back porch. They shared a joint and feasted on potato salad, cold baked beans, and lemonade.

"I want to watch the sunset."

Andy felt a mixing of joy and dread. "You sure?"

She nodded. "I'm healed now. It won't be like seeing him die anymore."

They braved the mosquitoes to get a panoramic view. Andy leaned against the gardener's cottage, Janine secure in his embrace.

Over a wash of gold, a cloud castle shimmered. A castle fit for a poet. How foolish she'd been. She'd used her father's dying words to plug their hourglass, hoping to 'keep' him.

The sunset was unchanged. It was peace. It was Heaven. *Sunsets will always be beautiful, Janine. Death isn't dark. Death is sun-shiny...*

She rested against Andy's chest, feeling his heartbeat...the center of her universe.

* * *

Hours later, as she showered, she held her face in the spray and let childhood pull her back. She weighed the ice cream truck's tinkling bell versus the vague outlines of the mother she'd never known. Happy and sad, juxtaposed on a playground seesaw.

Drowsiness tugged at her head, almost taking her down. Wobbling, she stepped out of the tub and into her terrycloth robe.

Andy stopped polishing the hallway mirror and hid his shock. "Hey, don't puddle my floor." He picked her up and carried her to bed…

Alone in the living room, he stretched out in the recliner and put on a headset. Occasionally, his chin would drop as he floated into nightmares of squirming indecision. Mainly, his eyes stayed open, watching the clock.

⋆ ⋆ ⋆

Two yellow eyes. Rectangular, flickering.

Janine gasped. Two became *four*, out-of-kilter and multi-dimensional, like a double-exposed photograph. On the peripheral, was a buzz. Like angry bees. Her head was too heavy to lift from the pillow. She opened her mouth. "What?"

Two windows popped into focus, her sun-catcher shattering beams of light into jittering rainbows. A pinprick sensation spread across her scalp, as if each hair was attached to her pillow.

The buzz again. Much louder.

He jumped on her chest, fire tipped claws extended. The roar from the black beast's throat was deafening.

She screamed until Andy's face replaced the cat's…

⋆ ⋆ ⋆

"It wasn't a dream." She stirred cinnamon into her oatmeal and studied Andy. "Why did you put that shirt back on? It has grass stains all over it." After waiting a few moments for an answer, she added. "You look *awful.*"

Andy rubbed at itchy stubble, a smile twitching the corners of his mouth. "I've always admired your bluntness. But then, I'm a real *twisted* bastard." A gulp of coffee burned his tongue. He struggled to keep from looking at his phone but took comfort in knowing he'd muted the ringer.

Janine's expression was alarming.

He caught and held her eyes, pouring himself into them. "I just fell

165

asleep in my clothes, that's all. *Really*." All the cards were dealt now. Except the blistering one, up his sleeve.

She left her breakfast and eased behind his chair. His shoulders were bunched. She massaged them, his earthy scent completing the photosynthesis of her besieged dream castle. *Beauty and brutality, intertwined...*

"I'm going back to bed, Andy. Headache. Play some music while you get ready, okay?"

Without a word, he pulled her hand to his mouth and kissed it. As her footsteps faded, tears rolled down his cheeks...

By the time she reached the gleaming hallway mirror, strains of her favorite song drifted up the stairs. She stooped, and Topaz leapt into her arms. The dull ache behind her eyes was already diminishing when she crawled into bed. *Pain had been her only prison.*

Topaz curled on Janine's chest and purred. The gentle vibration brought a smile...and *memories* of those times so long ago, when her father would sing her headaches to sleep.

* * *

The first ring pried open Andy's reddened eyes. The sun blazed, nearly overhead, but the covered back porch was cool and breezy.

"Hello...yes. The reports. Yes, Janine's latest results." His knuckles turned pale as he held the phone to his ear. "So... what you're saying is...to remove the tumor *may* prolong her life for *maybe* a year or two. But she'll likely still have seizures. And she's certain to go blind?" He numbed himself to the remainder, ending the call quickly...

He'd already prepared the syringe. *Morphine. Not quite the dose the doctor ordered.* After double-checking, he put the panel back in place and emerged from the stairwell. He re-set the player to track #1. *Box of Rain...*

The doctor's final sentences re-played in his head as he trudged up the stairs. *The seizures will increase, become nearly constant. She'll lose her sight either way, Andy...then, her life—but there's no predicting exactly how long that will take.*

The Long and the Winding

Jane was *so* hungry...

She shivered and jammed her hands deep in her pockets, snuggling into the linings to steal warmth. Crumpling her gloves with her fingers and squeezing them loosened the stiffness.

Greg's hand was seeking hers again.

"I'm too cold to even put my gloves on," she laughed. "My hands are staying in my pockets."

He found her knee instead. "Just as good."

"Well, you can use it as a gearshift soon, if I don't get something to eat. I'm starving!"

* * *

The sign was just plain huge:

The Waffle Palace

Her mouth watered. Fluffy scrambled eggs. No, an omelette. Pancakes...succulent blueberries topped with a generous dollop of whipped cream—what?"

"Huh? *What* what?" Greg's eyes were empty saucers.

Her stomach growled. "Should've called this place The Cracker Box." The crown of her skull thumped the headrest. "Just *look* up there. The sign's three times the size of the building," she cackled, through clenched teeth.

"I guess they want to make sure people spot it from the highway." Greg hesitated, eyeing her. His hand retreated from the dangling keys. "Well, Jane. What d'ya say? Going in?" He bumped her shoulder with his own.

She winced. *Maybe it was that God-awful glare off all that shiny chrome and glass.* "Ow."

"Ooh, *delicate* type, eh?"

"It's my eye, my left eye." She cupped a hand over the throbbing orbit. "Maybe it's a migraine coming on. I do feel weird. I'm prone to 'em when I go too long without a meal."

"Let's get *in* there, then." Greg switched off the engine.

* * *

Silence. No one had come to take their order. She lifted her head...

In the young man's motionless hand was a dripping spatula. His red and white striped shirt pulsated and screamed. His face bore no expression.

"No!"

Greg blinked, looked straight ahead, then back again. "Huh?"

"That guy over there, behind the counter," she said, minimizing lip movement.

Greg grinned. "Hat's kinda' funny, ain't it?"

"He's gouging my third eye!" She ducked and covered her head.

* * *

On the road again. Darkness swallowed the hills, releasing them one at a time into startled headlights. Despite the wide expanse of empty highway and fleeting glimpses of countryside, Jane felt caged... *confined.* The hunger was claustrophobic.

Static chewed her nerves like a jagged sawblade. "You sure like to play with those damned knobs, *don't* you?"

"Yep, every chance I get." Greg raised his voice over a crescendo of guitars, upping the volume even further. "Hey... do you know who this is?"

She hated it when he made her guess. "Just *tell* me. It's another 'eighties' band, right?"

"Ahh, your memory's slippin', eh?"

*Slippin'... slippin', slippin'...*her shoulder dipped into the swerve, but she righted herself immediately. "Gas?" She was peeved, and unsure why.

"Another one of those big-ass signs lookin' at you, baby," Greg chuckled. "Wow, listen to this." He dialed up the radio until the treble screeched. Her hands clamped over her ears...

He was out of the car and headed for the pay window, his lips puckered into a whistle. *She loved watching him from the back, those cute buttocks flexing—*

Sensory overload. Too much was coming at her at once. Yes, *this* sign was equally huge, its angry black licorice outlines shouting **GAS**. The plastic monstrosity teetered precariously, affixed to the roof of what resembled a white-washed glorified outhouse.

She sighed, and her hands slid slowly from her ears. Hank Williams' nasally serenade perched her on a barstool. She closed her eyes and let the sights and sounds soak in. *Salty fried pork rinds...*

"Whaaaaaat'ya got cookin'?"

She laughed out loud. Greg finished the chorus as he pumped the gas. "Hurry up. Ah'm hongry!" she wailed.

He stuck out his tongue and holstered the nozzle. Rubbing her frosty nose, she squelched the radio's rapid-fire commercial break and waited...

"Here y'are."

Dazed, she clutched a skinny cylindrical object thrust into her hand, her neck stretching to catch a glimpse through the dimness bordered by the pay window. She strained to make out the shape inside.

A bump in the driveway brought it into focus. A cowboy hat framed a featureless face. Slim fingers fluttered a lazy farewell.

Her eyes zig-zagged to her crimped knuckles. A stifled scream emitted as a pinched squeak. Red and white blinked, alternating... *merciless.*

"Nice guy," Greg said, leaning into the pedal. "Name's Hank. Said to give that peppermint stick to my lady."

It revolved like a Barber's pole. **Alive**. "Take it," she shuddered. "I need *real food*...not candy."

He bear-hugged her, then man-handled the wheel, zipping onto the highway ramp. "Accept no substitutes, huh? *My* kinda' woman, yep. I know just the place. Vittles and atmosphere, both. Hang on."

* * *

This was unfamiliar territory. She was an urbanite, damn it. She prayed Greg was headed toward home. *Her* home. John Denver was crooning now. She dove for the OFF switch.

It was missing.

Country road, take me home...

The miles unrolled like an endless chafing ribbon. Not another car in sight. *Desolate*. "I don't see any restaurants," she whimpered.

Patsy Cline warbled her *own* misery, the phrase lilting high above, silhouetted by the lacy mesh of tree-tops edging the moonlit sky. *Lonesome as I can be...*

Suddenly, there it was.

"You'll love it," Greg assured.

The sign was colossal. Proudly, it displayed three garish bubbling green letters:

EAT

"Delicious," she panted.

* * *

They slid into a cozy booth. She reveled in the clink of authentic silverware, but the black and white checkered floor tiles dizzied her. Averting her eyes, she devoured the quaint delicacies on her menu. *Ho-Made Chili...*

A rustle, liberally spliced with gum snapping, jerked her to attention.

"Howdy. You folks made up your minds yet?"

Jane's upward glance forced a double take. Horizontal red and white stripes exaggerated the woman's hourglass proportions.

"Yeah, I'll have a country fried steak and hash browns," Greg piped up. "Oh, and coffee. Long drive. Tryin' to stay awake."

"Uhh..." Jane was glued to the name tag. It read: **Waitress.** "Chili," she mumbled. "And strong hot tea."

"Right away, sugar, and did you want—"

"Yes. Sugar for my tea."

"I meant *crackers*, hon'." The waitress rolled her glassy doll-eyes. Cellophane packets spilled from her hand, reflecting the ceiling bulbs. "Be back in a flash with your drinks."

Jane pinched a knot of skin between her eyebrows and closed her lids as she massaged.

"You better take something for that headache," Greg reminded. "I'll bet this place sells aspirins."

"They don't work. I have my prescription stuff with me, but can't take it on an empty stomach. Hope it's not too late. Once a migraine takes hold, it can last for days. The timing's crucial."

Heyyyyyy, good lookin'...

Her eyes flew open, and Greg snickered.

"I don't believe it," she gasped. "Hank Williams again." She twisted all the way around. A flat black disk was spinning inside a juke box. Heavily adorned with glitz and glamour, flickering colors in its base kept rhythm with the tune. *Entrancing...*

"Are you gonna' eat? Thought you were starving."

She turned. "The food? Already? I didn't even hear the waitress."

"See how you are? Bet you weren't listening to me rattle on about high school either." Greg slathered butter on a roll.

A shimmering pool of orange grease encircled the chili. Nausea blunted her appetite. "Oh, I was listening...*really*."

"Sure." An enigmatic smile appeared. "There'll be a test, later." He winked and sopped up the pepper-speckled white flour gravy with his bread.

She grabbed her spoon and forced down a mouthful of chili, hoping the spices would clear her head. "Hot chili," she announced, giggling at the contradiction.

"So when are you going to *marry* me?" Greg asked. He reached across the table and offered her a metal-topped glass container.

Automatically, she accepted it. But an answer to his question wasn't available. Her smile frozen, she plunked her tea bag into her steaming cup and studied the container. It read:

SUGAR

She stirred the fragrant brew sluggishly, mulling over the meaning behind tonight's road trip. No doubt about it. Friendship had reached its destination. Greg had taken her to meet his mother...

Jane had a *relationship* on her hands.

The realization was as electric as a cattle prod. "Hmm. In sickness and in health?"

He nodded.

"I'm sick a *lot.*"

"I'm fearless."

She covered her eyes with her hands, soothing the ache with emollient blackness. "I guess I can take my medicine now."

He ordered a root beer, his voice *odd.* Distant, yet very close...

After midnight, searchin' for—

"Will you be havin' dessert tonight, folks?"

Jane's eyes bugged. "Wow...has anybody ever told you how much you resemble Patsy Cline?"

The waitress' pouty red lips parted, and out came bawdy laughter. "Every single time Patsy's playin' in the juke box! Ain't never failed *yet.* Right, Hank?"

Greg spoke up from behind his menu. "What? No 'pea-can' pie? Well, I'll be dipped in gravy!"

Jane's dizzy head swiveled back to "Patsy." For the first time, she noticed the patches on her uniform's breast pockets. The right side read: **TIP.** The left: **Please.** A guffaw slipped out—

Silence...

Everyone had turned. Everyone was staring. Gravy dripped from an old-timer's gray beard...

Jane rummaged frantically 'hrough her purse until her prescription bottle materialized. The only remaining trace of 'Patsy" was the guest check, so another glass of water seemed unlikely. Popping the cap, she shook two tablets into her palm.

"Well, I think I blew it." She sighed, then read the label aloud. "Ergotamine, seventy-five milligrams. Important: Take two tablets during pro-dromal phase to prevent migraine."

Background chatter had resumed, blending into a smeary buzz, but a voice from the opposite side of the booth broke through. "Beggin' your pardon, but what's a 'pro-dromal' phase?" Hank nudged her hand with his icy cold brown bottle. "You can wash 'em down with *this*, if y'like."

She doused a waffle with maple syrup, declining his proposal with a shake of her head. "It's also called an 'aura.' People have been known to experience vivid auditory and visual hallucinations during the stage just before a migraine hits full force."

"Hmmm..." Hank twirled a toothpick with his tongue. "Y'mean folks hear an' see things that ain't there?"

She unwrapped a chunky pat of butter and nodded vigorously. Her eyes rested on his string tie, which was held together by a glittery diamond studded guitar clasp. *He was adorable!* "Another waffle, Hank"?

"Yes, ma'am. Sure goes good with root beer, by golly." He took a hefty swig and cocked an eyebrow. "Ain't y'gonna' take your pills? Memory slippin', eh?"

Suddenly, he slammed his hat on the table. "Aw, shucks! Just an observation, but you're too purty for pain, lady. Kick its butt."

Amazing. The dull throb had already backed off since she'd started on the waffles. Triumphantly, she dropped the tablets back in the bottle and replaced the cap.

Hank responded with a dazzle of pearly whites. *Could be dentures,* Jane thought. At this point, it didn't matter. No doubt about it. Hank was by far the liveliest dead music legend she'd ever encountered. The romantic rogue type. The kind of man she'd always wanted to spend time with. A *lifetime*, perhaps.

Hank's hand appreciatively patted 'Patsy's' behind while he paid the check.

Well...maybe not.

* * *

Okay...so Hank was driving, and Jane had no idea where. She cuddled up close as he switched on the radio.

Her own voice oozed from the speakers: *The country? Sure! Nice place to visit, but I wouldn't want to live there.*

A sideways glance caught the lone road sign as they sped past. It read:

COMMITMENT Population...undecided.

Corrections

Darrow Elba was as grey as his surroundings. His eyes were battleship steel. Rarely did he recall his dreams but was certain he'd never dreamed in color. Craving zest, he pilfered it from others. A duty, not a crime. It was his *job*.

His fingers raked his thinning hairline. *Busy signal.* He slammed down the receiver. On his desk, Janice's studio portrait showcased her placid blue eyes. Happier times…back before she decided to make 'bitch' her career. He clutched the photo frame and turned it. Now she would face the wall.

* * *

The Yellow Pages shouted "Attorneys." Janice Elba waited, on hold, finger caressing the word 'divorce.' She heard a click, then the secretary's crisp voice. Janice hesitated, groping for the correct term. "Yes, I…I need a consultation, please. Just a consultation. I don't know the…*procedure.*"

* * *

Darrow punched out another series of numbers. "Let's see what Franck is up to, shall we?" His smile broadened with each ring, his pen tapping an erect column of business cards…

John Franck rolled over and snatched at the phone, toppling it from its base. It thrashed like a flounder and hit the floor. He recovered it, gripping tightly. "Yeah?"

"It's 8:30. Running late for work?"

Elba. "Uh, no luck yet." John chased his emotions with sheer will.

"Lots of applications in, but—"

"Then you're running late on your job *search*. Be here, 8 a.m. sharp. Tomorrow."

Click.

John's eyes were open wide. "The fucker with the wooden stakes," he grunted. "Must be pissin' himself to catch a sleeping vampire."

He trudged toward the kitchen, stopping momentarily. "You okay, mom? Gonna' fix some breakfast."

It was obvious she'd spent a sleepless night on the couch again. "I had another accident, honey...I'm so sorry." Her red-ringed eyes were shaded with guilt.

The air was pungent with urine. "No big deal," he muttered...

As he bathed her, she followed his directions like an obedient child. Toweling, clean pajamas, and a sluggish trip to her bed completed the routine.

Her voice cracked with defeat as she was positioned on the waterproof mattress pad. "I guess I'll try the 'old folks diapers'."

John's sigh expelled a mix of relief and sorrow. "Maybe there's some with Big Bird on 'em, eh?" His mother's scratchy giggle comforted the lump in his throat. "Got oatmeal with a little maple syrup. Sound good?"

She nodded, her head sinking into the freshly laundered pillowcase. "Thank you...oh, John—look!" Her eyes danced, reflecting the spectrum of colors streaming from the open blinds. "A pretty rainbow..."

The water came to a boil. Elba's card lurked on the counter-top, doing its best to provoke. "Sweet," John said, licking syrup from his fingers. "Sweet *revenge*, asshole. Later." He drizzled mom's warmed cereal with amber goo.

* * *

Darrow swabbed the signatures with White-Out, continuing at a machine's pace until he'd obliterated the woman's name from the entire stack of cards. Then he opened the droplet spattered window and waited for the fumes to clear.

A rainbow hung on the horizon, like a giant horseshoe thrown from fleeing hooves of thunder. "Hmm, lucky horseshoes and pots of gold. A change for the better?" A tacky gold embossed "2000" on the wall calendar mocked him. "Yeah, right. A new millennium. So far, same ol' shit."

When he returned to his chair, the white paste had dried. Small rectangles carpeted his desktop, ready to be personalized. He plucked the first card and inscribed "Darrow P. Elba" on the white-washed line below Board of Probations and Parole.

"Cheap bastards won't even spring for a fresh batch. Idiots. White-Out costs 'em *more*." He grimaced at the next card. Faint outlines of "Ms. Sherry Kincaid" were still visible.

Viciously, he scrubbed with the miniature paintbrush. "This is no place for bleeding hearts, babe. Hope they kept your job open at the Poodle Parlor."

A whiff of the chemical 'eraser' set off a round of sneezes. When the whirlwind abated, the mud tracked floor was a disaster area strewn with business cards. "Shit!" He snuffled dejectedly while he gathered...

The clock eyeballed him. Graham was five minutes late. Elba's hand went for the phone. It was stopped cold by a knock at the door.

"Who is it?"

"Er...Mark Graham."

"Get in here!"

The gangly kid bopped in, all elbows and knees, sporting a slept-in "Zig Zag Man" tee shirt and baggy shorts. He casually draped his jacket over the back of his seat.

Arrogant, naïve punk. "What's your story?" Darrow tidied his folders, opening one titled "Graham." Methodically, he wound his watch and straightened his tie. "*Well*?"

"Well...there was traffic—"

"I was referring to the fact that I couldn't reach you by phone yesterday—and the day *before* yesterday."

"...Oh. *That*. Sorry, man. Didn't know you left those messages 'til this morning. I was spending quality time with my woman." He smirked and executed several un-subtle pelvic thrusts. "You know how it is."

Darrow glared. "Spending the night anywhere but your own

residence is a violation. Let me give you another one of my cards. No, how about two? Just to be *sure* you have my number."

Mark's chin had dropped. "What? You kiddin'? My papers say to notify you if I *change* my residence. You're talkin' about House Arrest, when they put electronic ankle things on murderers...rapists. I got busted for a couple of *joints!*" Perspiration oozed. "My mom testified that I picked up those pain pills at the drug store for her. Her name was on the bottle. That's *proof!*"

But this humorless prick *owned* him. Elba's silence was making him nervous, *real* nervous. He yanked his attention from the condescending face and studied the cards. The asshole was always handing him cards...

Mark gaped, then burst into a fit of laughter. "Man, I never noticed this before." He wedged phrases into the spaces between guffaws. "Oh, man...like...wow...I can't believe it...these cards say 'Department *of of* Corrections'!"

He held his ribs. "Is that White-Out I smell? Wow, some people actually *huff* that shit, y'know? Okay, so kill me, Mr. Elba. It's fuckin' hilarious."

Elba was cracking a smile. A tiny one. The sight of it struck terror.

"Good reader, huh?" Darrow popped one knuckle at a time. "Do you read the Job Classifieds?"

"...Uh, hey...I've been mowing lawns," Mark wobbled.

"Doesn't qualify as employment. But...you *would* know your grass." Darrow's mouth stretched into a grin. "Yeah, that reminds me. You failed your piss test. Yeah, *you*, Funny Face. Shoulda' studied harder. Cannabis *and* codeine. That's *proof*, genius!"

He scribbled a notation, relishing The Comedy Kid's sudden stage fright. "You did graduate though. This isn't Juvenile Hall, and I'm not your mom. I take up where they left off. Oh, and you better hope your 'woman' isn't the fickle type. No conjugal visits at re-hab."

Mark located his voice. "But-but...what do you mean? I go there once a week, right?"

"Pack your pajamas this time."

* * *

The kid's simpering howl stayed with Darrow Elba for hours. He played it in his head every time he called Janice. It eased the pain of the busy signal.

But *nothing* could erase the humiliation of those damned cards! Mis-printed, re-cycled—*used*. They weren't just pieces of paper. They summed up his thankless job, his entire dysfunctional existence. What did he have to show for decades of planning, the sacrifices made for his family—the fact that he'd made the streets safer for *all* families?

* * *

Janice's tears sprinkled her untouched meal. Her gaze parted the organdy curtains above the kitchen sink.

The spectacular rainbow which had appeared earlier was gone. *Hope* had gone with it. Her world was shattered grey window glass, a jigsaw puzzle...and she'd never been good at games.

She spoke into the phone. "Carol, am I a whiner?"

"I haven't heard you whine since Kindergarten."

"I trusted. I put my signature on the line. Pre-nuptial agreements were the thing to do, remember?"

"You bet. The sensible approach, in *theory*."

"I didn't even read that contract. I *assumed* we had an equal partnership." Janice closed the curtains. "I raised the kids with fairness, as individuals, over-riding Darrow's military logic." Her eyes were dry now. Stinging. "He doesn't realize they stay out of trouble for the *right* reasons."

"Jan, you should try another lawyer. This doesn't sound legal."

"This *was* the second lawyer. It's clear cut. As his widow, I'd be provided for in the will. But that pre-nuptial document says if I leave this marriage, I leave with nothing. Somehow he made sure everything is in his name. There's no trace of me. I feel...*invisible*."

* * *

Darrow made a mental note to add this day to his Official Shit-List. He was tired...too tired to even lock his office. Nothing of value there anyway...

He feigned nonchalance, but the hairs on the back of his neck were rising, his shoe heels tapping out lonely echoes down the gangway. His eyes narrowed as he ducked into the parking garage.

Upon reaching his car, he lifted the hood and flicked on his flashlight. After a thorough inspection, he stooped to the ground and repeated the scrutiny. The beam slithered along undisturbed paths of brake lines.

A forced sigh did little to purge his anxiety. *Three weeks*...and the doctor's Magic Pills hadn't made the monsters blink. They ate at him. They gobbled up the Prozac, then gnawed on him some more. He squeezed behind the steering wheel—

He froze, his eyes riveted to the slip of paper tucked beneath the windshield wiper. Squinting, he patted his breast pocket, then cursed. He'd left his reading glasses behind. He began to sweat.

Threats. Ex-cons rarely made them to his face. Just the wannabe punks and three-time losers, and they were easy to dispose of. It was the seasoned, *quiet* 'career criminals' that made him sweat. Expressionless faces. No *conscience*. They played games with his head.

VIOLATION. The largest letters had jumped into focus.

"It's a ticket. Fuck!" The steering wheel dug into his gut, and a rusty screw in the door frame took a bite out of his scalp as he lunged.

"Hey!" He waved his fist of crumpled paper at a passing woman. She walked faster. "Please," he said, shadowing her. "I don't have my glasses. What does this say?"

The woman hurriedly unlocked her door, then brandished a black cylinder attached to her keychain. "Mace!" she screeched.

"Doris, it's *me*—put that away."

"Oh..." She lowered her weapon.

Darrow wondered if he'd imagined a trace of disappointment in her voice. "Putting in some overtime?" He handed her the ticket.

"Yep. The files are all screwed up again...hmm, this says your license plate's expired."

"What?"

Doris flinched. She regarded her empty hand, then Darrow's sputtering face.

His response was pushed out with great effort. "I'll find out...I'll find out who's behind this." He turned on his heel.

Taking her cue, Doris started her engine and darted toward the exit ramp. Her rear-view mirror showed an unraveled Darrow Elba giving his own bumper a kick...

He clicked his flashlight again, then planted himself on all fours. Yes, the sticker was *gone*, hastily peeled, a torn segment clinging to the plate.

He was sickened by his own rage, by the quandary of deciding which 'smoking gun' was the bigger worry. Obviously he was the *victim*, not the perpetrator. Even without his glasses, the evidence was plainly visible. The zealot with the badge had made a mistake. *Mistakes could be costly...*

A swirling wind-gust turned litter into tumbleweeds and chafed his clammy skin. The bottom line was undeniable: *Darrow Elba had let his guard down.* The sticker theft was the result of one of two possibilities. Random opportunism...or a client's vengeance.

Within seconds, he was revving the engine. A few minutes found him streaking down the highway toward home...

Suddenly, without knowing why, he merged into an exit lane. Many blind twists and turns, he realized he was on his way back to his office. The extra pair of reading glasses he'd stashed in the glove compartment lay on the seat where he'd flung them.

Beside them was the mangled ticket, wadded by Darrow's hand. He couldn't bear to look at it. *His name had been spelled incorrectly...*

* * *

Karen's phone was ringing as she lumbered up the stairway. Breathless by the time she reached the kitchen table, she deposited her groceries and sagged overtop them.

She laughed out loud. The man she loved was singing to her answering machine. Allowing his serenade to wind to a finish and begin an encore, she transferred the perishables to the refrigerator…

John wasn't a bad tune weaver, and he wasn't the best. But he loved to sing. Most of all, he loved *Karen.* She picked up the receiver.

"Hello, John."

"Hello, yourself. What's that panting all about? Had to chase your lover out the back door?"

"*You're* my lover, dummy. I just got home."

"Likely story."

Both were grinning. Their private jokes offset the bleakness of the miles separating them. The distance was physical reality. So was the ache.

"There's good news and bad news." John's smile retreated.

"Isn't there always?" She shook off the urge to open a beer. Maybe later. Almost *certainly* later.

"The car's fixable...for a thousand dollars."

"A thou—" She sat down. Over the span of three months, John's descent into a pit of rotten luck had increased relentlessly.

"And my P. O. told me to see him at eight, tomorrow. He can make me do that *every* morning, because 'Unemployment' isn't the same as having a job.' He's threatening to lock me up."

Karen exploded from her chair and paced the length of the kitchen. "That's Debtor's Prison."

"They call it 'parole violation'"

"But how can you *find* another job if you spend all your time trying to get to his office and back? Does he know your mother's *dying*? Does he know you worked six days a week until the car broke down? The state takes half your check. What more do they—"

"My *soul.* They get my blood, but I won't give 'em my soul."

Karen lapsed into silence. She slid a beer from the top shelf of the refrigerator. An icy blanket of barley and hops dampened the fire and evened her tongue. "What's this asshole's name? If I get a chance to kill him, I'd like to be sure it's the right asshole."

A wry smile tugged the corners of John's lips. "Darrow P. Elba."

"Darrell?" *Her sainted brother's name. This slimeball was tainting it.*

"No, Dar-*oh*. D-a-r-r-o-w. He's real picky about it. Keeps givin' out cards. Don't know why he bothers. Bet everybody just calls him 'asshole' anyway."

* * *

It wasn't so bad, John reasoned. Plenty of time to think. Hell, he could even discuss it with himself, out loud. *The importance of pieces of paper...*

"Money." He watched cars disappear over the hill. Turning, he walked backward, his thumb jerking toward his destination. Startled eyes met his, sized him up, then passed him by.

He stole a peek at his watch. *Three hours.* Well beyond the halfway point. His feet were protesting, and he'd removed his jacket despite the nip of mid-Autumn, but he was far from out of breath. "Not bad for an 'old man'"

The statement had been blotted by the roar from a spewing diesel, so he repeated it. He continued putting one foot in front of the other, and his thoughts careened amid the jangle of the morning rush. *Too much pride?* If he'd opened his mouth and asked for help, he'd be driving right now.

He shook his head. No... he'd been a burden to his sister long enough.

Roadside debris jotted artificial color on the landscape's palette. Candy wrappers tumbled aimlessly and fast-food cups screamed "Pepsi." Visions of birthday cakes and holidays swam by. Josh and Sean. He was no absentee father in *their* eyes.

But little pieces of paper had a way of disappearing. He'd trusted, even *after* the divorce. No reason to save all those check stubs...

The jail cell forced him to reconsider. He'd paced away his denial, but *shock* was a lifetime sentence. Receipts of child support payments. *Pieces of paper.* Without them, he was a felon. For *life...*

* * *

Janice Elba awoke. Frayed patches of nightmares were a binding quilt. She kicked free.

7:30 a.m. The alarm hadn't been set, but her internal clock had taken over. Darrow's side of the bed was cold, shocking to the touch. She took several deep breaths and let her eyes scan the room.

Fuzzy warm memories crowded out the panic... Those chilly mornings she'd cuddled the children beneath the covers after Darrow left for work. She could hear their bare feet scamper across the hardwood floor. She could feel their rounded bodies pounce, one on each side of her, like teddy bear book ends come-to-life. Her babies' clean smell of innocence would never leave her.

She reached for the phone on the nightstand. Then, she counted the rings at her husband's office. One...two...three...four--she smiled when she heard the tiny click.

Doris sounded harried. Janice strolled to the closet, the phone pressed to her ear.

"Um...well, Mrs. Elba, his first client isn't due until eight. He may be...sometimes he takes a little nap," Doris tittered. "I'll check the break room. I just made coffee. Hold on, alright?"

"Yes, thank you." Janice perused her suits before selecting the charcoal grey and a silky blouse of Robin's egg blue. Appropriate for a special day. She'd made a monumental decision. Freedom. There'd be papers to sign.

The hanger jerked at the sound. It was a scream, broken by indecipherable phrases. Robin's egg blue floated lazily, pooling on the floor as Doris' wailing approached, nearer and nearer...like a siren—

"Oh my God! Oh..."

"What is it? Doris!"

"H-he...oh, God. I have to call an ambulance!"

The line went dead.

* * *

After five hours of walking, John was ready to concede to the blisters. He would swallow his pride and call his son for the ride home.

A siren blared. The sun was full, *blinding*. A police car emerged from a side street and swerved, brushing John's jacket as he stood in the crosswalk. Forgetting his blisters, he galloped to the opposite corner.

Red and blue lights strobed at the end of the short block. "Fuck! I came all this way for *nothing* if the place is on fire." He quickened his pace. "They'll make me come back tomorrow, or-or...shit!"

Gruffly, he cleared a path through the gawkers in front of the building and hobbled up the stone steps. There, he was promptly escorted back to the sidewalk.

"Get behind the yellow tape!" bellowed the gent with the badge. "Go home and *call* about your appointment."

John wanted to stomp his blistered feet and watch the blood seep through his socks. He wanted to kick injustice in the teeth...if only he could attach the word to just one mortal entity.

His shoulders slumped. "Just more of the same," he told himself. "Your Hell raisin' days are over."

Just outside the perimeter of yellow, an armed guard stood by. Just *inside* was an image that would stick in John's mind for days.

An ambulance, door open wide. Three people clustered. The officer was mute, expressionless. The paramedic holding the clipboard handed a woman a pen. A calm, sedate woman. Her silky blouse was the color of the clear blue sky...

Elsewhere, inside the building, Doris was trembling. "Of course he got threats. No... I don't know. I didn't see him come in, and I just don't know anything else!" she sobbed. Her subconscious had made a decision. Her psyche required a low stress occupation. A job without contact with felons—

A paramedic sped past, altruism glazing his features. He skidded to a stop at Elba's door.

He was waved aside.

Beyond the threshold, immediacy had ebbed, but the medical team huddled around the prone form of Darrow Elba. His face was ashen, a match for his hair. He blended into the dingy carpet, almost invisible on first glance. But close-up inspection showed something had gone terribly wrong. It showed up in color, in the crimson froth that mottled his flaccid blue lips...

Ted Lakey's knees were cramping, his long legs folded beneath him. He coughed. "I hate to be a pest, but whoever's closest to the window—

open it!"

He swung his stethoscope over his shoulder, then spoke to the cop treading the hem of his starched white coat. "First priority was to see if there was a chance to resuscitate. Frankly, the possibility that *evidence* has been destroyed is remote, but dust and bag all ya' want. See the Medic Alert bracelet? Asthma, severe allergies. Smell the fumes? A lit cigarette woulda' set off a fuckin' *kaboom*."

The cop grimaced. "Yeah, I smell *somethin'*..."

"White-Out. Looks like he *erased* himself." Ted's pen scratched the word "anaphylaxis" on the top sheet of his report.

Flexible tubes receded into compact machines. The room swelled as more jacket clad officers squeezed through the doorway.

"People, try to keep the scene intact for the crime lab techs!" Ted's knees crackled as he hauled himself from the floor. He was formidable in size. Co-workers *expected* him to take charge...

Medical personnel were dispersing rapidly, and the lab techs advanced, zeroing in on peripherals. Short towers of business cards kept each other company on the desk, otherwise bare...except for a phone. And a framed photograph of Janice Elba.

On the floor, crushed cards lay, further insulted by the trampling of heavy shoes. They were crouton accents tossed with a salad of small plastic bottles, ball-point pens, and shredded heaps of file folders.

Angry slashes of White-Out gave the beige wall behind the desk a Picasso effect. An officer was studying the mess, back turned to the swarm of investigators.

Abruptly, his voice cut into the din.

"There's *writing* here!" he announced, pointing to a sizable chalky area. He bent forward, his nose even with the neat block letters. "What the...? It says 'My name is Darrow P. Elba. Fuck off'"

Nasty Habits

Jasmine's feet felt too big for her shoes on the way out, but the door's heft didn't trouble her shoulder like it had on the way in.

"Need a ride?"

Hoots and lewd giggles slid down her back, and a downpour washed her clean by the time she'd crossed the street. Golden Arches reflected briefly in splotched glass as she swung open an even heftier door, her shoulder providing a 'reminder' twinge.

The teen behind the counter glanced past her. "You don't look like a junkie," she said.

"I'll have two hamburgers...fries, regular, and a small coffee." Jasmine fingered her underweight coin purse. The girl looked familiar. *Cocoa brown hair. That mole above her eyebrow. Her voice.* "What does a junkie look like?" Jasmine asked her, dumping change on grey steel for an accurate count.

"Huh...well, they look all kinds of ways. Hey, if you ain't got enough money, I'll spot you this time, all right?"

Jasmine jumped as a hand covered hers. Next to it was a bulging paper bag, top neatly folded. "Wh-where did she go?"

"Who?" A woman with freckled skin scooped the coins and returned them to Jasmine's purse.

"That girl who took my order...uh, thanks. I'll have enough to pay for this tomorrow. I guess I answered her rude question with one of my own. I didn't mean it for you."

Laughter shook an ample figure in a downsized uniform. "No teen angels workin' night shift around here. Not unless they work the street, y'know?"

A grimace served as Jasmine's reply. Bag in hand, she tread carefully down a mud tracked aisle in search of a clean table. She settled for a booth. Its rusting bolts creaked and pulled slightly away from the wall, but no one appeared to notice.

"You bastard!"

The corner of Jasmine's eye caught a woman in a rain spattered jacket yelling into a phone. Beside her a small child was seated in a high chair.

"The cops'll get your ass and I'll be *glad*, you hear me?"

The toddler busied himself with his mother's beige canvas shopping bag. Clutching a felt marker in each fist, he scribbled angry colors on it. When the eyes in his ketchup smeared face met Jasmine's, he grinned.

Jasmine re-located to a filthy table next to the exit. Coffee. More coffee. Her first bite into solid food since early morning. She lifted the bun and drew a smiley face with mustard. Two hamburgers later, she hit the street, belly full of guilt. Cows had died for her sins.

Thunder rumbled, promising a second wave. The pavement had already forgotten the first, and the hide-and-seek sun would postpone nightfall another hour or so. Jasmine decided to walk...

Feral dogs and children chased each other in and out of alleys. A stagnant breeze followed, the smell of urine and sweat exacerbated by the heated cloudburst. Noise was everywhere. A voice filtered through: *are you old enough to smoke*? Jasmine felt a stab of panic and crossed the street. A cab slowed, shadowing the curb until it passed.

The hooded driver. Again. Her scalp prickled as she watched the cab turn at the next corner, but her breaths evened. "I should be afraid," she said.

"Yep. Sure should."

Jasmine's head spun. "Oh, it's you."

"Why didn't you call me?" her faithful cabbie scolded. "C'mon, get in."

Stale cigarette odor was dubious relief, but the AC snuffed the humid fog. "Just got an urge to walk tonight."

"My feelings are hurt."

She laughed. "That's your wallet throbbing...hey, by the way," she said as he navigated the intersection, "Do you know that guy?"

"What guy?"

"The cabbie wearing the hooded jacket. Well, I assume it's a guy. I've seen him several times, but only from behind. He never has a fare."

"Dunno who you mean."

"... He was right in front—you pulled over just as he passed me. You didn't see him?"

"I only have eyes for you, honey."

The fog encroached again, a menacing nudge. "Uh...I want to go over to Jim's house. Need to settle some things. Hope you aren't disappointed. I have my period. It's getting late anyway."

He made that combination snort-laugh that always annoyed her. "Since when is a period disappointing? Still early. Let him wait."

"I make my decisions," she said through gritted teeth. "You're going the wrong direction."

"Hey, I know where we...uh, I live."

"I'm not going there tonight. Don't worry, Dan, the cab fare'll go in *your* pocket this time."

The cab zig-zagged, then braked so fast, Jasmine's forehead slammed into the back of the passenger seat.

"I don't need the money, and I can make decisions too. I'm making one right now to un-involve myself. Let me know where to send your stuff when you're ready. Don't worry, I won't destroy it. I'm not vengeful, just tired. You know my number. Get out."

Jasmine trembled. The door handle felt like ice. "Involve? This arrangement was *your* idea." Dusk was catching up. The back of his head was blurring.

So was his voice. "*Arrangement.* Yeah, figures. Whores don't get involved with clients, and I need to learn to do the same." He sighed.

"Delete the idiotic 'whore' comment. It's not true, and I'm sorry I said it. By the way, I still keep Narcan in the glove compartment. *Also*…I love you, Jasmine." He paused and ran a hand through his hair. "Now get out."

The slippery curb challenged her numbing feet. "I didn't know," she said. She closed the door. "I didn't *know*, Dan." A bolt of lightning tore open the clouds and her tears merged with rain. The neighborhood was engrossed in its own fading discordant symphony. *She* was the conductor of absolutely nothing.

* * *

Jasmine was limping when she reached the two-story brick house. Taking pity, the wrought iron railing guided her to the porch. The aroma of cooked food sifted out the transom. She rang the bell and envisioned a pair of famished gargoyles flanking the mahogany door.

A rustle…then, footsteps thumped. Blinds parted, displaying Jim's eyes. Keys turned, a bolt was released. Thick wood groaned as it dragged across deep pile carpet.

"You're wringing wet—and your food is cold. I ate two hours ago. Do you know what time it is? Why are you so late?" Jim squinted at the street corner. "Where's the cab?"

"I felt like walking."

He looked wounded. "Guess you don't need the cab fare then," he said, cramming the bills in his pocket. "Why did you worry me? Don't you think about the crackheads and crazy fuckers out there?"

"Don't *you*? Seems like if you did, you'd get in your car and pick me up personally. You were worried? You don't *look* worried, just inconvenienced."

"Don't be dramatic. Sit down and eat. You still look like a skeleton."

"I already ate." Pain was her greedy doppelganger, fattened with dreams. *Her* dreams. Some days she dined on dreams and little else. "I gained a pound this week. They weighed me at the clinic."

"So you don't need food either. Well, we can just listen to the music. It's calming, y'know?" He looked wounded again, with an undercurrent of paranoia. His hands shook as his brain bubbled. She knew he wanted to throw the dishes in the trash...or break them over her skull. She was weary of what she knew about him.

Predictably, he upped the volume and stuck an unlit cigarette in his mouth. He chomped it while he leisurely cleared the table, doling out his personal brand of 'punishment.' She felt like telling him to go ahead and smoke in the house but wasn't up to the effort of projecting her voice over the blaring music.

He picked up his lighter and motioned toward the back porch, ending her suspense...for now. She sucked in a full breath when the screen door banged shut. After restoring the volume to a tolerable level, she paced from the hall through the dining room, into the living room and back again.

A collage of framed photographs stalked her, weak exhalations of Jim and Jasmine's History tickling the nape of her neck. On her second lap, she allowed them to wash over her: a tense series of poses, over-exposed by flash bulbs, cloistered inside a house always kept a little too cool, and much too dim. A 'mausoleum' fit for the King of Recluse.

No camera had captured the scene she treasured. One golden day outdoors, their holding-hands walk in the park...and Jim's voice. "I want to spend my life with you, Jasmine. I want to visit every place of beauty on this Earth with you."

No camera had witnessed that golden day. *It hadn't happened.* Jasmine wandered without purpose into Jim's bedroom.

A loose snapshot lay on the dresser, its border discolored from decades encased in its frame: an adoptive father wearing an Air Force uniform held a swaddled baby boy. He stood on the concrete stairway in front of an austere German orphanage. Peering out an opening in the blanket was a tiny face, seamless and uncorrupted. Jasmine's eyes moistened...

"Oh." Her face flushed. "I didn't hear you."

Jim resumed blotting her rain-soaked hair with a towel. An urge to back away yielded to gentle warmth. The terrycloth coddled her scalp while his fingers massaged their way to a truce. He drew her close to the radiator. "Here, let's dry your clothes," he said softly.

His hands peeled off her jacket and tee shirt, rubbing the chill from her skin in the same motion. Her eyes moistened again when she felt his lips touch her neck and travel down one shoulder. Next, he unhooked her bra...

Hypnotic. She was a spectator now. Her clothes wafted in comfort, draping the radiator, piece by piece...

She sank into the mattress, startled by a volatile mix of sensation. "Why, after all this time?"

"To celebrate. Because we *can* now."

"We can?" A grating whisper sounded in the distance, from a place she couldn't locate. *Bees flew into a jar of honey...*

"We can do anything together," Jim said.

Their bodies were matching puzzle pieces. The hope of creating something new and beautiful beckoned. He'd aimed a fan at the radiator, and the swaying motion of her clothing revived the wonder of her first dance. High school...the deaf boy everyone had ridiculed took her in his arms, closed his eyes and glided. *I feel vibrations in the soles of my feet.* She felt herself melt, interlocking a fuzzy past and present into the possibility of *future—*

Raw terror filled a blank space. She writhed inside a sticky hive of bees. *Hands that smelled like hamburger. A cruel lit cigarette—* "Stop! I can't do this anymore." She rolled onto her side, scorched and spastic. *Maggots squirmed inside the dead and dying. Scars closed out the living.*

"Do what?" Jim sat up.

"Sex. I... I didn't feel it when I was stoned." *And I didn't miss it when you were too stoned or drunk to even make an attempt,* she reminded herself.

"You didn't feel it? And now you do?" The lamp clicked on. "That's a problem? Jeez, thanks a lot."

You're welcome. "No, I meant...I don't know what I meant. If only

I could force an orgasm, just to make you happy."

"This is about making *you* happy. Guess I still can't. But how can I expect you to forget whoever knows how to give you orgasms?"

She imitated laughter. "Listen closely for a change, because I'm about to give your ego a boost. I've rarely had an orgasm with anyone but myself. Ironic that 'therapists' have told me I don't like myself, eh? Seriously, you do all the 'right' moves, but..."

His sarcasm deepened. "You've never spelled out this mystery ailment to me. Your current ailment is memory gaps, and lots of things can cause them. If this is physical, can't doctors fix it?"

"Something's never quite let you in emotionally either...and I'm starting to respect 'something's' judgment."

Jim retreated into 'silent mode' again. Jasmine retaliated in kind, her eyes seeking a distraction. The pillowcases were stained and pocked with cigarette burns, bringing an image of trampled marshmallows to mind. Her memory went on a childhood jaunt, down a narrow two-lane highway. *She watched daddy peel bark from slender twigs and sharpen the ends. Skewered marshmallows bubbled and blackened before they were withdrawn from the campfire. Her eager appetite awarded a singed lip...and she burst into tears. "I hurt when you hurt," daddy said. He placed an ice cube in his handkerchief and numbed the burn...*

Jasmine was compelled to break the silence. "My father believed in me, Jim. He was always 'there' and suddenly he wasn't anywhere. I have no idea what happened—and I—oh, everything's been so muddled for so long. I need closure."

"Obviously there's no such thing," Jim yelled, snatching his pants from the floor. "The ocean's deep and vast. Accept it and consider yourself lucky only *one* father let you down. I'm just a little bastard some nameless sperm machine didn't bother to claim."

The urge was so strong her fingers curled. They craved the dusty grip of a stick of charcoal—and equally—the sterile fuck of a syringe. "I made a decision." *She could do worse.* "I'm through with the clinic."

She'd done worse.

"Are you crazy?"

"I've weaned myself off the Methadone."

"It won't last. How can you be so stupid?"

"Your vote of confidence makes me even more determined to excise my biggest bad habit."

"You already did…or the Methadone did, rather."

"I wasn't referring to the heroin. And I meant 'through with the clinic' from a medical perspective only. The director bought four of my paintings. Two of them, both seascapes, are on the wall in the meditation room. He gave me referrals, too. I'm commissioned to do some work for the Brendt Aquarium, for starters."

He made a sour face. "Did the director pay you?"

"I get a check tomorrow." The scab over an old abrasion tingled. "You're happy for me…right?"

"I'm thirsty," he said on his way to the kitchen. As she yanked her clothes off the radiator, her phone dinged. She fished it from her purse. A text from Dan: *Jasmine, are you okay? Call asap. Please. I lost my mind. I've never been so sorry in my life.* She muted the phone and slipped it back in her purse. Her heart pounded.

A half-drained beer bottle returned with Jim. He waved it and sat on the bed. "I've got a twelve-pack. I'd better re-new my supply so I'm ready for the long nights by myself. You wouldn't marry me, won't even live with me since you started bunking at that 'shelter' next to the clinic." His fingers drummed the bedside table. "I'll keep busy remembering I was loved by the dad who adopted me…and I'll picture him after my 'mom' deserted him, stone-cold, next to bottles of bourbon and pills. But she's a famous artist. That's all that counts."

"Jim, it really is an endless loop, isn't it? A twisted legacy. Artists, writers, actors…remember what you said? Misfits—*losers*—who don't fit in the real world with real people. Tell me, where do *you* fit now? Methadone, heroin, Methadone, heroin—and most of all, booze. You're hooked on numbness. You love me only when I join in. Your uncle left you enough money to feed you and your true love for as long as you both shall live. As for me, I have a habit of worshiping wounds. I have to stop." She was fully dressed now, edging toward the hallway.

He rose, dropping his beer, and blocked the door. "No—I'm trying, can't you see? I won't go back, Jasmine. No heroin, ever. I'll stay on Methadone, I promise..." A fat tear coursed down his cheek, then another. "When I'm clean again, let's go back to smoking weed. Just weed, *only* weed…and a few beers. We were happy. Remember? Don't you understand? If you leave me, I'll die."

She'd watched the empty beer bottle roll to a stop. "Yeah…I remember being happy. Except for that constant terror underneath, always anticipating a drug bust. Federal agents bashing through the front door—maybe going to jail for decades—just because we had marijuana. That 'reefer-madness' gateway. Marijuana wasn't the fucking 'gateway' for you. The drug bust scenario opened that gate. A 'few' legal beers didn't numb your dread anymore. So you stocked your gun cabinet. I hated guns. Your guns, cops' guns. My arm became a masterpiece of evolving tattoos. Purple bruises mottled with blotches of red, yellow, and green as they aged. I stopped painting. Stopped caring. I'm the one who died! Did you even notice?"

Jim's eyes were huge. He stepped aside. "God, help me—no. It's time for the truth, no matter what it costs. Your memory blanks. I can fill them. I have to. The cigarette burns. It wasn't some random stranger in an alley. You were so out of it, I just let you tell yourself that. But it was *me*."

Jasmine was speechless. They'd advanced through the hallway, into the living room. Her daisy-embroidered pillow had fallen from the couch. She considered picking it up…

"It was almost a year ago. Are you listening, Jasmine? You were done with me and my nasty habits. Do you remember throwing the syringe— the whole kit—at me and heading for the door? *Do* you?"

"… No."

"You didn't make it. I stopped you—but the burns were an

accident." He turned off the music, and his words tumbled into the stark silence. "No, maybe not. How the fuck should I know? I can have memory blanks too." He gulped and leaned against the wall. "Who am I fooling? Those burns kept you with me."

"What? What are you talking about?" Her fingers probed the scars. The room swam. *The front door. Pain, searing pain.*

"The burns are like a brand. You fell hard against the door…and I didn't even realize I had a lit cigarette. See the burn spot in the carpet? I think a fear of something *worse* happening made you a prisoner here. You didn't leave the house for a month or so. Of course you don't remember. You were barely conscious most of the time."

Her head throbbed. "But…I remember going somewhere. We went somewhere—"

"The grocery store. We got food, and I cooked. Tried to get you to eat. You started eating more, and then you got restless. Went for walks, lots of walks. I knew you'd come back, but sometimes that cab driver brought you back. He said you were sleeping on benches but told him your address. He wouldn't accept money. But when you started staying at the shelter, I insisted you make him take money whenever he picked you up and brought you here. You agreed to 'visit' me, so I got my hopes up."

"Dan." *He'd carried her in his arms, into the Rehab Center…after reviving her with Narcan.*

"Who? Oh, yeah, the cab driver. He said always ask for him when I call a cab for you."

"Jim, what happened to my father? All you said was his empty cab was found in the river. What about before that? Are you going to tell me?"

"I don't know! We've been through all that. He kept calling, but I didn't want him to see you with an arm full of needle marks. You were sick, and you looked it. I told him you left me, without a word, a note…nothing. I even got a visit from the cops, but they just asked questions. They were satisfied with the same lie I told your father. They don't get search warrants to look for junkies. After that, you started disappearing for real, wherever those walks took you."

She felt an ice-cold chill. "It *was* you…I had this image in my mind of a stranger who terrified me. I was right about that. I'm looking right at him. I *know* I tried to call my father. Couldn't think of his number—or even where he lived. And his contact was gone from my phone. Coincidence? You just let him—"

"I need another beer."

"Wait, Jim." Patchy memories crawled from hiding places. "Another thing. I'm petrified of needles…I screamed when I got shots when I was a kid. Why do I have absolutely *no* memory of putting a needle in my arm?" She looked straight into his eyes. They evaded hers. "Is that just another 'lapse'? Well, *is* it?"

She saw tears streak his face as he turned and left for the kitchen. Her hands fumbled with the front door locks. The keys were missing. Of course, the keys were missing—

"Jasmine."

Her heart hammered.

Jim was seated in the black suede recliner. His 'comfy' chair, reserved for shooting up. In his hands was a phone. And keys. "Jasmine…you're free now. Don't fear me anymore—I can't stand it. I've loved you since we were sixteen." He stood and walked to the door, unlocking and unbolting in seconds. "I called a cab. It'll be here in a few minutes."

She felt his breath on her face as his fingers smoothed her hair.

"Don't touch me!" Her hand stung. She reeled backward, realizing she'd hit him. "Never touch me again. You *forced* that needle into my arm. Not once, but over and over until I started begging for it. I remember *everything* now. You loved me? And you did *that*?" Her voice was hoarse. "Are you going to admit it?" she yelled.

"I…I just…*yes*. I did. I'm sorry, baby. Go to the shelter. I know you can't ever forgive me. But let me send you money. Will you let me? Just give me an address when you have one. I worry about you." His voice broke. "I *do* love you."

"It isn't enough, Jim. It never was. Money can't fix this." She whooshed past the hungry gargoyles. The cab was already in sight…

She saw the hooded driver as she approached the cab, but she didn't even slow down. She ducked into the back seat.

"Where to?" he said.

"Home, I hope. First, I have to make a phone call to someone I think I love. *The shelter. The "shelter" was Dan's apartment, Jim! She wished she'd screamed it out loud.* "Please, just drive while I think. Anywhere."

"It shall be done, m'lady. Let your saddle rest."

His voice was a horse and buggy ride… She drifted. The city was blanketed with humidity and the temperature had plummeted. A sizzling mist escaped the manholes, but the rain had stopped. The sky was an odd shade of violet. A star fell to Earth and perished. It was beautiful and sad, and she wanted to cry. A soft tune swirled from the radio. *In the sweet by and by…we shall meet on that beautiful shore.* She shut her drowsy eyes and rested her head on the back of the seat, riding a low tide.

The cab paused. She glanced up, a vivid scene cutting through her torpor. Steps of pearl white led up a steep hill, to a church's blood red doors. On the lawn, frenzied moths swarmed above floodlights like inebriated fighter jet pilots. The cab accelerated again.

*What an image to preserve at her easel…*a robed figure, arms raised, silhouetted against blinding light. Suicidal moths darted and dove, morphed into fireflies. *Shooting stars.*

Her heartbeat quickened. Guilt flogged. Today was Father's Day, and she'd forgotten…

A turn onto the main thoroughfare daubed the windows with reflections. Jasmine did a jerky double take. Beside her, a young waitress hoisted a tray of burgers, her face illuminated in yellow flashing caution lights. The image freeze-framed on the smeared glass. Above the teen's left eyebrow, partially hidden in cocoa brown hair, was a mole.

"I remember now," Jasmine whispered. "It was my first job." Her fingers probed beneath a sprinkling of dyed red bangs...and exposed the burn scars on her forehead, above her left eyebrow, next to the mole. "That's where I first met Jim." If only she could hate him. Knowing his *self*-hatred would soon destroy him would be less painful…

The voice from the front seat cart-wheeled through a blurred year. "I was afraid you were dead, Jazzy, but I never stopped searching for you. At first, Jim wouldn't open that door at all. After that, he opened up…to show me the gun in his pocket. I told another cabbie—Dan, that's his name—that the cops closed the case on my missing daughter after questioning her boyfriend once. Just once. Dan said he thought maybe he'd seen you, might know where you were…"

Jasmine froze, stunned…listening.

The voice continued. "In my dreams, I lured Jim into my cab, and drove straight to the beach, to the Moonlight Drop-Off—and I kept driving. In reality, my cab slid off the icy bridge…"

"You—*daddy?* They found your cab, *only* your cab. That's what Jim told me. I didn't know you were alive!" She grabbed his shoulder and pulled herself forward…then fell back, eyes doing lazy pirouettes, a stricken ballerina…

* * *

Jasmine stood alone, as calm as the sea. The shoreline was beautiful. Her palette offered infinite possibilities. In her mind, she loaded a brush with starlit blue paint. *"You're safe now, Jazzy"* still echoed from the blank void inside the hood.

Her phone lit up as she tapped out a number. "Dan, I hope you can believe this." She held her breath…

She heard him exhale.

"*Try* me, Jasmine."

About the Author

Jane Gwaltney's favored moniker, "Poe's Sparrow", is an amalgamation of two loves.

Mr. Poe has long inspired her imagination and haunted her dreams. Edgar is clearly the victim of the incessant nagging of a majestic raven.

In contrast, Jane is blessed by tender memories of a lowly orphaned sparrow. She raised Mr. Bird, and he shared her home and heart for ten years.

A raven and a sparrow, so very different. Nevertheless, the mysterious fluttering of wings provokes fanciful tales from both quill and keyboard.

www.ingramcontent.com/pod-product-compliance
Lightning Source LLC
Chambersburg PA
CBHW061349310726
48974CB00001B/265